The Ugly Swans

TRANSLATED FROM THE RUSSIAN BY

Alice Stone Nakhimovsky and

Alexander Nakhimovsky

THE UGLY SWANS

Arkady Strugatsky and

Boris Strugatsky

Macmillan Publishing Co., Inc.
NEW YORK

Collier Macmillan Publishers
LONDON

Macmillan Publishing Co., Inc.
866 Third Avenue, New York, N.Y. 10022
Collier Macmillan Canada, Ltd.

Library of Congress Cataloging in Publication Data
Strugatskiĭ, Arkadiĭ Natanovich.
    The ugly swans.

    Translation of Gadkie lebedi.
    I. Strugatskiĭ, Boris Natanovich, joint author.   II.
Title.
PZ4.S919Ug   1979 [PG3476.S78835]   891.7'3'44
ISBN 0-02-615190-1   78-31895

First Printing 1979

Printed in the United States of America

SF

Y. A.

acc'd
10-79

The Ugly Swans

Chapter I

Irma left the room, carefully closing the door behind her. She was a thin, long-legged girl with a wide mouth and her mother's red lips; she smiled politely, like an adult. When she had gone, Victor attacked his cigarette. "That's no child," he thought, stunned. "Children don't talk like that. It's not even rudeness, it's cruelty, no, not even cruelty—she simply doesn't care. You'd think she was proving some theorem to us. She made her calculations, completed her analysis, and duly communicated the results. And then she left, serenely swinging her pigtails."

Victor got over his uneasiness and looked at Lola. Her face had broken out in red spots. Her red lips trembled as if she were about to cry, but of course she had no intention of crying; she was furious.

"You see," she said in a high voice. "A little snot-nosed bitch. Nothing's sacred to her, every word is an insult—as if I weren't her mother but a doormat for her to wipe her feet on. I can't face the neighbors. The little brat."

"Right," thought Victor. "I lived with this woman. I went for walks with her in the mountains, I read Baudelaire to her, I trembled when I touched her, I remembered her fragrance. I even got into fights over her. To this day I don't understand what was going through her mind when I read her Baudelaire. No, it's just amazing that I managed to get away from her. It boggles the mind—how did she let me? No doubt I wasn't any prize myself. No doubt I'm still no prize, but in those days I

1

drank even more than I do now, and, what's worse, I considered myself a great poet. . . ."

"Of course, this wouldn't mean anything to you, how could it?" Lola was saying. "Big city life, ballerinas, actresses . . . I know everything. Don't think that people here don't know. Your money, and your mistresses, and the constant scandals. If you want to know the truth, I'm completely indifferent to all of it. I haven't bothered you, you lived the way you wanted to."

". . . the thing that spoils her is that she talks a lot. When she was younger she was quiet, reticent, mysterious. There are women who know from birth how to carry themselves. She knew. In fact, she's not so bad now, either. When, for example, she sits on the couch holding a cigarette, silent, her knees on display. . . . Or when she suddenly puts her hands behind her head and stretches. A provincial lawyer would be terribly impressed by it." Victor imagined a comfortable tête-à-tête: an end table next to the couch, a bottle, champagne fizzing in crystal glasses, a box of chocolates tied up with a ribbon, and the lawyer himself, all starched up and wearing a bow tie. Everything just as it's supposed to be, and then Irma walks in. "Awful," thought Victor. "She must be really unhappy."

"I shouldn't have to explain to you," Lola was saying, "that it's not a matter of money. Money won't help now." She had already calmed down; the red spots had disappeared. "I know in your own way you're an honest man, capricious and disorganized, but not mean. You've always helped us financially and in this respect I'm not making any demands on you. But now I need a different sort of help. . . . I can't say I'm happy, but you never succeeded in making me unhappy either. You have your life, and I have mine. I'm still young, you know, I still have a lot ahead of me."

"I'll have to take the child," thought Victor. "Apparently she's already decided everything. If Irma stays here, it'll be sheer hell. All right, but what will I do with her? Let's be honest," he said to himself. "You have to be honest here, these aren't toys we're playing with." He very honestly recalled his life in the capital. "Bad," he thought. "Of course, I can always get a housekeeper. That means renting an apartment. But that's beside the point. She has to be with me, not with a housekeeper. They say that the best children are the ones brought up by their fathers. And I like her, even though she's very strange. And anyway, it's my duty. As an honest man, as a father. And I feel guilty about her. But all this is playacting. What if I'm really honest? If I'm really honest, then I have to admit that I'm frightened. Because she's going to stand in front of me, smiling like an adult with her wide mouth, and what will I be able to tell her? Read, read more, read every day, you don't have to do anything else, just read. She knows that without me, and I have nothing else to say to her. Which is why I'm frightened. But that's not completely honest either. I don't feel like it, that's what it is. I'm used to being alone. I like being alone. I don't want it any other way. That's the way it looks, if I'm honest. It looks disgusting, like any other truth. It looks cynical, egotistical, and low. If I'm honest."

"Why aren't you saying anything?" asked Lola. "Are you planning to just sit there and not say anything?"

"No, no, I'm listening," said Victor, hastily.

"Listening to what? I've been waiting half an hour for you to deign to respond. After all, I'm not her only parent. . . ."

"Do I have to be honest with her too?" thought Victor. "She's about the last person in the world I want to be honest with. Apparently she's decided that I can settle that sort of question right here, not leaving my seat, between cigarettes."

"Get it into your head," said Lola, "I'm not saying that you should take her. I'm well aware that you wouldn't, and thank God you wouldn't, you're no good at it. But you have connections, friends, you've still got a name. Help me set her up somewhere. There are exclusive schools, boarding schools, special institutes. After all, she's talented; she's got a gift for languages, and math, and music."

"A boarding school," said Victor. "Yes, of course. An orphanage. . . . No, I'm not serious. It's worth thinking about."

"What's there to think about? Most people would be glad to put their children in a good boarding school or special institute. Our boss's wife—"

"Listen, Lola," said Victor. "It's a good idea, I'll try and do something. But it's not that simple, it takes time. Of course I'll write—"

"You'll write! That's just like you. It's not writing you have to do, you have to go there, ask in person, beat down doors. You're not doing anything anyway! All you do is drink and hang out with sluts. Is it really that difficult, for the sake of your own daughter?"

"Oh, damn," thought Victor, "try and explain things to her." He lit another cigarette, stood, and walked around the room. Outside it was getting dark. As before, the rain was coming down in large drops, heavy and patient. There was a lot of it and it clearly wasn't hurrying anywhere.

"God, am I sick of you," said Lola with unexpected spite. "If only you knew how sick I am of you."

"Time to go," thought Victor. "It's starting in—sacred maternal wrath, the fury of the abandoned, and so forth. At any rate, I can't give her an answer today. And I'm not making any promises."

"I can't count on you for anything," she was saying. "A worthless husband, a talentless father—one of your popular writers. Couldn't bring up his own daughter. Any peasant understands people better than you do. Just what am I supposed to do now? You're no help. I'm knocking myself out all alone, and I can't get anywhere. To her I'm a nothing, a zero; any slimy is a hundred times more important to her than I am. Never mind, you'll find out. And if you don't teach her, then they will. Pretty soon, she'll be spitting in your face the way she does with me."

"Drop it, Lola," said Victor, wincing. "Somehow, you know,

you're. . . . I'm her father, true, but, after all, you're her mother. You're throwing the blame on everybody else."

"Get out," she said.

"Look," said Victor. "I have no intention of quarreling with you. But I also have no intention of making rash decisions. I'll think it over. And you—"

She was standing stiffly erect, all but trembling, savoring the intended rebuke and anticipating her entrance into the fray.

"And you," he said quietly, "try not to worry. We'll think up something. I'll call you."

He walked out into the foyer and put on his raincoat. The raincoat was still wet. Victor went into Irma's room to say good-bye, but she wasn't there. The window was wide open, and rain beat down on the windowsill. A sign in big red letters was hanging on the wall: "Please don't ever close the window." The sign was wrinkled, with dark stains on it and frayed edges, as if it had been torn down more than once and trampled underfoot. Victor closed the door softly.

"Good-bye, Lola," he said. Lola didn't answer.

Outside it was already dark. Rain drummed on his shoulders and the hood of his raincoat. Victor bent over and dug his hands deeper into his pockets. "This is the park where we kissed for the first time," he thought. "This house wasn't built yet, there was just an empty lot, and behind the lot was a garbage dump—we used to go after cats there with slingshots. There used to be a hell of a lot of cats in this town and now for some reason I never see any at all. In those days we never opened a goddamned book, and now Irma has a roomful of them. What was a twelve-year-old girl in my time? A freckled giggler. Snow White, ribbons and dolls, pictures of bunnies, whispering in twos and threes, paper cones full of candy, bad teeth. Goody-goodies and tattletales, but the best of them were like us: scraped knees, wild bobcat eyes, masters of kicks in the shin.

"So the times have finally changed, have they? No," he

thought. "It's not the times. That is, it's the times too, of course. Or maybe I've got a prodigy on my hands. There are such things as prodigies, after all, and I am the father of one. An honor, but a bother, and more of a bother than an honor—in fact, it's no honor at all. . . . I always liked this alley because it's so narrow. And wouldn't you know it, there's a fight. We just can't get along without fights, without fights we simply can't manage. Since time immemorial. And two against one."

There was a streetlight at the corner. A car with a canvas top dripped in the rain at the edge of the illuminated space. Next to the car two men in shining raincoats were forcing a third one, wearing something black and wet, down to the gutter. The three of them were stumbling along the cobblestones, awkward and strained. Victor stopped short, then moved closer. It wasn't clear exactly what was going on. It didn't look like a fight—no one was throwing any punches. Even less did it look like a scuffle from an excess of youthful energy—there was no wild whooping and braying. Suddenly the one in black, trying to tear himself free, fell on his back. The pair in raincoats jumped on top of him. Victor noticed that the doors of the car were wide open; either they had just dragged the one in black out of it, or they were trying to shove him in. Victor went up close to them and barked, "Stop!"

The pair in raincoats turned. For a split second they stared at Victor from under their pulled-up hoods. Victor noticed only that they were both young and that they were panting from the strain. Then with unbelievable speed they dove into the car, slammed the doors, and sped off into the darkness. The man in black slowly lifted himself up. Victor looked at him and took a step backward. It was a patient from the leprosarium—a "slimy," or "four-eyes" as they were sometimes called because of the yellow circles that rimmed their eyes like eyeglasses. The lower half of his face was completely covered by a black bandage. He was breathing heavily and painfully; vestiges of eyebrows were raised in a look of suffering. Water streamed down his bald head.

"What happened?" said Victor.

The four-eyes wasn't looking at him, but past him. His pupils widened. Victor wanted to turn around, but at that moment something hit him in the back of the head.

When he came to, he found himself lying face up under a drain pipe. Water was gushing into his mouth; it was warm and tasted rusty. Spluttering and coughing, he moved away and sat up with his back against the brick wall. Water that had collected in his hood poured under his collar and trickled down his body. Bells, horns, and drums reverberated in his head. Through the noise, Victor made out a thin, dark face in front of him. A boy's face. Familiar. "I've seen him somewhere. Before my jaws got smashed together." He moved his tongue around and shifted his jaw. His teeth were okay. The boy collected a handful of water from the pipe and splashed him in the face.

"Thanks, pal," said Victor. "That's enough."

"I thought that you still hadn't regained consciousness," the boy said seriously.

Carefully, Victor placed his hand under his hood and felt the back of his head. There was a lump—nothing terrible, no shattered bones, not even any blood.

"Who got me?" he asked, thoughtfully. "Not you, I hope."

"Will you be able to walk by yourself, Mr. Banev?" the boy asked. "Or should I call someone? The truth is, you're too heavy for me."

Victor remembered who it was.

"I know you," he said. "You're Bol-Kunats, my daughter's friend."

"Yes," said the boy.

"Fine. No need to call anyone and no need to say anything to anyone. Let's just sit here for a minute and pull ourselves together."

Now he could see that Bol-Kunats wasn't completely all right either. There was a fresh gash on his cheek, and his upper lip was swollen and bleeding.

"I think I'd better call someone," said Bol-Kunats.

"Why should you?"

"The truth is, Mr. Banev, I don't like the way your face is twitching."

"Really?" Victor felt his face. It wasn't twitching. "It just seems that way to you. So. Now we're going to get up. What is essential in order to get up? In order to get up, it is essential to pull your feet in under you." He pulled in his feet, which did not quite seem to belong to him. "Next, moving slightly away from the wall, shift the center of gravity in the following manner." He couldn't manage to shift his center of gravity; something was holding him back. "How did they do it?" he thought. "A good job, really."

"You're stepping on your raincoat," the boy offered, but Victor had already unraveled the mysteries of his arms, his legs, his raincoat, and the orchestra under his skull. He stood up. At first he had to support himself against the wall, but then it got better.

"Aha," he said. "So you pulled me over here, up to the pipe. Thanks."

The streetlight was still there, but the car and the four-eyes were gone. Everybody was gone. Only little Bol-Kunats was carefully stroking his cut with a wet hand.

"Where could they have gone?" asked Victor.

The boy didn't answer.

"Was I here by myself?" asked Victor. "Nobody else was around?"

"Let me accompany you," said Bol-Kunats. "Where would you prefer to go? Home?"

"Wait," said Victor. "Did you see how they wanted to make off with that four-eyes?"

"I saw someone hit you."

"Who did it?"

"I couldn't tell. His back was to me."

"And where were you?"

"The truth is, I was lying there around the corner."

"I don't get it," said Victor. "Or maybe it's my head. What were you doing lying around the corner? You live there?"

"The truth is, I was lying there because they got me even before they got you. Not the same one that got you; another one."

"The four-eyes?"

They were walking slowly, trying to keep to the roadway and avoid the runoff from the roofs.

"N-no," said Bol-Kunats, thinking. "I don't think any of them were wearing glasses."

"Oh, God," said Victor. He put his hand under his hood and felt his lump. "I'm talking about the lepers, people call them four-eyes. You know, from the leprosarium? Slimies—"

"I don't know," said Bol-Kunats shortly. "In my opinion they were all perfectly healthy."

"Come on," said Victor. He felt a little uneasy and even stopped. "Are you trying to convince me that there wasn't a leper there? Wearing a black bandage, dressed all in black?"

"That's no leper!" said Bol-Kunats with unexpected vehemence. "He's healthier than you are."

For the first time, something boyish had appeared in him. It disappeared immediately.

"I don't quite understand where we're going," he said after a short silence, in his former serious, almost impassive tone. "At first it seemed as though you were going home, but now I see that we're walking in the opposite direction."

Victor was still standing in place, looking down at him. "Two peas in a pod," he thought. "He made his calculations, completed his analysis, but decided not to communicate the results. So he's not going to tell me what happened. I wonder why not. Was it a crime? No, not likely. But maybe it was? Times have changed, you know. Nonsense, I know what criminals are like nowadays."

"Everything is under control," he said and started walking. "We're going to the hotel, I live there."

The boy walked next to him, stiff, severe, and wet. Victor

overcame a certain indecisiveness and put his hand on the boy's shoulder. Nothing special happened; the boy tolerated it. Although, most likely, he'd simply decided that his shoulder was needed for utilitarian purposes, to hold up someone in shock.

"I must say," remarked Victor in his most confiding tone, "that you and Irma have a very strange way of expressing yourselves. When we were kids we didn't talk that way."

"Really?" said Bol-Kunats politely. "And how did you talk?"

"Well, for example, with us your question would have sounded something like this: Whaaa?"

Bol-Kunats shrugged his shoulders. "Do you mean to say that it would be better like that?"

"God forbid! I only meant that it would be more natural."

"It is precisely that which is most natural," Bol-Kunats observed, "that is least fitting for man."

Victor felt a chill deep inside himself. An uneasiness. Or even fear. As if a cat had laughed in his face.

"The natural is always primitive," Bol-Kunats continued. "But man is a complex being, and naturalness is not becoming to him. Do you understand me, Mr. Banev?"

"Yes," said Victor. "Of course."

There was something incredibly false in the fatherly way he had placed his hand on the shoulder of this boy, who wasn't a boy. His elbow even began to ache. He carefully removed his hand and put it in his pocket.

"How old are you?" he asked.

"Fourteen," said Bol-Kunats absentmindedly.

"Oh."

Any ordinary boy in Bol-Kunats's place would have certainly been intrigued by the irritatingly indefinite "oh," but Bol-Kunats was not an ordinary boy. He said nothing. Intriguing interjections left him cold. He was reflecting on the interrelationship of the natural and the primitive in nature and society. He regretted having come upon such an unintelligent companion, the more so one who'd just been hit over the head.

They came out onto the Avenue of the President. Here there were many streetlights, and pedestrians, men and women hunched up under the incessant rain, hurried past. Store windows were lit up, and under an awning by the neon-bathed entrance to a movie house stood a crowd of young people of indeterminate sex, in shining raincoats down to their heels. And above everything, through the rain, shone incantations in blue and gold: "Our President is the Father of His People," "The Legionnaire of Freedom is the True Son of the President," "The Army is Our Awesome Glory."

Out of inertia they continued to walk in the roadway. A passing car honked and chased them back onto the sidewalk, splashing them with dirty water.

"And I thought you were about eighteen," said Victor.

"Whaa?" asked Bel-Kunats in a repulsive voice, and Victor laughed, relieved. All the same, this was a boy, one of your ordinary prodigies who had devoured Geibor, Zurzmansor, Fromm, and maybe even coped with Spengler.

"When I was a kid," said Victor, "I had a friend who got the idea of reading Hegel in the original. He did it, but he turned into a schizophrenic. At your age, you undoubtedly know what a schizophrenic is."

"Yes, I know," said Bol-Kunats.

"And you're not afraid?"

"No."

They reached the hotel.

"Maybe you'll come up to my room and dry off?" proposed Victor.

"Thank you. I was just about to ask your permission to come up. First of all, there is something I have to tell you, and second, I have to make a telephone call. You don't object?"

Victor didn't object. They went through the revolving door past the doorman, who took off his cap to Victor, past the sumptuous statues with their electric candelabra, and into the completely empty vestibule, permeated with odors from the restaurant. Victor felt a familiar excitement. He anticipated the coming evening, when he would be able to drink and shoot his mouth off irresponsibly and shove off onto tomorrow all of today's leftover irritations. He looked forward to seeing Yul Golem and Dr. R. Quadriga. "And maybe I'll meet someone else, and maybe something will happen—there'll be a fight, or I'll get an idea for a story. Tonight I think I'll have some marinated eel, and everything will be just fine, and I'll take the last bus to Diana's."

While Victor was getting his keys from the porter, a conversation started behind his back. Bol-Kunats was talking with the doorman.

"What the hell are you doing here," hissed the doorman, "hanging around restaurants?"

"I am having a conversation with Mr. Banev," said Bol-Kunats. "The restaurant does not interest me."

"As if a restaurant could interest you, you little punk. In one minute I'll send you packing."

Victor got his key and turned around. "Uh," he said. He had forgotten the doorman's name. "The young fellow's with me, everything's okay."

The doorman didn't answer, but he was obviously annoyed.

They went up to his room. With great enjoyment, Victor threw off his raincoat and bent over to untie his soggy shoes. The blood went to his head, and he felt painful, intermittent throbs coming from the vicinity of his lump. The lump itself was heavy and round, like a leaden egg. He straightened out immediately and, holding onto the doorjamb, pushed off one shoe with his other foot. Bol-Kunats stood next to him, dripping wet.

"Take off your things," said Victor. "Hang everything on the radiator, I'll get you a towel."

"If you don't object, I'll make a phone call," said Bol-Kunats, not budging from the spot.

"Go to it." Victor kicked off his other shoe and went to the bathroom in his wet socks. Undressing, he could hear the boy talking quietly and calmly. He couldn't make anything out. Only once, the boy said loudly and clearly, "I don't know." Victor rubbed himself dry and threw on a robe. He found a clean bath towel and went back into the room.

"This is for you," he said and saw immediately that there was no need for it. As before, Bol-Kunats was standing by the door, and as before he was dripping wet.

"Thank you," he said. "The truth is, I have to be going. There's just one more thing I'd like to—"

"You'll come down with a cold," said Victor.

"No, don't worry, thank you. I won't come down with a cold. There's just one more matter I'd like to clarify with you. Irma hasn't told you anything?"

Victor threw the bath towel on the couch, squatted down in front of the liquor cabinet, and pulled out a bottle and a glass.

"Irma has told me a lot of things," he answered rather sullenly. He poured some gin into the glass.

"She didn't pass on our invitation?"

"No. She didn't pass on any invitations. Here, have a drink."

"Thank you, I'd rather not. Since she didn't tell you, then I will. We would like to meet with you, Mr. Banev."

"Who's 'we'?"

"The pupils of our school. The truth is, we have read your books and would like to ask you a few questions."

"Hm," said Victor doubtfully. "You're sure that everybody would be interested in this?"

"I think so."

"I don't exactly write for middle-school students," Victor reminded him.

"That doesn't matter," said Bol-Kunats with gentle persistence. "Will you accept?"

Victor thoughtfully stirred the transparent liquid in his glass.

"Maybe you'll have some anyway?" he asked. "Best way to avoid a cold. No? Then I will." He downed the glass. "All right,

I accept. Only no posters, no announcements. A small group. You and your friends, and me. When will it be?"

"Whenever it's convenient for you. It would be best to have it this week. In the morning."

"Let's say two days from now. Only not too early. Let's say Friday at eleven. Is that all right with you?"

"Yes. Friday at eleven, at the school. Should we remind you?"

"By all means," said Victor. "I always do my best to forget about soirees and banquets, not to mention meetings, receptions, and conferences."

"Good, I'll remind you," said Bol-Kunats. "And now, with your permission, I'll go. Good-bye, Mr. Banev."

"Wait, I'll take you down," said Victor. "So the doorman doesn't insult you. For some reason he's out of sorts today, and doormen being doormen, as you know—"

"Thank you, don't trouble yourself," said Bol-Kunats. "He's my father."

And he left. Victor poured himself some more gin and fell into an armchair. "So," he thought. "The poor doorman. What on earth is his name? It's awkward. Still, he and I are comrades in misfortune, colleagues. I'll have to talk with him, share experiences. No doubt he's had more experience. But what a concentration of prodigies in my dank little hometown. Maybe from the increase in humidity." He threw his head back and winced from the pain. "That bastard, how did he do it, anyhow?" He felt his lump. "Very likely a hard rubber nightstick. Although how would I know what you get from a hard rubber nightstick. I know what you get from a Danish modern chair in the Grilled Pegasus. From the butt of a submachine gun, or, for example, the handle of a pistol. From champagne bottles with and without champagne. I'll have to ask Golem. All in all, it's a strange business. I'd like to know what's going on." He started to think about it, in order to drive away the thought about Irma that was surfacing from some secondary level—the necessity of giving something up, accepting some limitations, or else sending off letters and asking for favors. " 'Sorry to bother you, old man, but I've got this daughter here. She's a bit over twelve, a terrific little girl, but her mother's a fool and her father's a fool too, so it would be good to set her up somewhere far away from such stupid people.' I don't want to think about it today, I'll think about it tomorrow." He looked at his watch. "Anyhow, I've done enough thinking. Enough."

He got up and began to dress in front of the mirror. "I'm getting a paunch, damn it, why should I be getting a paunch? I was always the lean, sinewy type. It's not even a paunch, exactly, your noble, working paunch from a life of moderation and good food. Just a lousy little paunchlet, a dissident's tummy. I'm sure Mr. President's is quite different. Mr. President's, I'm sure, is a noble, glossy, draped-in-black dirigible." He straightened his tie, moved his face closer to the mirror, and thought suddenly, "Observe this confident strong face, so beloved by women of a certain sort. Not a handsome face. Rather the courageous face of a fighter, with a square chin. And what did this face look like at the end of the historic encounter? . . . The face of Mr. President is also not lacking in courage or rectangularity, but at the end of the historic encounter it looked, if we come right out with it, between you and me, like a wild boar's snout. Mr. President had been pleased to work himself up into a terrible state. Spit was flying from his tusked maw, and I took out a handkerchief and conspicuously wiped off my cheek. It was probably the most courageous act of my life, if you don't count the time I fought three tanks at once. But I don't remember how I fought the tanks, I only know about it from the stories of eyewitnesses. But I got out my handkerchief consciously and with full awareness of what I was headed for. . . . The papers didn't write about it. Our honest and courageous papers reported with sober frankness that belletrist V. Banev sincerely thanked Mr. President for the observations and explanations made in the course of their talk."

"It's strange how well I remember it all." He discovered that his cheeks and the tip of his nose had turned pale. "That's the way I looked then—who wouldn't go after a guy who looked like that? The old wreck couldn't have known that I wasn't turning pale from fear but from anger, like Louis XIV. But let's stop waving our fists after the fight. What difference does it make what I was turning pale from? Okay, we'll stop. But in order to calm down, in order to get things under control before appearing in company, and return a homely but courageous face to its normal color, I must observe, Mr. Banev, and I must remind you, that if you hadn't flaunted your handkerchief in front of Mr. President, at the present moment you would be biding your time in our glorious capital, under the most pleasant conditions, and not in this wet hole."

Victor finished off the gin and went down to the restaurant.

Chapter II

"Of course they could have been muggers," said Victor. "Only in my day no mugger would think of taking on a four-eyes. To throw a stone at one—well, all right. But to grab one, drag him around, and above all touch him. . . . We were all afraid of them, we thought it was catching."

"I'm telling you, it's a genetic disease," said Golem. "You can't catch anything from them."

"What do you mean you can't," said Victor. "They give you warts, just like toads. Everybody knows that."

"You can't get warts from toads," said Golem expansively. "You can't get them from slimies either. You should be ashamed of yourself, my dear writer. Though writers en masse are notoriously dense."

"Like all masses. The masses are dense, but they are wise. And if the masses declare that toads and slimies give warts—"

"If it isn't my inspector coming toward us," said Golem.

Pavor walked over to them. He was wearing a wet raincoat, right from the street.

"Hello," he said. "I'm soaked to the skin, I want a drink."

"He smells like slime again," grumbled Dr. R. Quadriga, awakening from an alcoholic trance. "He always smells like slime. Like a pond. Duckweed."

"What are you drinking?" asked Pavor.

"It depends," said Golem. "I, for one, am drinking cognac. As usual. Victor is having gin. And the doctor is having one of everything."

"Shame!" muttered Dr. R. Quadriga. "Scales. And gills."

"A double cognac," Pavor shouted to the waiter.

His face was wet from the rain. His thick hair hung in clumps, and shining rivulets flowed down from his temples along his smoothly shaven cheeks. "Another hard face," thought Victor. "A lot of people must envy him. How did a health inspector get a face like that? A hard face. I can see it. The rain is pouring, there are searchlights. Shadows flash along the wet trains and break off. Everything is dark and glittering, nothing but darkness and glitter. No discussions, no bullshit, only orders, and everyone obeys. It doesn't have to be a train, maybe an airplane, the airfield, and later nobody knows where he came from. Girls are falling over backwards, and men feel like doing something manly. Like straightening their shoulders and pulling in their stomachs. Take Golem. It wouldn't hurt Golem to pull in his stomach. But it won't work, where could he pull it, there's no room left. Or Dr. R. Quadriga. But he wouldn't be able to straighten his shoulders, he's been bent over for a long time, forever. In the evening he's bent over the table, in the morning he's bent over a basin, and during the day he's bent over because his liver hurts him. So I'm the only one capable of pulling in my stomach and straightening my shoulders. But I think I'll direct my manliness toward this glass of gin."

"Nymphomaniac," moaned Dr. R. Quadriga to Pavor. "Mermaidomaniac. And seaweed."

"Pipe down, Doctor," said Pavor. He was wiping his face with paper napkins, which he then crumpled up and threw on the floor. Then he started to wipe his hands.

"You've been fighting," said Victor. "Who with?"

"Raped by a slimy," remarked Dr. R. Quadriga, trying desperately to focus his pupils which had wandered off toward his nose.

"Not with anyone yet," answered Pavor. He gave the doctor a long look. The doctor failed to notice it.

The waiter brought the cognac. Pavor slowly drained his glass and stood up.

"I think I'll go get washed," he said in an even voice. "Nothing but mud in the country, I've got shit all over me." He left, colliding with the chairs.

"Something is happening to my inspector," said Golem. He flicked a wet napkin off the table. "Something of universal proportions. You wouldn't happen to know what exactly?"

"You should know better than I do," said Victor. "He's inspecting you, not me. And then you know everything. Incidentally, Golem, how did you get to know everything?"

"Nobody knows anything," objected Golem. "Some people have their suspicions. Very few—those who want to. But you can't ask how they have their suspicions. Where is it raining to? What does the sun come up with? Would you forgive Shakespeare if he wrote something like that? Actually, you probably would. We can forgive Shakespeare a lot, he's not Banev. But listen, my dear man of letters, I've got an idea. I'll polish off my cognac, and you finish this gin. Or are you already plowed?"

"Golem," said Victor, "did you know I'm a man of iron?"

"I suspected as much."

"And what follows from that?"

"You're afraid of rusting."

"Well, okay," said Victor. "But that's not what I mean. I mean that I can drink a lot and at length without losing my moral equilibrium."

"Oh, I see," said Golem, pouring himself cognac from a decanter. "We'll take up this topic again."

"I can't seem to recall," said Dr. R. Quadriga suddenly in a clear voice. "Have I introduced myself to you gentlemen? My pleasure: Rem Quadriga, artist, doctor honoris causae, honorable associate. . . . You I remember," he said to Victor. "We were in school together, etc., etc. As for you, excuse me. . . ."

"My name is Yul Golem," said Golem carelessly.

"S'my pleazhure. A sculptor?"

"No. Physician."

"Surgeon?"

"The chief physician of the leprosarium," Golem explained patiently.

"Oh, yes," said Dr. R. Quadriga, shaking his head like a horse. "Of course. Sorry, Yul. Only why the big front? You're no doctor. You're breeding slimies. I'll get you an introduction. We need people like you. Excuse me," he said suddenly. "I'll be right back."

He got out of his armchair and wandered off toward the exit through a maze of empty chairs. A waiter hurried over to him, and Quadriga threw his arms around his neck.

"It's the rain," said Golem. "We're breathing water. This city has been breathing water for three years. But we're not fish, and either we're going to die, or we're going to get out of here." He looked at Victor seriously and sadly. "And the rain will fall on an empty city, it will wash the pavements, soak through the roofs, the rotting roofs. Then it will wash everything away, the city will dissolve into primordial earth, but it still won't stop, it will keep falling and falling."

"The apocalypse," said Victor, in order to say something.

"Yes, the apocalypse. It will rain and rain and the earth will drink its fill. The earth will be sown anew and as never before, and there shall be no weeds among the grain. But we won't be around to enjoy it."

"If only he didn't have those gray bags under his eyes," Victor thought, "and that soft sagging belly. If only his great Semitic nose looked a little less like a topographical map. Only, if you think for a minute, prophets have always been drunkards, because it's so depressing: you know everything, and nobody believes you. If we made a government position out of it, then our state prophet would have to have a rank no less than Secret Councillor in order to strengthen his authority. And still it probably wouldn't help."

"For his systematic pessimism," Victor said aloud, "which has subverted professional discipline and undermined faith in a rational future, I hereby order Secret Councillor Golem to be stoned in the executing chamber."

Golem snorted.

"I'm only a collegiate councillor," he said. "And then, what kind of prophets do we have nowadays? I don't know a single one. A lot of false prophets and not a single real one. In our times you can't predict the future—it's a linguistic impossibility. What would you say if you saw in Shakespeare something like 'predict the present'? Can you predict a bureau in your own bedroom? But I believe that's my inspector coming. How are you this evening, inspector?"

"Wonderful," said Pavor, taking a seat. "Waiter, a double cognac! Our artist is in the lobby surrounded by four big men. They're trying to tell him where the entrance to the restaurant is. I decided not to intrude. He doesn't believe anyone and he's in a fighting mood. But what bureaus were you talking about?"

He was dry, elegant, fresh; he smelled of cologne.

"We were speaking about the future," said Golem.

"What sense does it make to talk about the future?" objected Pavor. "The future isn't talked about, the future is made. Here's a glass of cognac. The glass is full. I will make it empty. Like this. A wise man once said that you can only invent the future, you can't predict it."

"Another wise man," observed Victor, "said that the future doesn't exist, there's only the present."

"I don't like nineteenth-century philosophy," said Pavor. "Those people couldn't and wouldn't do anything. They just liked to sit around and reason, in the same way as Golem likes to sit around and drink. The future is just a thoroughly cleaned-up present."

"I always feel funny," said Golem, "when I hear a civilian reasoning like a soldier."

"Soldiers don't reason," objected Pavor. "All they have are reflexes and a little bit of emotion."

"You could say the same thing about most civilians," said Victor, stroking the back of his head.

"Right now nobody has time for reasoning," said Pavor. "Neither soldiers nor civilians. We barely have time to cope. If you're interested in the future, then invent it quickly, on the run, according to your reflexes and emotions."

"The hell with inventors," said Victor. He felt drunk and a little giddy. Everything was as it should be. He didn't want to go anywhere, he wanted to stay where he was, in the half-darkness of this empty, not quite dilapidated hall, with its stained walls, loose floorboards, and kitchen smells. Especially since it was raining outside, raining over the whole world, over the cobblestoned pavements and the peaked roofs, over the hills and valleys. "Someday the rain will wash everything away, but that won't happen for a while . . . although, if you think about it, you can't say that it would be very long either. Yes, my friends, the time is long past when the future was nothing but a repetition of the present and changes hovered on a far horizon. Golem's right: there's no future anymore, it's merged with the present, and now you can't tell the difference."

"Raped by a slimy," said Pavor maliciously.

Dr. R. Quadriga appeared at the restaurant door. For a few seconds he stood in place, staring heavily at the rows of empty tables. Then his face brightened. In a sudden burst of speed, he made for his seat.

"Why do you call them slimies?" asked Victor. "Did they get moldy from all the rain?"

"Why not?" said Pavor. "What would you prefer?"

"Four-eyes," said Victor. "A good old word. Since time immemorial."

Dr. R. Quadriga was approaching. In front he was sopping wet—somebody had probably washed him over a sink. He looked tired and disillusioned.

"Goddamnit," he grumbled, still some distance away. "That never happened to me before. There wasn't any entrance. No matter where you turn, nothing but windows. . . . I seem to have made you wait, gentlemen." He fell into his chair and saw Pavor. "He's here again," he informed Golem in a confidential whisper. "I hope he's not disturbing you. But you know, the most amazing thing just happened to me. They got me all wet."

Golem poured him some cognac.

"Much obliged," said R. Quadriga, "but I think I'll skip a few rounds. I've got to dry out."

"In general," said Victor, "I'm for good old things. Let four-eyes stay four-eyes. And in general I don't want to see any changes. I'm a conservative. Attention!" he said in a loud voice. "I propose a toast to conservatism. One minute." He poured himself some gin and stood up, leaning on the back of the chair. "I'm a conservative," he said. "And every year I get more conservative, only not because I'm getting older, but because I feel that way."

Pavor, sober, his glass suspended in midair, was looking at him with pointed attention. Golem slowly ate his marinated eel, and Dr. R. Quadriga seemed overwhelmed by the problem of who was talking. Everything was fine.

"People love to criticize the government for being too conservative," Victor continued. "People love to extol progress. This is a new tendency, and it's stupid, like everything else that's new. People should pray God for the most sluggish, backward, conformist government possible."

Now even Golem raised his eyes and looked at him, and Teddy stopped wiping bottles at the bar and strained to listen. But then the back of his head began to ache, and he had to put down his glass and rub his lump.

"The government apparatus, gentlemen, has throughout time considered its primary task to be the maintenance of the status quo. I don't know to what extent this was justified before, but now it's absolutely necessary. I would formulate it as follows: do everything possible to prevent the future from extending its feelers into our own time, chop off these feelers, or sear them with hot iron. Make it hard for inventors, but encourage windbags and pedants. Institute an exclusively classical education in all schools. All candidates for the highest government posts should be old codgers burdened with families and debts, minimal age fifty, to foster bribe-taking and sleeping at committee meetings."

"What's all this bullshit for, Victor," said Pavor reproachfully.

"Why, what's wrong with it?" said Golem. "It's a rare pleasure to hear a speech of such moderation and loyalty."

"I haven't finished yet, gentlemen! Talented scientists should be turned into highly paid administrators. All inventions are to be accepted and then shelved. Inventors must be poorly paid. Draconic taxes should be extracted for all commercial or industrial innovations." "Why am I standing up anyway," thought Victor suddenly and sat down. "Well, how do you like it?" he asked Golem.

"You are absolutely right," said Golem. "We have nothing but radicals around here. Even the director of the middle school. Conservatism is our only salvation."

Victor tossed off his gin. He was starting to get pathetic. "There isn't going to be any salvation. Because all these idiot radicals don't only believe in progress, they love it, they think they can't live without it. Because progress, in addition to everything else, means cheap cars, domestic gadgets, more for less. So every government is forced to use one hand—that is to say, not a hand, of course—to use one foot to step on the brakes and the other to step on the gas. Like a racing car driver on a curve. The brakes keep you from losing control and the gas keeps you from losing speed, so that some demagogic champion of progress doesn't shove you out of the driver's seat."

"It's difficult to argue with you," Pavor said politely.

"Don't," said Victor. "It's a bad idea. Arguments may, God forbid, yield truth." He tenderly stroked his lump. "However, this is no doubt the result of my ignorance. All scientists are champions of progress and I'm not a scientist. All I am is a not unknown versifier."

"Why do you keep poking at the back of your head?" asked Pavor.

"Some bastard lit into me," said Victor. "With brass knuckles. Am I right, Golem? Brass knuckles?"

"Looks like it," said Golem. "Although it could have been a brick."

"What are you talking about?" said Pavor. "What brass knuckles? In this backwoods?"

"So you see," said Victor in a didactic tone. "Progress. Let's have another drink to conservatism."

They had another drink to conservatism. The clock struck nine. A familiar pair appeared in the hall, a young man with thick glasses and his lanky companion. They took their accustomed seats, lit the table lamp, meekly glanced around the room, and set to studying the menu. The man in glasses had, as usual, come with his attaché case, which he put on an empty armchair next to him. He was always very kind to his attaché case. The two dictated their order to the waiter, straightened up, and stared silently into space. "A strange pair," thought Victor. "An astonishing lack of correspondence. As though you were seeing them through bad binoculars—as soon as one comes into focus, the other fades out, and vice versa. Complete incompatibility. You could have a chat about progress with the one in glasses, but not with the lanky one. Whereas the lanky one could slug me with a set of brass knuckles, but not the one in glasses. But now I'm going to bring you both into focus. Only how? Well, let's see. . . . The cellar of some government bank. Cement, concrete, a security system. The lanky one works on the combination lock and the steel block rotates, revealing the entrance to the depository. The two enter, the lanky one works on a second combination lock, the doors of the safe roll back, and the one in glasses is up to his elbows in diamonds."

Dr. R. Quadriga suddenly burst into tears and grabbed Victor's hand.

"Sleep," he said. "My place. All right?"

Victor rushed to pour him some more gin. Quadriga gulped it down and wiped his chin.

"My place. My villa. There's a fountain. All right?"

"A fountain—that's a good one," said Victor, putting him off. "What else?"

"A cellar," moaned Quadriga. "Footprints. Frightening. It's awful. Want to buy it?"

"Make it a gift," said Victor.

Quadriga blinked. "Can't do it," he said.

"Tightwad," Victor reproached him. "Comes from your childhood. Can't spare your villa. Well, go choke on it."

"You don't like me," said Dr. R. Quadriga bitterly. "Nobody likes me."

"What about Mr. President?" Victor was getting aggressive.

"The president is the father of his people," said Quadriga, livening up. "A sketch in gold tones. 'The President in the Trenches.' A fragment from a painting: 'The President in the Trenches During the Shelling.' "

"What else?" inquired Victor.

" 'The President in a Cloak,' " said Quadriga quickly. "A panel. Panorama."

Victor got bored. He cut himself a slice of marinated eel and started listening to Golem.

"I'll tell you what, Pavor," Golem was saying. "Leave me alone. What else can I do? I showed you our books. I'm ready to sign your report. If you want to make a complaint about the soldiers, go ahead. If you want to make a complaint about me—"

"I don't want to write about you," said Pavor, pressing his hands to his heart.

"Then don't."

"Then tell me what to do. Can't you give me some idea of what to do?"

"This is deadly, gentlemen," said Victor. "I'm taking off."

Nobody paid attention to him. He pushed the table aside and stood up. Feeling very drunk, he moved toward the bar. The bald barman was wiping bottles. He looked at Victor without curiosity.

"The usual?" he said.

"Wait," said Victor. "What did I want to ask you . . . Oh, yes. How's it going, Teddy?"

"It's raining," said Teddy shortly and poured him some hundred-and-fifty-proof.

"Lousy weather we're having," said Victor and leaned against the bar. "What does your barometer say?"

Teddy stuck a hand under the bar and got out his weatherwhiz. The three pins were pressed tightly against the shining, almost lacquered handle.

"No clearing," said Teddy, studying the weatherwhiz. "The devil's own invention." He thought for a minute and added: "But who knows, it might have broken a long time ago. How many years has it been raining?"

"Take a trip to the Sahara," proposed Victor.

Teddy smirked. "It's funny," he said. "This friend of yours, Pavor, a funny business, offered me two hundred crowns for this hunk of wood."

"He was probably drunk," said Victor. "What does he need it for?"

"That's what I told him." Teddy turned the weatherwhiz in his hands and held it up to his right eye. "I won't give it away," he declared. "Let him get one for himself." He shoved the weatherwhiz under the bar, looked at Victor playing with his glass, and added, "That Diana of yours stopped by."

"A long time ago?" asked Victor carelessly.

"Around five. I gave her a case of cognac. Rosheper is on a binge, he can't stop. He's sending his whole staff out for cognac. The filthy bastard. A member of parliament. Aren't you worried about her?"

Victor shrugged. He suddenly saw Diana standing next to him. She took shape next to the bar in a wet slicker with the hood pulled down. She wasn't looking in his direction. He saw only her profile, and he thought that of all the women he had ever known, she was the most beautiful and that in all likelihood he would never have another one like her. She was leaning against the table, her face was terribly pale and terribly indifferent, and she was the most beautiful—everything about her was beautiful. And always. When she cried, when she laughed, when she got mad, and when she didn't give a damn, and when she was freezing cold, and especially when she was in one of her moods. "God am I drunk," thought Victor, "I probably reek of liquor, like Quadriga." He stuck out his lower lip and exhaled. "Can't tell."

"The roads are wet and slippery," Teddy was saying. "It's foggy . . . and then, you know this Rosheper is a real womanizer, a dirty old man."

"Rosheper is impotent," objected Victor, mechanically swallowing his hundred-and-fifty-proof.

"Did she tell you that?"

"Drop it, Teddy," said Victor. "Forget it."

Teddy stared at him for a moment and sighed. Grunting, he squatted down, rummaged around under the bar, and came up with a bottle of liquid ammonia and an opened packet of tea. Victor glanced at the clock, then started watching Teddy slowly get out a clean glass, fill it with club soda, add a few drops of ammonia, and in the same deliberate manner stir the mixture with a swizzle stick. Teddy pushed the glass toward Victor. Victor drank it and made a face, holding his breath. The repulsively fresh stream of ammonia exploded in his brain and spread somewhere behind his eyes. Victor drew in a slow breath of air that had become unbearably cold, and stuck his fingers into the packet of tea.

"All right, Teddy," he said. "Thanks. Charge everything to my account. They'll tell you how much. I'm going."

Concentrating on chewing the tea leaves, he returned to his table. The young man in glasses and his lanky companion were wolfing down their dinner. The single bottle on the table was local mineral water. Pavor and Golem had cleared away a place on the tablecloth and were playing dice, and Dr. R. Quadriga was holding his shaggy head and muttering over and over again: " 'The Legion of Freedom is the Backbone of the President.' A mosaic. . . . 'on the Happy Anniversary of Your Highnesses' Birth.' 'The President is the Father of His Children.' An allegorical painting. . . ."

"I'm leaving," said Victor.

"Too bad," said Golem. "However, I wish you good luck."

"Say hello to Rosheper," said Pavor, winking.

"Member of Parliament Rosheper Nant," Quadriga perked up. "A portrait. Not too expensive. Waist-length."

Victor picked up his lighter and pack of cigarettes and left. Behind him Quadriga pronounced in a clear voice: "I believe, gentlemen, that it's time we became acquainted. The name is Rem Quadriga, doctor honoris causae, but as for you, my dear sirs, I can't seem. . . ." At the door, Victor bumped into the fat coach of the soccer team Brothers in Reason. The coach was wet and looked worried. He let Victor pass.

Chapter III

THE BUS STOPPED. "Here we are," said the driver.

"Is this the health resort?" asked Victor. Outside the bus, the fog was dense and milky. The beam of the headlights dissolved into it, and nothing could be seen.

"The resort, what else?" muttered the driver, lighting a cigarette.

Victor walked toward the exit. "Some fog," he said, stepping off the bus. "Can't see a thing."

"You'll get there," the driver promised indifferently. He spit out the window. "They really picked a good place for a health resort. Fog all day, fog at night. . . ."

"Have a nice trip back," said Victor.

The driver didn't answer. The engine whined, the doors slammed shut, and the huge, empty bus made its turn, its glass lit up from inside like a department store closed for the night. No more than a dull spot of light, it sped off to the city. Victor felt his way along the iron railing, found the gate, and stumbled along the path. Now that his eyes had gotten used to the darkness, he could distinguish the brightly lit windows of the right half of the building and the impenetrable darkness of the left half, where the Brothers in Reason slept soundly after a full day's action in the rain. Through the fog, as though through cotton wadding, you could hear the usual health resort din: the sound of a stereo, the clank of dishes, somebody's hoarse shout. Victor forged ahead, trying to keep to the middle of the sandy path so as not to knock into some plaster vase.

He kept the bottle of gin clasped to his breast and was very careful, but, all the same, he tripped over something soft and had to stumble ahead on all fours. From behind him came a halfhearted curse and a suggestion that he should have turned the lights on. In the semidarkness Victor fumbled for the fallen bottle, again clasped it to his breast, and went on, feeling his way with his free hand. He collided with a parked car, maneuvered around it, and collided with another one. Nothing but goddamned cars in this place. Victor, cursing, wound his way through them as though through a labyrinth, and for a long time could not get near the murky glow that indicated the entrance to the lobby. The smooth sides of the cars were wet from the condensed fog. Somewhere close there was romping and giggling.

This time the lobby was empty. Nobody was playing blindman's buff, nobody was jiggling his fat ass in a game of tag or sleeping in the armchairs. Everywhere there wore crumpled raincoats, and some joker had put a hat on a rubber tree. Victor climbed the carpeted staircase up to the second floor. Music blared. On the right half of the corridor, the doors leading to the Member of Parliament's suite were wide opened, exuding a rich odor of food, smoke, and overheated bodies. Victor turned left and knocked on the door to Diana's room. Nobody answered. The door was closed, but the key was in the keyhole. Victor walked in, turned on the light, and put the gin on the night table. He heard footsteps and looked out. A tall man in a dark evening suit was retreating along the corridor with a firm, wide step. He stopped at the mirrored landing, and, craning his neck, fixed his tie. Victor had time to observe his swarthy, faintly yellow eagle's profile with its sharp chin. And then something happened to the man: he let his shoulders sag, leaned slightly on one foot, and, swaying his hips in a repulsive manner, disappeared into one of the opened doors. "Fop," thought Victor, not quite sure of himself. "Went to take a puke." He looked to the left. It was dark.

Victor took off his raincoat. He left the room, locked the

door, and went to look for Diana. "I'll have to look in at Rosheper's," he thought. "Where else could she be?"

Rosheper had a three-room suite. The first one contained the remains of a recent feast. The tables were covered with soiled cloths and piled up with dirty plates, ashtrays, bottles, and crumpled napkins. There was nobody left, except a single solitary bald head, dripping with sweat and snoring away into a gravy dish.

In the adjoining room all hell had broken loose. Half-naked girls, imported from the capital, were kicking their legs on Rosheper's enormous bed. They were playing some strange game with an apoplectically purple gentleman, his honor the burgomaster, who was diving into them like a pig into a pile of acorns, kicking and grunting with enjoyment. Among the other guests were his honor the police chief, out of uniform, his honor the city judge, eyes popping from nervous exhaustion, and some unknown hustling type dressed in lilac. The latter were competing furiously in a game of miniature billiards that had been propped up on a dressing table, while in the corner, slumped against the wall and arrayed in a filthy state uniform, sat the director of the middle school, smiling idiotically, his legs spread wide apart. Victor was on his way out when someone grabbed at his trouser leg. He looked down and took a step backwards. Beneath him, on all fours, was the Knight of the Orders, author of a widely circulated project for fish breeding in the Kitchigan Reservoirs, Member of Parliament Rosheper Nant.

"I want to play horsey," whined Rosheper. "Let's play horsey! Giddy-yap!" He was beside himself.

Victor delicately freed his leg and glanced into the next room. There he saw Diana. At first he didn't even realize that it was her, and when he did he didn't like it. "Very nice," he thought. The room was full; men and women, all vague acquaintances, were standing in a circle and clapping. In the center of the circle Diana was engaged in a wild dance with the sallow-faced fop, the owner of the eagle's profile. Her eyes burned, her cheeks burned, her hair flew above her shoulders, the devil himself was no match for her. The eagle's profile was trying his best to keep up.

"Funny," thought Victor. "What's going on?" Something was not quite right. "He's a good dancer, he's just a terrific dancer. He could teach dancing. He's not just dancing, he's demonstrating how it should be done. He's not even a teacher, he's a student at an exam, and he really wants an A. No, that's not it. Listen, pal, you're dancing with Diana! Can you really be unaware of that?" Victor made his habitual imaginative leap. "An actor is dancing on the stage, everything is fine, everything is the way it should be, without any wrinkles, while at home there is suffering . . . no, not necessarily suffering, they're just waiting for him to return, and he's also waiting for the curtain to fall and the lights to go out . . . and he's not even an actor, he's an outsider, playing an actor who's playing another outsider, this time a real one. Can't she feel it? This is false. He's a mannequin. There's no closeness between them, not a drop of seduction, not a shadow of desire. They're saying something to one another, it's impossible to figure out what. Chitter-chatter. 'Aren't you hot?' 'Yes, I've read it, it's marvelous. . . .' "

Then he saw Diana pushing aside the guests and running toward him.

"Let's dance," she shouted when she was still far away.

Someone barred her path, someone else grabbed her hand, and she tore herself free, laughing, but Victor kept on looking for her sallow-faced companion. He couldn't find him, and that disturbed him.

Diana finally reached him, hooked her fingers in his sleeves, and dragged him into the circle.

"Come on, come on! They're all ours—boozers, whoozers, losers. Show them how to do it! That fledgling can't do a thing."

She dragged him into the circle. Someone in the crowd shouted, "Hurrah for our writer Banev!" The stereo, silent for a moment, once again groaned and clattered. Diana pressed against him and then moved back; she smelled of perfume and wine, her body burned, and Victor was blind to everything but her face, aroused and beautiful, and her streaming hair.

"Dance!" she shouted, and he started dancing. "I'm glad you came."

"Right."

"Why are you sober? You're always sober when you shouldn't be."

"I'll get drunk."

"Today I need you drunk."

"You'll have me."

"So I can do whatever I want to with you. Not you with me, but me with you."

"Right."

She laughed, satisfied, and they danced in silence, seeing nothing and not thinking about anything. As in a dream. Or a battle. That's the way she was now—like a dream, like a battle. Diana in one of her moods. Around them people were clapping and shouting, and somebody tried to cut in but Victor pushed him out of the way, and Rosheper gave a drawn-out cry: "Oh, my poor drunken people!"

"He's impotent?"

"Completely. I give him his bath."

"Well?"

"Nothing happens."

"Oh, my poor drunken city!" moaned Rosheper.

Victor took her by the hand and led her away. The boozers and whoozers made way for them, stinking of liquor and garlic. At the door a thick-lipped punk with flushed cheeks said something rude, itching for a fight, but Victor told him, "Later, later," and the punk disappeared. Holding hands, they ran along the empty corridor. Without letting go of her hand, Victor opened the door, and, without letting go of her hand, locked it again from the inside. It was hot, it had become unbearably hot and close. The room pulsated around them, and then it became narrow and confining, and Victor got up and threw open the window. The damp black air poured onto his naked shoulders and chest. He got back onto the bed, fumbled in the darkness for the bottle of gin, took a swig, and handed it to Diana. Then he stretched out. To his left was a stream of cold air, and to his right it was warm, silky, and soft. Now he could hear that the carousing was still going on—the guests were singing in chorus.

"How long are they going to keep at it?" he asked.

"At what?" said Diana sleepily.

"At this howling."

"I don't know. What difference does it make?" She turned on her side and put her cheek on his shoulder. "I'm cold," she complained.

They disentangled and crawled under the blanket.

"Don't sleep," he said.

"Uhuh," she mumbled.

"Are you happy?"

"Uhuh."

"What if we try your ear?"

"Uhuh. . . . Leave me alone, it hurts!"

"Look, do you think I could stay here for a week?"

"Sure."

"Where?"

"I want to sleep. Let a poor drunken woman get some sleep."

Victor fell silent but didn't move. Diana was already sleeping. "So that's what I'll do," he thought. "It'll be nice and quiet here. Except at night. Or maybe even at night. He's not going to booze it up every night. After all, he's taking a cure here. Stay here for three or four days . . . or five or six. Drink less . . . not drink at all . . . and get some work done. It's been a long time. To start working, you have to get really bored, so bored that you don't feel like doing anything else." He dozed off, then jerked awake. "Oh, yeah, Irma. I'll write to Rots-Tusov, that's what I'll do. If only he doesn't squirm out of it, the coward. Owes me nine hundred crowns. When it comes to Mr. President, nothing really matters, we all turn into cowards. Wonder why? What are we all so afraid of? Change, that's what. No more going into the writers' bar and polishing off a glass of hundred-and-fifty-proof, no more bows from the doorman, no more doormen—they'll make you the doorman. If they send you to the mines, that's really bad. But that's an exception, times have changed, a weakening of morals. I've thought about it a hundred times, and a hundred times I've decided that there's nothing to be afraid of, but I still am. Because it's a blind force," he thought. "It's a terrible thing when there's a blind, pigheaded, pig-bodied force pitted against you, impervious to logic and emotion. No Diana either."

He dozed off and woke up again. Through his open window came loud talk and hoarse animal laughter. Branches were snapping.

"I can't lock them up," said the drunken voice of the police chief. "There's no law for that."

"There will be," said the voice of Rosheper. "Am I a legislator or not?"

"Where is the law that says there has to be a hotbed of infection right outside of town?" barked the burgomaster.

"There will be," said Rosheper stubbornly.

"They're not infectious," bleated the falsetto of the middle-school director. "I mean medically speaking."

"Hey, middle school," said Rosheper. "Don't forget to pull your zipper down."

"Where is the law that says you can bankrupt honest citizens?" barked the burgomaster. "Where does it say that?"

"There will be, I'm telling you," Rosheper said. "Am I a legislator or not?"

"What can I throw at those assholes?" Victor thought.

"Rosheper!" said the police chief. "Aren't we buddies anymore? I nursed you along, you son of a bitch. I elected you, you son of a bitch. And now those germs are all over the place, and I can't do anything. There's no law, understand?"

"There will be," said Rosheper. "Take my word for it. In view of the poisoning of the atmosphere—"

"Moral atmosphere," put in the middle-school director. "Moral and ethical."

"What are you talking about? I'm telling you, in view of the poisoning of the atmosphere and taking into account the poor spawning of fish in the neighboring reservoirs, the germs are to be liquidated and reestablished in a remote province. How's that?"

"How about a kiss from me?" said the police chief.

"Good boy," said the burgomaster. "What a mind. From me too."

"Peanuts," said Rosheper. "Nothing to it. Want to sing? On the contrary, I don't. Let's have another drink and go home."

"That's right. Another drink, and back home."

Once again there was a sound of snapping branches, and Rosheper said from somewhere in the distance, "Hey, middle school, you forgot to zip it up." Then there was silence. Victor dozed off again, slept through an insignificant dream, and then the telephone rang.

"Hello," said Diana hoarsely. "Yes, it's me. . . ." She cleared her throat. "Never mind, I'm listening. . . . Everything's fine, I think he liked it. . . . What?"

Her body was stretched across Victor's, and he suddenly felt her tense up.

"Strange," she said. "All right, I'll give a look. . . . Yes. . . . All right, I'll tell him."

She hung up, climbed over Victor, and lit the lamp.

"What happened?" asked Victor sleepily.

"Nothing. Sleep, I'll be right back."

Through his screwed-up eyes he could see her picking up her

underwear from the floor, and her face was so serious that he got worried. She dressed quickly and left the room, straightening her clothes on the run. "Rosheper got sick," he thought, listening intently. "Drank too much, the old geezer." The huge building was silent, and he distinctly heard Diana walking down the corridor, but instead of going to the right, to Rosheper, she made a left. A door creaked, and the footsteps broke off.

Victor turned on his side and tried to go back to sleep, but it was impossible. He realized that he was waiting for Diana and that he wouldn't be able to sleep until she got back. He sat up and lit a cigarette. The lump on the back of his head started to throb, and he made a face. Diana didn't return. For some reason he remembered the sallow-faced dancer with the eagle's profile. "What's he doing here?" thought Victor. "An actor playing another actor who's playing a third actor. The thing is, that was the room he came out of, the one on the left, where Diana went. Went to the landing, looked in the mirror, and turned into a fop. First he played the man about town, then a worn-out gigolo." Victor listened again. "God, is it quiet, everybody's sleeping . . . someone's snoring."

Then a door creaked again, and he could hear footsteps coming closer. Diana walked in. Her face was serious as before. Nothing concluded; await further developments. Diana walked up to the telephone and dialed a number.

"He isn't there," she said. "No, he went out. . . . So did I. . . . No, don't worry about it, of course. . . . Good night."

She hung up. For a few seconds she stood looking into the darkness beyond the window, then she sat down on the bed next to Victor. She was holding a flashlight. Victor lit up a cigarette and gave it to her. She smoked in silence, turning something over in her mind.

"When did you fall asleep?" she asked.

"I don't know, it's hard to say."

"But after I did?"

"Yes."

She turned to face him.

"Are you sure you didn't hear anything? A brawl, fighting?"

"No," said Victor. "I think it was very peaceful. First they sang, then Rosheper and company urinated under our window, then I fell asleep. They were already getting ready to go back."

She threw her cigarette out the window and stood up.

"Get dressed," she said.

He snickered and stretched out a hand for his shorts. "Your order is my command," he thought. "Obedience is a fine thing. No questions asked, ever." "Are we driving or walking?" he asked.

"What? First we'll walk, then we'll see."

"Somebody get lost?"

"Looks like it."

"Rosheper?"

He suddenly felt her glance on him. There was doubt in it. She was already regretting that she'd asked him to come. She was asking herself, who is he anyway that I should take him along?

"I'm ready," he said.

She was still vacillating, playing with her flashlight.

"Well, all right, let's go." She didn't move from the spot.

"Maybe I should break a leg off the chair?" proposed Victor. "Or the bed?"

She woke up.

"No. It won't do any good." She opened the desk drawer and pulled out a huge black pistol. "Take it," she said.

Victor braced himself, but it turned out to be nothing more than a low-caliber hunting pistol. It didn't even have a cartridge.

"Let's have some cartridges," he said.

She looked at him absent-mindedly, then looked at the pistol.

"No. We don't need any. Let's go."

Victor shrugged and stuck the pistol in his pocket. They went down to the lobby and walked out onto the porch. The fog had thinned out; it was drizzling weakly. There weren't any cars at the entrance. Diana turned into a small path between the wet bushes and turned on the flashlight.

"What an idiotic position," thought Victor. "You're itching to ask what's going on, and you can't. Got to find out some way of asking. Beat around the bush. An observation with a query in the subtext. Maybe I'll have to fight? Don't feel like it. Not today. I'll hit him with the pistol. Right between the eyes. How's my lump doing?" His lump hadn't moved. It hurt slightly. "Funny duties the nurses have in this institution. But I've always felt that Diana was a woman with a secret. From the first glance and all five days. . . . Ugh, is it damp, should have taken a swig of something before I left. As soon as I get back, I'll have something. Aren't I being good?" he thought. "No questions asked. Your order is my command."

They circled around their half of the building, crawled through the lilac bushes, and wound up near the fence. Diana shone the flashlight on it. One of the iron rails was missing.

"Victor," she said softly. "We're going to turn onto a trail. You'll follow. Watch your feet, and don't step off the trail. Got it?"

"Got it," said Victor submissively. "A step to the right, a step to the left, and I shoot."

Diana squeezed through first, then held the flashlight for Victor. They made their way very slowly down the hill. It was the eastern slope of the health resort hill. All around them unseen trees were rustling in the rain. Diana slipped, and Victor barely had time to grab her shoulders. She freed herself impatiently and went on. Every minute she repeated, "Watch your feet. Follow me." Victor obediently watched Diana's feet, flickering in the dancing pool of light. At first he kept on waiting for a blow on the back of his head, right on his lump, then he decided it was unlikely. It didn't fit together. Probably it was just some nut who snuck off, or Rosheper had had a tantrum and they'd have to march him back, frightening him with an empty pistol.

Diana stopped short and said something, but her words didn't reach Victor's consciousness. Within a second, at the side of the trail, he saw someone's shining eyes—immobile, huge, and staring intently from under a wet, protruding forehead. Only eyes and a forehead, nothing more: no mouth, no nose, no body, nothing. Just the heavy, damp darkness and in a pool of light, shining eyes and an unnaturally white forehead.

"Bastards," said Diana. There was a catch in her voice. "I knew it. The bastards."

She fell to her knees. The beam of the flashlight skimmed along the black body, and Victor caught sight of a glistening metallic arc and a chain in the grass. "Quick," commanded Diana, and Victor crouched down next to her. Only then did he see that it was a trap, and that there was a man's leg caught in it. He put both hands into the iron jaws and tried to force them apart. They gave way just a little bit and then snapped back into place.

"Idiot!" shrieked Diana. "Use the pistol."

He clenched his teeth, got a better grip, and strained his muscles until his shoulders cracked. The jaws came apart.

"Pull," he said hoarsely. The leg disappeared. The iron arcs snapped together, catching his fingers.

"Hold the flashlight," said Diana.

"I can't," said Victor guiltily. "I'm caught. Get the pistol out of my pocket."

Diana, swearing, felt for his pocket. He wrenched the trap apart another time, she put the handle of the pistol between the jaws, and Victor freed himself.

"Hold the light," she repeated. "Let me look at the leg."

"The bone is shattered," said a strained voice in the darkness. "Carry me to the resort and call for a car."

"Right," said Diana. "Victor, give me the flashlight, and you take him."

She shone the flashlight down. The man was sitting in the

same place as before, leaning against a tree. The lower half of his face was hidden behind a black bandage. "An owl," thought Victor. "A slimy. How did he get here?"

"Hurry up, take him," said Diana. "On your back."

"Right away," he answered. He remembered the yellow circles around the eyes. A lump rose in his throat. "Right away." He crouched down next to the slimy and turned his back toward him. "Grab me around the neck," he said.

The slimy turned out to be thin and light. He didn't move and it seemed as though he wasn't even breathing. He didn't moan when Victor stumbled, but every time it happened a shudder went through his body. The trail was much steeper than Victor had thought, and when they reached the fence he was completely out of breath. Getting the slimy through the gap in the fence proved difficult, but in the end they managed.

"Where to?" asked Victor when they had reached the entrance.

"Into the lobby for now," answered Diana.

"Don't," said the slimy in the same strained tone. "Leave me here."

"It's raining," objected Victor.

"Stop jabbering," siad the slimy. "I'm staying here."

Victor didn't say anything and started walking up the steps.

"Leave him," said Diana.

Victor stopped.

"Goddamnit, it's raining," he said.

"Don't be a fool," said the slimy. "Leave me . . . here. . . ."

Victor, not saying a word, strode up the steps three at a time, reached the door, and walked into the lobby.

"Cretin," whispered the slimy and dropped his head on Victor's shoulder.

"You dolt," said Diana, catching up with Victor and grabbing his sleeve. "You'll kill him, idiot! Get him out of here right away and put him back under the rain. Right away, you hear? What are you standing here for?"

"You're all crazy," sputtered Victor.

He turned around, kicked the door open, and went out onto the porch. The rain seemed to be waiting for his return. Before it had been drizzling lazily, and now it poured down in torrents. The slimy moaned softly. He raised his head and suddenly began panting like a hunted animal. Victor was still dawdling, instinctively looking around for some shelter.

"Put me down," said the slimy.

"In a puddle?" asked Victor, sarcastic and bitter.

"That's unimportant. Put me down."

Victor carefully lowered him onto the ceramic tiles of the porch. The slimy stretched out his arms and legs. His right leg was twisted unnaturally; in the strong light of the porch lamp his great forehead seemed blue-white. Victor sat down next to him on the steps. He really felt like going back into the lobby, but that was unthinkable—to leave an injured man in a heavy rain and seek shelter in a warm place.

"How many times have I been called a fool today?" he thought, wiping his face with his hand. "Pretty often. And there's a grain of truth in it too, insofar as a fool, alias dolt alias cretin and so on, is an ignoramus, persisting in his ignorance. Look at that, he's doing better in the rain. His eyes are opened, they're not so terrible looking. A slimy," he thought. "Really, a slimy rather than a four-eyes. How the hell did he get himself into a trap? And how come there are traps around here? It's the second slimy I've met today, and both of them in trouble. They get in trouble and they get me in trouble."

Diana was in the lobby on the phone. Victor listened.

"The leg. . . . Yes. The bone is shattered . . . Okay. . . . All right. . . . Quickly, we're waiting."

Through the glass door Victor saw her hang up the phone and run upstairs. "Something's gone wrong with the slimies in this town. Too much fuss around them. For some reason they've gotten into everyone's way, even the middle-school director's had it with them. Even Lola," he remembered suddenly.

"It seems she also had something to say about them." He looked down at the slimy. The slimy was looking at him.

"How do you feel?" asked Victor. The slimy didn't answer. "Do you need anything?" asked Victor, raising his voice. "A sip of gin?"

"Don't yell," said the slimy. "I can hear you."

"Does it hurt?" Victor sympathized.

"What do you think?"

"An exceptionally unpleasant man," thought Victor. "However, the hell with him—we'll go our separate ways. And he's in pain."

"Don't worry," he said out loud. "Try to stand it for a few more minutes. They're coming for you."

The slimy didn't answer. Wrinkles appeared on his forehead; his eyes closed. He looked like a corpse—flat and immobile in the pouring rain. Diana ran out onto the porch with a doctor's bag, sat down next to them, and started to do something with the injured leg. The slimy groaned softly, but Diana didn't say anything comforting, as doctors usually do in cases like that.

"Can I help you?" asked Victor.

She didn't answer. He stood up. "Stay for a minute, don't go away," said Diana, not turning her head.

"I'm not going anywhere," said Victor. He watched her deftly putting on a splint.

"We'll need you," said Diana.

"I'm not going anywhere," said Victor again.

"As a matter of fact you can run upstairs. Run up to the room, take a slug of something while there's still time, but come right back down."

"Forget it," said Victor. "I'll manage."

From somewhere behind the screen of rain came the rumble of a motor and the flash of headlights. Victor could make out a jeep carefully turning into the gates. The jeep drove up to the porch, and Yul Golem, in his ill-fitting raincoat, clambered out. He climbed up the steps, bent over the slimy, and took his hand.

"No injections," said the slimy in a hollow voice.

"All right," said Golem and looked at Victor. "Help me with him."

Victor took the slimy in his arms and carried him to the jeep. Golem ran ahead of them, threw open the door, and crawled inside.

"Let's have him here," came his voice from the darkness. "No, feet first. Don't be afraid. Hold him by the shoulders."

Golem, breathing heavily, arranged things in the car. The slimy groaned again, and Golem said something incomprehensible, like "six angles on the neck," or maybe he was cursing. Then he crawled out, slammed the door shut, and, getting behind the wheel, asked Diana, "Did you call them?"

"No," answered Diana. "Should I?"

"It's not worth it anymore," said Golem, "They'll seal the place up. Good-bye."

The jeep started moving, drove over a flower bed, and sped off down the path.

"Let's go," said Diana.

"Let's swim," said Victor. Now that it was all over he felt nothing more than irritation.

In the lobby Diana linked her arm in his.

"Never mind," she said. "You'll change your clothes, have some vodka, and everything will be all right."

"I'm dripping like a wet dog," said Victor. He was angry. "And now perhaps you'll explain to me at long last what was going on?"

Diana gave a weary sigh.

"Nothing in particular was going on. He shouldn't have left his flashlight behind."

"Setting traps all over the place is nothing in particular? Is that the way you see it?"

"The burgomaster does it, the bastard."

They reached the second floor and walked along the corridor.

"Is he crazy?" asked Victor. "It's a criminal offense. Or is he really crazy?"

"No. He's just a bastard and he hates the slimies. Like everyone else in town."

"I've already noticed. We don't like them either, but as for traps. . . . What did the slimies do to them?"

"They have to hate somebody," said Diana. "In some places they hate Jews, in other places they hate blacks, and we hate slimies."

They stopped in front of a door. Diana turned the key, entered, and turned on the light.

"Wait a minute," said Victor, looking around. "Where are we?"

"This is the lab," said Diana. "I'll just be a second."

Victor waited at the door and watched her walk around the large room and close all the windows. There were puddles on the floor.

"And what was he doing there in the middle of the night?" asked Victor.

"Where?" asked Diana, not turning around.

"On the trail. You knew he was there, didn't you?"

"Well, you see," she said, "they have a hard time with medical supplies in the leprosarium. So sometimes they come here to request. . . ."

She closed the last window and took a quick walk around the room, checking the tables, the instruments, and the glassware.

"The whole thing is shitty," said Victor. "What a government. No matter where you look, there's some dirty business going on. Let's get out of here, I'll freeze to death.

"One second," said Diana.

She took a dark piece of clothing off a chair and shook it out. It was a man's evening suit. She hung it neatly in the wardrobe for lab coats. "What's that suit doing here?" thought Victor. "I've seen it somewhere."

"All right," said Diana. "I don't know what you want to do, but I'm going to take a hot bath."

"Listen, Diana," said Victor carefully. "Who was that . . . with a nose like this, yellowish face? The one you were dancing with?"

Diana took him by the hand.

"As a matter of fact," she said after a short silence, "he's my husband. My former husband."

Chapter IV

"I HAVEN'T SEEN YOU for a while," said Pavor. He had a cold.

"Not that long," objected Victor. "Only two days."

"May I join you, or would you prefer to be alone?" asked Pavor.

"Please," said Diana politely.

Pavor took a seat across from her and looked for the waiter. "A double cognac!" he called out. It was getting dark; the doorman was letting down the blinds over the windows. Victor switched on the table lamp.

"I really admire you," Pavor turned to Diana. "To live in a climate like this and maintain such a rosy complexion." He sneezed. "Excuse me. These rains will be the end of me. How's the work going?" he asked Victor.

"Not too good. I can't work when it's gray out—all I want to do is have a drink."

"What about this scene you pulled at the police chief's?" asked Pavor.

"A lot of crap," said Victor. "I was seeking justice."

"What happened?"

"That bastard of a burgomaster was hunting slimies with traps. One of them got caught and hurt his leg. I took the trap, went to the police station, and demanded an investigation."

"I see," said Pavor. "And then?"

"They have some odd laws in this town. Insofar as the victim did not file a complaint, in legal terms there was no crime at all, but only an accident, in which nobody but the victim was to blame. I told the police chief that I'd take note of that. He declared that that was a threat—which is where we left it."

"Where did all this happen?" asked Pavor.

"Around the health resort."

"Around the health resort? What would a slimy be doing around the health resort?"

"I think that's none of anybody's business," said Diana curtly.

"Of course," said Pavor. "I was simply surprised." He frowned, screwed up his eyes, and gave a loud sneeze. "Goddamn," he said. "Excuse me."

He stuck a hand in his pocket and pulled out a huge handkerchief. Something fell to the floor with a bang. Victor bent over. It was a pair of brass knuckles. Victor picked them up and handed them to Pavor.

"What are you doing with these?" he asked.

Pavor, burying his face in his handkerchief, fixed his reddened eyes on the brass knuckles.

"It's all because of you," he said in a strained voice and blew his nose. "You frightened me with your story. Incidentally, they say there's some sort of local gang operating here. Either a gang, or an offshoot of organized crime. It's not to my taste to get beaten up."

"Do they beat you up often?" asked Diana.

Victor looked at her. She was sitting in an armchair with her legs crossed, and she was smoking. Her eyes were lowered. "Poor Pavor," thought Victor. "Now you're in for it." He stretched out a hand and tugged her skirt over her knees.

"Me?" asked Pavor. "Do I look like a man who gets beaten up often? I'll have to do something about that. Waiter, another double cognac! So the next day I went to see a locksmith, and he fixed me up with these." He looked over his brass knuckles with a satisfied expression. "A fine piece of equipment, even Golem liked it."

"So they didn't let you into the leprosarium?" asked Victor.

"No. They didn't let me in, and they aren't planning to either. I've already lost hope. I've sent written complaints to three departments, and now I'm sitting and writing my report. How much money the leprosarium spent on underwear over the past year. Men's and women's separately. Wildly amusing."

"Write that they're having a hard time getting medicine," advised Victor. Pavor raised his eyebrows, and Diana said lazily, "Better drop your scribbling, have a glass of mulled wine, and go to bed."

"Got it," sighed Pavor. "Time to go. You know which room I'm in?" he asked Victor. "Stop by sometime."

"Two twenty-three," said Victor. "I'd be glad to."

"Good-bye," said Pavor, getting up. "Have a nice evening."

They watched him go up to the bar, take a bottle of red wine, and walk toward the exit.

"You have a big mouth," said Diana.

"It's true," said Victor. "Sorry. You know, for some reason I like him."

"I don't," said Diana.

"Neither does Dr. R. Quadriga. I wonder why?"

"He has an ugly face," said Diana. "A blond beast. I've seen it before. A real he-man type. No honor, no conscience, lord of the fools."

"What do you think of that," said Victor. "And I thought you liked men like that."

"There aren't any men now," said Diana. "They're either fascists or old women."

"What about me?" said Victor with interest.

"You? You're too fond of marinated eel. Though you do like justice."

"Exactly. But I think that's good."

"It's not bad. But if you had to choose, you'd take the marinated eel, that's what's bad. You're lucky you've got talent."

"How come you're so spiteful today?" asked Victor.

"That's the way I am. You've got talent and I've got spite. If you took away your talent and my spite, we'd be two copulating zeros."

"There are zeros and zeros," said Victor. "Even as a zero you wouldn't be too bad. A shapely, beautifully proportioned zero. Besides, if you took away your spite you'd become kind, which is not bad either."

"If you took away my spite I'd be a jellyfish. In order to be kind, you have to replace spite with kindness."

"Funny," said Victor. "Usually women don't like to reason. But once they get started, they become amazingly dogmatic. Where did you get the idea that you completely lack kindness? It doesn't work that way. You have kindness, too, it's just hidden behind the spite. Every person has a little bit of everything mixed up in him and life decides what will appear on the surface."

A group of teenagers burst into the hall, and it immediately got noisy. Their behavior was quite informal—they swore at the waiter and sent him running off for beer, then took over a table in a far corner, and started talking and doubling over with laughter. Some thick-lipped, red-cheeked oaf danced over to the bar, snapping his fingers. Teddy handed him a glass of something which he accepted with two fingers, pinky raised. He turned his back to the bar, leaned his elbow on it, and, crossing his feet, surveyed the empty hall. "Greetings to Diana!" he yelled. "How's life?" Diana gave him an indifferent smile.

"Who's that creep?" asked Victor.

"A certain Flamen Juventa," answered Diana. "One of the police chief's little relatives. The nephew."

"I think I've seen him somewhere," said Victor.

"The hell with him," said Diana impatiently. "All people are jellyfish and there's nothing to them. Once in a while you find some real ones, who have something of their own—kindness, talent, spite—but if you take that away from them, then there's nothing left, they turn into jellyfish like everyone else. Do you really think I liked you because of your passion for marinated eel and justice? Nonsense! You're talented, you're famous, you've written books, but aside from that you're the same hopeless sloth that everyone else is."

"What you're saying," said Victor, "is so far from the truth that I'm not even offended. But go on, it's interesting to watch your face change as you talk." He lit up a cigarette and gave it to her. "Go ahead."

"Jellyfish," she said bitterly. "Stupid slippery jellyfish. They swarm, they crawl, they kill, they don't know what they want, they don't know how to do anything, they don't really love anything. Like worms in a privy."

"That's indelicate," said Victor. "The image is striking— but it's decidedly unappetizing. And in general, you're giving me nothing but banalities. Diana, sweetheart, you're not a thinker. In the last century, in a small town, this might have gone over—at the very least, the social world would have been sweetly shocked, and pale youths with burning eyes would have followed at your heels. But today all these things are truisms. Today everybody knows what man is. The problem is what to do with him. And even that one's been talked to death."

"And what about the jellyfish?"

"What do you mean? What are the jellyfish doing?"

"I mean what are we doing with them?"

"As far as I know, very little. I think we can them."

"All right, enough," said Diana. "Have you managed to get anything written over the last couple of days?"

"Have I ever! I wrote an incredibly touching letter to my friend Rots-Tusov. If after this letter he doesn't get Irma into a boarding school, then I'm really good for nothing."

"And that's all?"

"That's it," said Victor. "The rest I threw out."

"Terrific," said Diana. "And for that I looked after you, tried not to bother you, chased away Rosheper . . ."

"Gave me a bath," Victor reminded her.

"Gave you a bath, kept you supplied with coffee . . ."

"Wait," said Victor. "I gave you a bath too."

"That doesn't count."

"What do you mean, it doesn't count? You think it's easy to work after giving you a bath? I wrote six variants describing the process and none of them are any good."

"Let me read them."

"For men only," said Victor. "Besides I threw them out, didn't I tell you? Anyway, they were lacking in patriotism and national self-awareness, so I couldn't show them to anyone."

"Tell me how you do it—do you write first and stick in the national self-awareness later?"

"No," said Victor. "First I immerse myself in national self-awareness to the very depths of my soul. I read the speeches of Mr. President, memorize heroic sagas, go to party meetings. Then, when I start to throw up—not when I start to get nauseous, but when I start to throw up—I go to work. Let's talk about something else. Like what we're going to do tomorrow."

"Tomorrow you have a meeting with the middle-school students."

"That won't take any time. And then?"

Diana didn't answer. She was looking past him. Victor turned around. A slimy was walking towards them, in all his magnificence: black, wet, and with a bandage on his face.

"Good evening," he said to Diana. "Golem hasn't returned yet?"

Victor looked in amazement at the change in Diana's face. It was a face from out of an old painting, a face from an icon. The same strangely immobile features, which you stare at not quite sure what got them there, an artist's master stroke or a hack's clumsiness. She didn't respond. She was silent, the slimy looked at her in silence, and there was no awkwardness in it. They were together, and Victor and everybody else was excluded. Victor was not amused.

"Golem is probably on his way," he said in a loud voice.

"Yes," said Diana. "Why don't you sit down and wait."

Her voice was normal, and she smiled at the slimy with her usual indifferent smile. Everything was normal—Victor was with Diana and the slimy and everybody else was excluded.

"Please," said Victor cheerfully, pointing to Dr. R. Quadriga's armchair.

The slimy took a seat, putting his black-gloved hands on his knees. Victor poured him some cognac. With an accustomed, careless gesture, the slimy took the glass, tipped it from side to side as if weighing it, and put it back on the table.

"I hope you haven't forgotten?" he said to Diana.

"No," said Diana. "No, I'll bring it right away. Victor, give me the key to the room, I'll be right back."

She took the key and hurried to the exit. Victor lit up a cigarette. "What's with you, pal?" he said to himself. "You've been imagining too much the last couple of days. Have you really gotten so sensitive? Jealous. And for what? None of this has anything to do with you, all these former husbands and strange acquaintances. Diana is Diana and you are you. Rosheper is impotent. Impotent. And let's leave it at that."

He knew that it wasn't that simple, that he'd already tasted the poison, but he told himself that enough was enough and for the moment, for the time being, he managed to convince himself that it was.

The slimy sat across from him, immobile and frightening, like a stuffed bird. He smelled of mildew and of something else as well, some medicine. "Who would have thought that someday I'd be sitting in a restaurant sharing a table with a slimy? Progress, gentlemen, is slowly creeping ahead. Or are we the ones that have changed and become accepting? Has it finally dawned on us that all men are brothers? Humanity, my friend, I am proud of you. And you, sir, would you let your daughter marry a slimy?"

"Banev," said Victor, introducing himself. "How is the health of your—uh—injured colleague? The one who fell into a trap?"

The slimy quickly turned toward him. "He's facing me across the trenches," thought Victor.

"Satisfactory," said the slimy drily.

"If I were him I'd file a complaint with the police."

"It doesn't make any sense," said the slimy.

"Why not?" said Victor. "You don't have to go to the local police; you can go to the regional office."

"We don't need that."

Victor shrugged.

"Every crime which goes unpunished leads to a new one."

"Yes. But that doesn't interest us."

There was a short silence. Then the slimy said, "My name is Zurzmansor."

"An illustrious name," said Victor politely. "You wouldn't be a relative of Pavel Zurzmansor, the sociologist?"

The slimy squinted.

"Not even a namesake," he said. "They tell me, Banev, that you're giving a talk at the middle school tomorrow."

Victor didn't have a chance to answer. A chair moved behind him, and he heard a sprightly baritone.

"Get out of here, you filthy germ."

Victor swung around. Towering above him was the thick-lipped Flamen Juventa, or whatever his name was—in a word, the nephew. Victor looked at him for no more than a second, but he felt incredibly annoyed.

"Just who are you addressing, young man?" he inquired.

"Your friend," said Flamen Juventa politely. He turned away. "I'm talking to you, you soggy bastard."

"One moment," said Victor and stood up.

Flamen Juventa, smirking, looked down at him. A young

Goliath in a ski jacket glittering with innumerable emblems, the paragon of the national *sturmführers*, the backbone of the nation, with a nightstick in his hip pocket. The terror of the left wing, the right wing, and the center. Victor lightly touched Juventa's tie. "What is it you've got there?" he asked, feigning concern and curiosity. And when the young Goliath instinctively inclined his head to see what it was he had there, Victor grabbed Goliath's nose.

"Hey!" Juventa yelled, stunned, and tried to free himself. But Victor wouldn't let him. For quite some time Victor got an icy satisfaction from turning and twisting Juventa's insolent and muscular nose.

"Behave yourself, you puppy, you spoiled brat, you lousy storm trooper, you son of a bitch."

Victor's position was ideal. The young Goliath was kicking desperately, but there was an armchair between them; the young Goliath beat his fists in the air, but Victor's arms were longer and he kept on twisting and turning until a bottle flew over his head. He looked behind him. The whole gang was crashing its way toward him, kicking aside tables and knocking over chairs. There were five of them in all, and two were huge. For a moment everything stopped, as in a film freeze: Zurzmansor, all in black, calmly reclining in his armchair; Teddy, hanging in a half-completed leap across his bar; Diana with a white package in the middle of the hall. In the background, by the doors, the furious mustachioed face of the doorman, and, right next to Victor, five churlish faces with fangs bared. Then the freeze ended and the film resumed.

The first gorilla was neatly disposed of with a hook to the jaw. He took off and didn't reappear for some time. The second gorilla got Victor in the ear. Someone landed a karate chop on his cheek, apparently aiming at the throat. And someone else—the freed Goliath?—jumped him from behind. The backbone of the nation was nothing more than a street gang. Only one of them knew boxing and the others didn't want to fight so much as maim, gouge out the eyes, rip open the mouth, kick the groin. Had Victor been alone, they would have mutilated him. But along came Teddy, bounding in from the rear, devout observer of the bouncer's golden rule to squelch all fights at their very outset. From the flanks appeared Diana, Diana Enraged, fiery with hatred, unlike herself, wielding a heavy wickered bottle in place of her white package. And last but not least, the doorman, an old-timer but, to judge from his grip, a former soldier. The doorman moved in with his keychain, swinging it like a soldier's belt with a bayonet hanging from it. Thus, by the time the two waiters ran in from the kitchen, there was nothing left for them to do. The nephew took off, abandoning his transistor radio. One of his pals remained in prone position under the table, felled by Diana's bottle. Victor and Teddy took care of the remaining four. Rallying one another with war whoops, they literally pounded their victims out of the hall, chased them through the lobby, and kicked them through the revolving doors. Out of inertia they followed them onto the street, and only there, under the rain, did they acknowledge their victory and calm down.

"Lousy punks," said Teddy, lighting two cigarettes at once, one for himself and one for Victor. "They've hit on something new—a fight every Thursday. Last week I turned around for a minute and they broke two chairs. And who has to pay for it? Me!"

Victor felt his swollen ear.

"The nephew left," he said, disappointed. "I didn't get to give him what he deserved."

"Just as well," said Teddy matter-of-factly. "Better not get involved with that thick-lipped bastard. His uncle is you-know-who and he himself—Backbone of the Motherland, Backbone of Law and Order, or whatever they call it. And you, my dear writer, have learned how to fight. You used to be a pushover—one blow and there you were under the table. Good for you."

"It's my profession," sighed Victor. "A product of the struggle for existence. That's the way we do it—every man for himself. And Mr. President backs everyone."

"Does it really come to blows?" asked Teddy innocently.

"What did you think happens? They give you a good review, they say you're chock full of national self-awareness. You go to find the critic and he's already got his friends with him, and they're all hot-tempered young musclemen, Sons of the President."

"You don't say," sympathized Teddy. "And then what?"

"It depends. You win some and you lose some."

A jeep drove up to the entrance. The doors opened, and the young man in glasses, carrying his attaché case, came out into the rain. Behind him, sheltered under the same raincoat, was the lanky companion. The driver crawling out from behind the wheel was Golem. The lanky companion watched with keen, almost professional interest as the doorman booted the last hood, still slightly dazed, out the revolving door.

"Too bad that one wasn't with us," whispered Teddy, eyeing the companion. "A far cry from you. A real professional—know what I mean?"

"Got you," Victor whispered back.

The young man with the attaché case and the lanky companion jogged past them and disappeared into the entrance. Golem, unhurried and smiling at Victor, was about to follow suit. But Mr. Zurzmansor, holding a white package, blocked his path. Zurzmansor said something in a low voice, after which Golem stopped smiling and went back to the car. Zurzmansor got in the back and the jeep took off.

"Hey," said Teddy. "We were fighting the wrong battle, Mr. Banev. People are shedding their blood for him, and he gets into somebody's car and drives off."

"Come on, you're overdoing it," said Victor. "A sick, unhappy man, today it's him, tomorrow it'll be you. You and I are going to go in for a drink, and he's being taken back to the leprosarium."

"We know where they're taking him!" said Teddy, intransigent. "You writers don't understand our life."

"Lost touch with the nation?"

"The hell with the nation, it's our life you don't know. Try living with us: how many years has this rain been coming down, everything's rotted in the fields, the children are out of control. Just look what's going on—not a single cat is left in town, the mice have taken over. Ugh," he said, waving his hand. "Let's get going."

They returned to the lobby. "How much did they ruin?" Teddy asked the doorman, who had by now resumed his post.

"Not so bad," said the doorman. "You came through all right. They broke a lamp and messed up a wall. I took the money from—uh—from the last one. Here, take it."

Teddy went back to the restaurant, counting the money on the way; Victor followed. Quiet had returned to the hall. The young man in glasses and his lanky friend were lost in boredom over a bottle of mineral water. In front of them was their ever-present supper, which they chewed melancholically. Diana was back in her seat. She was very animated and terribly pretty. She even managed to smile at Dr. R. Quadriga as he took his seat, although on most occasions she couldn't stand him. Opposite R. Quadriga was a bottle of rum, but he was still sober and for that reason looked peculiar.

"To the victor," he intoned mournfully. "A pity that I wasn't present even as a midshipman."

Victor collapsed into his chair.

"Some ear," said R. Quadriga. "Where'd you get it? Like a cockscomb."

"Cognac!" demanded Victor. Diana poured him some cognac. "To her and her alone do I owe my victory," he said, pointing to Diana. "Did you pay for the bottle?"

"It didn't break," said Diana. "What do you take me for? But did he fall! Boy, did he ever come crashing! I wish all the bastards would—"

"Let us proceed," intoned R. Quadriga, pouring himself a full glass of rum.

"He tipped over just like a mannequin," said Diana. "Like a bowling pin. Victor, are you all in one piece? I saw how they were kicking you."

"The pièce de résistance is still intact," answered Victor. "I watched out for it."

Dr. R. Quadriga gurgled down the last drops of rum from his glass like a kitchen sink gurgling down the dishwater. His eyes immediately got glassy.

"We're already acquainted," said Victor hurriedly. "You are Dr. Rem Quadriga, and I am the writer Banev."

"Forget it," said R. Quadriga. "I'm completely sober. But I'll get there. That's the only thing I'm sure of now. You can't imagine, but when I came here six months ago I was an absolute teetotaler. My liver is bad, my intestines are inflamed, and there's something wrong with my stomach. Drinking in my condition is absolutely forbidden, and here I am getting drunk day in and day out. Absolutely nobody needs me. This has never happened to me before. I don't even get any letters, because my old friends are in the camps without writing privileges and my new ones are illiterate."

"No government secrets," said Victor. "I don't have security clearance."

R. Quadriga poured himself another glass and started sipping the rum as though it were lukewarm tea.

"It works faster that way," he informed them. "Try it, Banev. It may help. And you don't have to stare at me," he snapped at Diana. "I beg you to hide your feelings. If you don't like—"

"Relax, relax," said Victor, and R. Quadriga cooled down.

"They don't understand a goddamned thing about me," he complained. "Nobody. Only you understand a little. You always understood me. Only you're awfully crude, Banev, and you always wounded me. I'm wounded all over. They don't dare denounce me now, all they can do is praise me. And as soon as one of those bastards praises me, I get a wound. Another bastard praises me; another wound. But now all that's behind me. They don't know that yet. Listen, Banev! You have a great woman. I beg you . . . ask her, let her come to my studio. No, you fool! A model! You don't understand anything, I've been looking for a model like that for years."

"An allegorical painting," Victor explained to Diana. " 'The President and the Eternally Young Nation.' "

"Fool," whimpered Quadriga. "You all think I'm selling myself. It's true, I sold myself. But I'm not painting presidents any more. A self-portrait! Understand?"

"No," confessed Victor. "I don't understand. You want to paint your portrait as Diana?"

"Fool," said R. Quadriga. "It will be the face of the artist—"

"Modeled on my ass," said Diana.

"The face of the artist!" repeated R. Quadriga. "You're an artist, Victor. And so are all the people sitting in the camps without writing privileges. And so are all the people lying in their graves without writing privileges. And so are all the people living in my house, that is to say, not living. You know, Banev, I'm afraid. I told you, come, live with me for just a little while. I have a villa. A fountain. But the gardener ran away. Coward. Only I can't live there, I'm better off at the hotel. You think I drink because I sold out? Bullshit! This isn't some fashionable novel. Live with me for awhile and you'll see. Maybe you'll even come to know them. Maybe they aren't my friends at all, maybe they're yours. Then I'd know why they refuse to recognize me. They walk around barefoot . . . they laugh." His eyes filled with tears. "Ladies and gentlemen!" he said. "How lucky we are that Pavor isn't with us! Your health."

"Cheers," said Victor, exchanging glances with Diana. Diana looked at R. Quadriga with fastidious anxiety. "Nobody here likes Pavor," he continued. "Only I am some sort of monster."

"A still pond," pronounced Dr. R. Quadriga. "A frog jumping. Blatherer. Always silent."

"He's just stewed, that's all," Victor said to Diana. "Nothing to worry about."

"Gentlemen!" said Dr. R. Quadriga. "Madam! Allow me to introduce myself! Rem Quadriga, doctor honoris causae."

Chapter V

VICTOR ENTERED THE MIDDLE SCHOOL a half hour before the appointed time, but Bol-Kunats was already waiting for him. Fortunately, the boy was tactful. He told Victor only that the meeting would take place in the auditorium and then excused himself, citing some pressing business. Left alone, Victor wandered along the corridors, looking into the empty classrooms, breathing in the scent of ink, chalk, and dust that never settled. The smell of fights "till the first blood" and the smell of exhausting interrogations at the board. The smell of prison, the smell of arbitrariness, and the smell of lies, elevated to a moral code. He kept trying to call forth sweet memories of childhood and youth—his knighthood, his friendships, his first pure love. But nothing came of it, although he tried hard, ready to melt at the first opportunity. Everything was the way it always had been: the bright, stuffy classrooms and the scratched-up boards, the desks with their colored initials and apocryphal inscriptions about boys and handy toys. The thick fortress walls, painted halfway up in a cheerful shade of green, and the plaster chips in the corners. Everything was the way it had always been—hateful and vile, inspiring malice and despair.

He found his old classroom, though not right away. He found his seat by the window, though the desk was new. But on the windowsill you could still see the deeply-etched emblem of the Legion of Freedom, and he vividly remembered the suffocating enthusiasm of those times. The white and red neckerchiefs, the tin piggy banks "for the Legion Fund," the desperate, bloody fighting with the Reds and the portraits. The portraits in every newspaper, in every textbook, and on every wall: that face which then seemed handsome and important, but had since turned flabby—a wild boar's snout, punctuated by a huge, tusked, saliva-spraying mouth. They had been so young, so uninteresting, so identical . . . and so stupid. You couldn't feel good about that stupidity now, you couldn't feel happy that you'd grown smarter. There was only a burning shame for what you were then, an efficient little gray fledgling which imagined itself bright, irreplaceable, and chosen. And your shameful childish desire, your agonizing fear before a girl you'd already boasted about so much there was no way of getting out of it. And the next day, your father's deafening anger and your burning ears, and all this is what they call the happy years—grayness, desire, fanaticism.

"Bad deal," he thought. "What if fifteen years from now I look back and see that today I'm just as gray and subjugated as I was in my childhood, only worse, because now I consider myself grown up, knowing enough and having lived through enough to have a basis for self-satisfaction and the right to judge.

"Modesty and only modesty, right down to self-abasement . . . and nothing but the truth, never lie, at least never to yourself. But it's terrible, abasing yourself when you're surrounded by so many idiots, lechers, and self-centered liars; when even the best of them are marked with spots, like lepers. Do you want to be young again? No. But would you like to live another fifteen years? Yes. Because to live is good. Even when you get hit. As long as you have the chance to hit back. All right, enough. Let us conclude on the thought that the present life is a means of existence permitting the bearer to hit back. And now let's see what's become of the children."

There was a good crowd in the auditorium and the usual hum of voices, which ceased when Bol-Kunats led Victor onto the stage. He sat him down under a huge portrait of the president—a gift of Dr. R. Quadriga—at a table covered with a red and white cloth. Then Bol-Kunats walked to the front of the stage.

"Today we have with us the well-known writer Victor Banev, a native of our town." He turned to Victor. "How would you like to do it, Mr. Banev? Should the questions be delivered from the audience directly, or would you like to read them first?"

"Makes no difference," grinned Victor. "As long as there are a lot of them."

"In that case, we are at your service."

Bol-Kunats jumped off the stage and took a seat in the first row. Victor scratched his eyebrows and looked over the hall. There were about fifty of them, girls and boys ranging in age from ten to fourteen, and they were looking at him with quiet expectation. Nothing but prodigies here, flashed through his mind. He caught sight of Irma in the second row and smiled at her. She smiled back.

"I was a student in this school," Victor began, "and once I even got to play Osric on this stage. I didn't know my part, and I had to make it up as I went. That was the first thing I ever made up when not under threat of an F. They say that school has gotten harder than it was in my day. They say that you have new subjects, and that what we did in three years you have to cover in a year. But you probably don't notice that it's gotten harder. Scientists speculate that the human brain is capable of taking in a lot more information than the ordinary person would think at first glance. All you have to do is be able to cram the information—" "Right," thought Victor. "Now I'll tell them about hypnopedia." But Bol-Kunats handed him a note: "Don't talk about the achievements of science. Talk with us as equals. Valeryans, Grade 6."

"So," said Victor. "Here is a certain Valeryans from the sixth grade who proposes that I talk with you as equals and asks me

not to outline the achievements of science. I must confess,
Valeryans, that I was really intending to say a few words about
the achievements of hypnopedia. But I shall willingly restrain
myself, although I consider it my duty to acquaint you with
the fact that the majority of my equals have only the foggiest
understanding of it." It was uncomfortable for him to talk
sitting down; he stood up and walked the length of the stage.
"I must confess to you, my young friends, that I've never been
fond of meeting with my readers. As a rule, it's completely
impossible to figure out what kind of reader you're dealing
with, what he needs from you and what exactly interests him.
For that reason I try to turn my appearance into a question-
and-answer session. Occasionally this becomes quite amusing.
So let's begin, and I'll start the questioning. So. . . . Have you
all read my works?"

"Yes," responded the childish voices. "We've read them . . .
all of them. . . ."

"Fine," said Victor, a bit troubled. "I'm flattered, but nonetheless surprised. Well, all right, let's see. Would the group like
me to tell how one of my novels was written?"

There was a short silence, after which a thin pimply-faced
boy in the center of the hall stood up, said "No," and sat
down.

"Fine," said Victor. "All the better, since despite certain
widely held views, there is nothing particularly interesting in
learning how a novel was written. Let's move on. Would my
respected audience like to hear about my creative plans?"

Bol-Kunats stood up. "The truth is, Mr. Banev," he said
politely, "that questions closely related to the technique of
your work would better be discussed toward the end of our
meeting, when the general picture will have been clarified."

He took his seat. Victor put his hands into his pockets and
retraced his steps along the stage. It was getting interesting, or,
in any case, unusual.

"Perhaps you would prefer literary anecdotes?" he asked ingratiatingly. "How I hunted with Hemingway. How Ehrenburg gave me a Russian samovar. Or what Zurzmansor told me when I met him in a streetcar."

"Did you really meet Zurzmansor?" came from the hall.

"No, I'm joking," said Victor. "So what's the decision on literary anecdotes?"

"Will you take a question?" said the pimply-faced boy, getting to his feet.

"Of course."

"How would you like to see us in the future?"

"Without pimples," flashed in Victor's head, but he pushed the thought aside because he felt that things were getting hot. The question was a tough one. "If only someone would tell me how I would like to see myself in the present," he thought. But he had to answer.

"Intelligent," he said at random. "Honest. Kind. . . . I would like you to love your work . . . and to work only for the good of mankind." ("I'm laying it on," he thought. "But what else can you do?") "Something on that order."

A murmur ran through the hall. Then someone asked from his seat, "Do you really think that a soldier is more important than a physicist?"

"Do I think that?" Victor flared up.

"That was my understanding of your novella *Misfortune Comes at Night*."

The speaker was a little towheaded bug about ten years of age. Victor took in his breath. *Misfortune* could be a bad book and it could be a good book, but it was in no way a children's book. It was so far from being a children's book that not a single critic could figure it out—they all took it for pornographic trash which undercut morality and national self-awareness. And the worst of it was that the towheaded bug really had a basis for believing that the author of *Misfortune* considered a soldier "more important" than a physicist, in certain respects, at any rate.

"The thing is," said Victor with feeling, "that—how can I put it to you—everything's possible."

"I wasn't referring to physiology," objected the towheaded bug. "I was talking about the general conception of the book. Perhaps 'important' is the wrong word."

"I wasn't referring to physiology either," said Victor. "I mean that there are situations in which knowledge is insignificant."

Bol-Kunats picked up two notes from the audience and handed them to Victor. "Can a person who works for the military-industrial complex be considered honorable and kind?" and "What is an intelligent man?" Victor started with the second question—it was easier.

"An intelligent man," he said, "is someone who acknowledges the imperfection and incompleteness of his knowledge, strives to overcome it, and is successful in this. Do you agree with me?"

"No," said a pretty little girl, half-rising.

"Why not?"

"Your definition is not functional. Any fool, using your definition, might consider himself intelligent. Especially if other people support him in his opinion."

"Right," thought Victor. He was seized by a light panic. "This isn't one of your talks with your pen-wielding colleagues."

"In a sense you are right," he said, surprising even himself by his respectful tone. "However, in general the concepts of 'fool' and 'intelligent person' are historical and, ultimately, subjective."

"It follows that you yourself would not take on the task of distinguishing a stupid person from a smart one?"

The question came from the back rows, a dark creature with beautiful biblical eyes and a shaved head.

"Why not?" said Victor. "I would. But I'm not convinced that you would always agree with me. There's an old aphorism: a fool is just someone who thinks differently." Usually this saying made the audience laugh, but this time the auditorium waited silently for him to continue. "Or someone who feels differently," Victor added.

He had a sharp sense of the audience's dissatisfaction but he didn't know what else to say. There hadn't been any contact. As a rule, the audience would easily adopt the position of the speaker, and agree with all his judgments. What was meant by "fools" would be clear to everyone—with, of course, the understanding that in the present company there weren't any. If worse came to worse, the audience wouldn't agree and would look for a confrontation. But even then it was easy, because you could always use ridicule and sarcasm. And it's not hard to take on a group singlehandedly, since your opponents contradict each other and you can always pick out the loudest and the stupidest and trample him underfoot to the general delight.

"I don't completely understand," said the pretty little girl. "You would like us to be intelligent, that is, to put it in terms of your aphorism, to think and feel the same way as you do. But I've gone through all your books and find only negativism in them. There is no affirmative program. On the other hand, you would like us to work for the good of mankind. That is, literally, for the good of those dirty, unpleasant types who fill up your books. After all, your books are realistic, aren't they?"

Victor felt that he had finally touched bottom.

"You see," he said, "by work for the good of mankind I have in mind transforming people into clean and pleasant types. And this wish of mine bears no relationship to my creative work. In my books I attempt to depict everything as it is, not to preach or show what should be done. At most I indicate the pressure point, draw attention to what it is we have to fight. I don't know how to change people—if I did I wouldn't be a writer. I'd be a superb pedagogue or an eminent psychosociologist. Literature is not the place for teaching, for proposing specific paths or concrete methodologies. Look at our greatest writers. I bow down before Tolstoy, but only to the point where he remains an individual, uniquely reflective of reality.

As soon as he starts teaching me to go barefoot and turn the other cheek, I'm seized with pity and boredom. The writer is an instrument which indicates the condition of society, and is only to an infinitesimal degree a weapon for transforming it. History shows that society is not transformed by literature, but by reforms and machine guns, or, recently, by science as well. At best, literature shows whom to shoot at or what needs changing." He paused, thinking that he'd forgotten about Dostoevsky and Faulkner. But while he was figuring out how to bring in literature as a tool for studying the individual psyche, a voice came from the back of the hall.

"Excuse me, but all this is rather trivial. This isn't the point. The point is that the objects you have depicted in no way desire to be changed. And then they're so unpleasant, so neglected, so hopeless, that one doesn't even want to change them. You understand, they're not worth it. Let them rot away by themselves, they don't have any role to play. So for whose good are we to work, in your opinion?"

"Now I'm beginning to see," said Victor slowly.

It had suddenly dawned on him: "My God, these wet-nosed kids really think I only write about the scum of the earth, that I think everyone belongs there. But they haven't understood a thing, and how could they have, anyway—they're only children, strange children, sure, intelligent to the point of sickness, but with a child's experience in life and a child's understanding of people plus whatever they've gotten from all their books. With a child's idealism and a child's desire to put everything into pigeonholes with the labels 'bad' and 'good.' Just like my pen-wielding colleagues."

"I've been deceived by your way of talking like grown-ups," he said. "I even forgot that you weren't grown-ups. I understand that it's pedagogically bad to talk this way, but I'm afraid it's necessary, or we'll never find our way out of this. The whole problem is that you, apparently, can't understand how a man who is unshaven, unstable, and eternally drunk can be

an excellent person, a person it's impossible not to love, someone you'd bow before and whose hand you'd be honored to
shake, because this man has been through an unimaginable
hell, and yet remained a human being. You consider the
heroes of my novels to be dirty bastards, but that's half-
forgivable. You consider that I relate to them the same way
as you do. And that's unforgivable. Unforgivable in the sense
that we'll never understand each other."

God only knows what kind of a reaction he expected from
his well-intended lecture. Either that they'd start exchanging
embarrassed glances, or that their faces would light up with
understanding, or that a sigh of relief would flood through the
hall as a sign that the misunderstanding had passed and they
could begin again on a new, more realistic basis. In any event,
none of this occurred. In the back of the hall, the boy with the
biblical eyes stood up and asked, "Would you mind telling us
how you define progress?"

Victor felt insulted. "Of course," he thought. "And then
they'll ask if a machine can think and whether there's life on
Mars. Everything."

"Progress," he said, "is the movement of society toward a
state in which people don't kill, trample, and torment one
another."

"And how do they fill their time?" asked a fat boy to the
right.

"They drink liquor and nibble *quantum satis,*" mumbled
someone to the left.

"And why not?" said Victor. "The history of mankind has
seen very few times when people could drink liquor and nibble
quantum satis. For me, progress is the movement of society
toward a state in which people don't trample one another and
don't kill. And how they'll fill their time then is, in my opinion, not that important. For me, it's the necessary conditions
of progress that are paramount; the sufficient conditions can
wait."

"May I interrupt?" asked Bol-Kunats. "Let us look at the following scheme. Automation proceeds at the same pace as today. It follows that in a few decades the vast majority of the active population of the Earth will be thrown out of industry and the service professions because of obsolescence. Picture how good it is: nobody's hungry, trampling your neighbor makes no sense, nobody bothers anybody—and nobody needs anybody either. There are, of course, a few hundred thousand persons inventing new machines and insuring the uninterrupted work of old ones, but the remaining billions are of no use to one another. Is that good?"

"I don't know," said Victor. "Of course it's not completely good. It's somehow insulting. But I have to say that it's still better than what we're seeing now. So that there still would be definite progress."

"And would you yourself like to live in that world?"

Victor thought.

"You know," he said, "I don't picture it very clearly, but to be honest with you, it wouldn't be bad to give it a try."

"And could you picture someone who would categorically refuse to live in a world like that?"

"Of course I could. There are people, I've seen them, who would be bored there. No room for power, nobody to order around, no reason to trample your fellow man. Naturally, they'd be unlikely to turn down that rarest of all opportunities—turning heaven into a pigsty . . . or into a barracks. They would be delighted to destroy that world. So, as a matter of fact, no, I couldn't imagine such a person."

"And what about your heroes, the ones you're so fond of. Would a future like that suit them?"

"Of course. They'd get the peace they deserve."

Bol-Kunats sat down, but the pimply-faced boy stood up and shook his head sadly.

"This is the whole problem. The problem is not whether we understand real life or not, but that for you and your heroes a future like that would be completely acceptable, while for us it would be death. The end of hope. The end of humanity. A dead end. That's why we say that we don't want to waste our strength working for the good of those types, your types, who are longing for peace and up to their ears in filth. It's no longer possible to instill in them the energy for real life. And whatever you might have intended, Mr. Banev, still, in your books—in your interesting books, I'm all for them—you didn't show us any pressure point in the human race, you showed us rather that no such pressure point exists, at least in your generation. You've fed on one another—excuse the expression—you've exhausted yourselves with your infighting and your lying and the war against lying which you carry out by thinking up new lies. It's like your song: 'Truth and lies, you aren't so far apart, yesterday's truth becomes a lie, yesterday's lie becomes tomorrow's purest truth, tomorrow's ordinary truth.' So you swing from lie to lie. You simply can't get it into your heads that you're already dead men, that by your own hands you've created a world which has become your headstone. You've rotted in the trenches, you've thrown yourselves under tanks, and who has it helped? You've criticized the government and criticized law and order as if you didn't know that your generation is, well, simply unworthy of anything better. You've been beaten on the head, excuse the expression, and you persist in repeating that man by nature is good, or, even worse, that the name 'man' has a proud ring. And think of the people you've called 'men'!"

The pimply-faced orator waved his hand and sat down. Silence reigned. Then he stood up again. "When I said 'you,' I did not mean you personally, Mr. Banev."

"Thank you," snapped Victor.

He felt irritated—this pimply-faced puppy had no right to talk with such finality, it was sheer insolence . . . give him a shove and throw him out of the room. He felt awkward—much of what was said was true, and he himself felt the same way, and now he found himself in the position of defending something that he hated. He felt himself at a loss. He didn't know what to do next, how to continue the conversation and whether it was worth continuing. He glanced around the auditorium and saw that they were waiting for his answer, that Irma was waiting for his answer, that all these rosy-cheeked, freckled monsters shared the same thoughts, and the insolent kid with the pimples had merely expressed the general consensus. And he had expressed it sincerely, with deep conviction, not because he had just read some forbidden pamphlet. They really didn't feel the tiniest bit of gratitude or the most elementary respect for him, Victor Banev, for having enlisted in the hussars and attacked tanks on horseback, for having nearly died of dysentery when they were surrounded or for having cut down a guard with a homemade knife. Or for what he did later on, when he got home—for slapping a security recruiter in the face and refusing to sign a denunciation. And then wandering around with a hole in his lung and without work, dealing in black-market fruit even though he'd been offered the most lucrative positions. "And when you come down to it, why should that make them respect me? Because I moved on a column of tanks with a bared saber? You have to be an idiot in order to have a government that would get the army into such a mess." He shuddered, imagining the huge labor of thought these fledglings must have gone through in order to arrive, completely independently, at the same conclusions that adults reach after laying bare their very skins, shattering their souls, and ruining their own lives and most of the lives around them. And not even all adults, but only some of them. The majority to this day believes that everything was right, everything was just terrific, and if the need should arise they'd be ready to start in all over again. Has a new age really dawned? He glanced at the audience with something approaching fright. It seemed that the future had really managed to extend its feelers into the very heart of the present, and that that future was cold and pitiless. It couldn't care less about the virtues of the past, both the real ones and the imaginary ones.

"Look," said Victor. "You young people probably haven't noticed it, but you're cruel. You're cruel out of the best possible motives, but it's cruelty just the same. And it can't bring anything except fresh grief, fresh tears, and fresh baseness. That's what you have in mind. And don't think that you're saying something very new. To destroy the old world and build up a new one on its bones is a very old idea. And never once has it brought the desired results. The same thing that calls forth the desire for merciless destruction in the old world quickly adapts itself to the process of destruction, to cruelty and mercilessness. It becomes essential to this process and always gets retained. It becomes the master of the new world and, in the final analysis, kills the bold destroyers themselves. A crow won't peck out the eye of its brother; you can't fight cruelty with cruelty. Irony and pity, my young friends. Irony and pity!"

The audience suddenly stood up. It was completely unexpected, and the mad thought flashed through Victor's mind that he had finally managed to say something that struck the imagination of his listeners. But then he saw a slimy walking into the auditorium, thin and light, as immaterial as a shadow. The children were looking at him, and not only looking, they were being drawn toward him. He made a polite bow to Victor, mumbled an excuse, and took a seat at the side of the hall, next to Irma. The children also took their seats. Victor looked at Irma and saw that she was happy, that she was trying not to show it, but the contentment and joy were bursting out of her. But before he could get his wits together, Bol-Kunats spoke.

"I'm afraid you've misunderstood us, Mr. Banev," he said. "We're not cruel at all, and if we are cruel from your point of view, then it's only theoretical. After all, we're not intending to destroy your old world. We intend to build a new one. It's you that are cruel: you can't imagine building the new without destroying the old. And we can imagine this very well. We'll even help your generation to build its heaven, and you can drink liquor to your heart's content. We're building, Mr. Banev, only building. We're not destroying anything, only building."

Victor finally tore his eyes off Irma and pulled his thoughts together.

"Yes," he said. "Of course. Go to it, build. I'm all for you. You've overwhelmed me today, but I'm still with you—maybe for that reason alone. If I have to, I'll even give up my share of the pie. Only don't forget that old worlds have had to be destroyed because they got in the way . . . got in the way of the new—didn't like it, crushed it."

"The present old world," said Bol-Kunats enigmatically, "will not get in our way. It will even help us. Past history has come to an end, there's no need to refer to it."

"Well, then, all the better," said Victor, tired. "I'm glad that it's working out so well for you."

"Terrific boys and girls," he thought. "Strange, but terrific. But I'm sorry for them. They'll grow up, climb on top of one another, multiply, and begin working for their daily bread. No," he thought with despair. "Maybe they'll manage without that. They're not at all like we were. Maybe they'll manage without it." He swept the notes off the table. There were a lot of them. "What is a fact?" "Can someone who works for the military-industrial complex be considered honest and kind?" "Why do you drink so much?" "Your opinion of Spengler?"

"I have a bunch of questions here," he said. "I don't know if it's still worth—"

The pimply-faced nihilist stood up.

"As it happens, Mr. Banev, I don't know what questions you have there but the point is, in fact, it doesn't really matter. We simply wanted to become acquainted with a well-known contemporary author. Every well-known author expresses the ideology of his society or of a part of that society, and we needed to learn the ideology of contemporary society. Now we know more than we knew before our meeting with you. Thank you."

There was a rustling in the hall; people began to talk. "Thank you. Thank you, Mr. Banev." Children were getting up and leaving their seats. Victor stood, crumpling the notes in his hand, feeling like an idiot. He knew that he was red in the face, that he looked lost and pathetic, but he took himself in hand, stuffed the notes into his pocket, and left the stage.

The hardest part was that he hadn't figured out how he should relate to these children. They were unreal, they were impossible. Their statements, their attitudes toward what he wrote and what he said had nothing in common with their flying pigtails and disheveled curls, their unwashed necks, their thin, scratched-up hands and the high-pitched din all around. It was as if some power, on a whim, had merged a kindergarten with a dispute in a research laboratory. The merging of the unmergeable. That's probably what the cat felt in the experiment: they gave her a piece of fish, scratched her behind the ear, and at the same moment hit her with an electric shock, fired a cartridge under her nose, and blinded her with a floodlight. "I know," sighed Victor to the cat, whose condition he could picture very clearly. "Our psyches are not made for shocks like that; I could even see us dying from them."

Suddenly he realized that he was stuck. They had surrounded him and wouldn't let him pass. For a moment panic and terror overtook him. He would not have been surprised if they had quietly and matter-of-factly stretched him out on the floor and started doing an autopsy for the purpose of ideological investigation. But they didn't want to do an autopsy on him. They were holding out their opened notebooks, cheap pads, little bits of paper. They were murmuring, "Could we have your autograph," squealing "Here, please." Their voices were breaking. "Could you please, Mr. Banev?"

He got out his fountain pen and started taking the cap off, following his feelings with the curiosity of an outsider. He was not surprised to find that he was proud. These were the phantoms of the future, and to be popular with them was still pleasant.

Chapter VI

BACK IN HIS ROOM he headed straight for the bar, poured himself some gin, and drank it down in one gulp, like medicine. Water streamed down his face and down his collar (apparently he had forgotten to put on his hood). His pants were soaked to the knees and stuck to his legs (he had probably walked along without looking, straight through the puddles). More than anything he craved a cigarette. It seemed that he hadn't had a smoke in over two hours.

"Acceleration," he declared to himself as he threw his wet raincoat right onto the floor, changed his clothes, and wiped his head with a towel. "It's nothing but acceleration," he comforted himself, lighting a cigarette and taking the first greedy drags. "There it is, acceleration in action," he thought with horror, recalling the self-assurance of those childish voices making their impossible pronouncements. "Lord save the grownups, save their parents, enlighten them and make them smarter, now's the time. For Thy own good I pray Thee, Lord, or they'll build themselves a Tower of Babel, a monument on the grave of all those idiots you put on this earth to be fruitful and multiply. You never did think through the consequences of acceleration, did you? Not too bright of you, brother."

Victor finished his cigarette, spit the butt onto the carpet, and lit up a new one. "What am I getting so worked up about?" he thought. "My imagination's gotten out of hand. So I saw some kids, so they're old beyond their years. Is this the first time I've looked at kids who were old beyond their years? Where did I get the idea that they thought it all up by themselves? All this local filth got to them. They read a lot of books, they oversimplified, and, naturally, they came to the conclusion that it was imperative to build a new world. And not all of them are that way. They have their chiefs, their ringleaders—Bol-Kunats, the one with the pimples, and then that pretty little thing. Instigators. And the rest were just kids, they sat there, they listened, and they got bored." He knew that it wasn't true. "Well, suppose they didn't get bored, suppose they were interested—still, a provincial town, a famous writer. . . . No way you would have caught me reading my books when I was their age. And you wouldn't have gotten me to go anywhere, except to a cowboy film or a traveling circus, to gawk at the tightrope walkers' thighs. I didn't give a shit about the old world or the new world either, I didn't even know there was such a thing. I knew how to exhaust myself playing soccer. I knew how to unscrew light bulbs and explode them against a wall, or how to get hold of some momma's boy and cream him." Victor fell into his armchair and stretched out his legs. "We have all these rosy memories of our happy childhoods, and we're sure that that's the way it's always been and always will be, ever since the days of Tom Sawyer. That it has to be that way. And if it isn't, then the child is abnormal. If you don't know him well, you feel sorry for him, and if you do, you're overcome with pedagogical indignation. And the child looks mildly at you and thinks, 'Of course you're a grown-up, you've got muscles, you could flog me. But you've been a fool ever since you were a child, you're going to stay a fool and you're going to die a fool. And that's not enough for you, you want to make me into a fool, too.' "

Victor poured himself some more gin and started remembering what it had been like, and he had to take a sudden gulp to keep from howling with shame. How he had pushed himself on those kids, self-assured and self-satisfied, looking down on them, a fashionable blockhead. How he had started right in with platitudes, well-meaning nonsense, and pseudo-masculine clucking. They put him in his place, but he didn't lay off, he continued to demonstrate his extreme intellectual insufficiency. They did their honorable best to get him back on the right path, they warned him, but he kept on going with his banalities and trivialities, imagining that mere momentum would carry him through, that never mind, he'd make it. And when they finally lost patience and let him have it for real, he burst into cowardly tears and started complaining that they weren't treating him nicely. And when, out of pity, they started asking for his autograph, he felt disgracefully triumphant. Victor let out a moan, realizing that with all his self-imposed honesty he would never have the courage to tell anyone what had happened. Within a half hour or so, in the interests of preserving his spiritual balance, he would deviously rework the facts, turning his utter collapse into an unusual success, or, if worse came to worse, into an ordinary and not overly inter-esting meeting with a bunch of provincial prodigies. Prodigies who were after all—what do you expect?—only children, and didn't understand all that much about literature or life. "I should go into the Department of Education," he thought hating himself. "They always need people like that. There's one consolation, though. There aren't too many of them yet and if acceleration continues even at its present pace, then by the time there get to be a lot of them, I will, God willing, be safely dead. What a nice thing—to die in time!"

There was a knock at the door. Victor shouted, "Come in!" and Pavor came in, disheveled, nose swollen, wrapped in an imitation Bukhara robe.

"At long last," said Pavor in a nasal voice, taking a seat across from Victor. He retrieved a huge, wet handkerchief from the area of his bosom and started sneezing and blowing his nose. It was a piteous sight—little remained of the former Pavor.

"What do you mean, at long last?" asked Victor. "Do you want some gin?"

"Oh, hell, I don't know," sniffed Pavor. "This town is driving me crazy. He-he-hep chuuu! Oh, hell."

"Gesundheit," said Victor.

Pavor turned his watery eyes on him.

"Where have you been keeping yourself?" he asked peevishly. "I came around three times, I wanted to get something to read from you. I'm going to pieces, the only thing to do around here is sneeze and blow your nose. There's not a soul in the hotel. I even tried the doorman, but all the old ninny could offer me was a telephone book and some old brochures. 'Visit our sunny city!' Do you have anything to read?"

"Not really," said Victor.

"What do you mean, not really. It's your profession. Oh, I understand, you don't read anyone else, but you must leaf through your own stuff at least occasionally. That's all anyone here talks about, Banev this, Banev that. What's the title? *Death in the Afternoon? Midnight After Death?* I can't remember."

"*Misfortune Comes at Night,*" said Victor.

"That's it. Lend it to me."

"I can't. I don't have it," said Victor decisively. "And even if I did I wouldn't give it to you. You'd sneeze all over it. And you wouldn't understand it either."

"Why not?" objected Pavor, indignant. "They say it's all about homosexuals, what's there to understand?"

"You yourself . . ." said Victor. "Forget it, let's have a drink. You want it with tonic or straight?"

Pavor sneezed. He muttered something, cast a despairing look around the room, then threw back his head and sneezed again.

"A headache," he complained. "Right here. And where have you been? They said you were meeting your readers. The local homosexuals."

"Worse," said Victor. "I was meeting the local prodigies. You know what acceleration is?"

"Acceleration? That's something connected with premature maturation, isn't it? I've heard about it. At one time there was a lot of talk on the topic. But then our department appointed a commission which proved that it was simply a part of Mr. President's personal concern for the coming generation of lions and dreamers. So everything snapped into place. But I do know what you're talking about, I've seen our local prodigies. God save us from lions like that. They belong in a cabinet of curios."

"Or maybe we do," objected Victor.

"Maybe," agreed Pavor. "At any rate, acceleration has nothing to do with it. Acceleration is a biological and physiological phenomenon. An increase in birth weight, after which the subjects shoot up six feet, like giraffes, and at twelve they're ready to reproduce. What we've got here is something else—a system of education. The kids are absolutely normal. Whereas their teachers. . . ."

"What about the teachers?"

Pavor sneezed.

"The teachers are, well, unusual" he said in a nasal voice.

Victor remembered the school director.

"What's so unusual about the teachers here?" he asked. "That they forget to zip their flies?"

"What flies?" asked Pavor, taken aback. He stared at Victor. "They don't have any flies."

"What else?" asked Victor.

"In what sense?"

"What else is so unusual about them?"

Pavor started blowing his nose. Victor sipped at his gin and looked at him with pity.

"I can see you don't know a damn thing," said Pavor, examining his dirty handkerchief. "Mr. President was quite right when he observed that the main characteristic of our writers is their chronic ignorance of life and estrangement from the interests of the nation. Take yourself. You've been here awhile. Have you been anywhere besides the bar and the resort? Have you spoken to anyone besides that drunken sot Quadriga? God knows what you're getting paid for."

"All right, enough," said Victor. "I get enough of that from the papers. Some authority you are—a runny-nosed critic, a teacher with no fly."

"You don't like it?" said Pavor with satisfaction. "Have it your way, I'll stop. Tell me about your meeting with the prodigies."

"There's nothing to tell," said Victor. "Run of the mill prodigies."

"Well?"

"Well, I got there. They asked me some questions. Interesting questions, very mature." Victor was silent for a moment. "To be honest with you, they really gave me a hard time."

"What kind of questions?" asked Pavor. He looked at Victor with sincere interest, and, it seemed, with sympathy.

"It's not the questions," sighed Victor. "To tell the truth, what struck me most was that they acted like adults, and not like any adults either. Like superior ones. The incongruity was diabolical, almost sick." Pavor nodded sympathetically. "In a word, it was bad," said Victor. "I don't want to think about it."

"Of course," said Pavor. "You weren't the first and you won't be the last. The parents of a twelve-year-old are always rather pitiful creatures, beset by a multitude of concerns. But our local parents are something else. They remind me of the rear of an occupying army in a region of stepped-up partisan attacks. Anyhow, what kind of things were they asking?"

"Well, they asked me what progress was. And to their minds it's very simple: Herd us all onto a reservation so that we won't be running around underfoot and they can be free to study Zurzmansor and Spengler. That was my impression, at any rate."

"Why not, it's perfectly plausible," said Pavor. "Like master, like man. You're talking acceleration, Zurzmansor. But do you know what the nation is saying?"

"The what?"

"The nation! The nation is saying that the problem is with the slimies. The kids have gotten warped because of the slimies."

"That's because there aren't any Jews around," said Victor. Then he remembered the slimy who came into the hall, and how the children all stood up, and the expression on Irma's face. "Are you serious?" he asked.

"It's not me," said Pavor. "It's the voice of the nation. Vox populi. The cats all ran away, and the children are in love with the slimies. They hang around the leprosarium, they spend whole days and nights with them. They're out of control, they don't obey anyone. They steal their parents' money and buy books. They say that at first the parents were very happy about it—the kiddies weren't tearing up their pants climbing fences, they were sitting home quietly and reading books. The more so because of the bad weather. But now everybody sees what came of it and who was responsible. Nobody's happy about it any more. Only they're still afraid of the slimies, they only mutter about them behind their backs."

"The voice of the nation," thought Victor. "The voice of Lola and his honor the burgomaster. We've heard it before. Cats, rain, television programs. The blood of Christian babies."

"I don't understand," he said. "Are you serious or is it just that you're bored?"

"It's not me!" repeated Pavor with feeling. "That's what they're saying in town."

"I'm aware of what they're saying in town," said Victor. "But what do you make of it?"

Pavor shrugged.

"The flow of life," he said mysteriously. "One part bullshit, one part truth." He peered at Victor from under his handkerchief. "Don't take me for an idiot," he said. "Think about the

children. Where have you ever seen children like that? Or
at any rate, so many children like that?"

"Right," thought Victor, "children like that. The cats can
do as they damn please, but that slimy in the hall is another
story. Not just one of your part-cats part-rain stories. There's
an expression, a face lit up from within. That's what Irma's
face looked like then. And when she talks to me it's only lit
up on the outside. And her mother she doesn't talk to at all,
she just sputters at her condescendingly. If what he says is
right, if it's really the truth and not just dirty gossip, then it
looks extremely distasteful. What do they want with the children? They're sick people, they're doomed. And anyway, it's a
dirty business, turning children against their parents, even parents like Lola and me. We had enough trouble with Mr. President: the Nation Above and Beyond the Family, the Legion
of Honor is your Father and Your Mother, and before you know
it the kid marches to the nearest post and declares that his
father called Mr. President a strange man and his mother called
the Legion marches a waste of money. And now on top of that
some slimy in a black suit comes along and with no grounds
whatsoever declares that your father is a mindless drunk and
your mother is a stupid whore. It may even be true, but it's
still dirty. This is not the way it should be done. And it's none
of their goddamned business, it's not their responsibility, no
one asked them to engage in educational activities. It's pathological. And what if that's not all? A child opens its rosy little
mouth and starts lisping about progress and saying terrible
cruel things. And it doesn't understand what it's saying, but
still, from the depths of its young being it's getting used to intellectual cruelty, to the most terrible cruelty imaginable. And
there they are, peeling faces wrapped in black cloths, standing
backstage and manipulating the strings. It's not a new generation, it's just an old game of marionettes, and I was an ass
for taking it to heart. What a foul joke it is though, this
civilization of ours."

". . . who has eyes and sees," Pavor was saying. "They don't let us into the leprosarium. Barbed wire, soldiers. All right. But some things you can see right here in town. I saw the slimies talking with some boys, and I saw how those boys were behaving with them, what little angels they turned into. But go ask one of them how to get to the factory and you'll be dripping from head to toe with his scorn."

"They don't let us into the leprosarium," thought Victor. "They've got barbed wire there. But the slimies go wherever they want. And it's not Golem who's behind this. That bastard," he thought suddenly. "The Father of the Nation. That son of a bitch. So this is his doing, too. The Best Friend of Children. Highly possible, it's just like him. You know, Mr. President, if I were you I would try to vary my methods somewhat. It's too easy to distinguish your hind quarters from everyone else's. Barbed wire, soldiers, and passes: the unmistakable sign of Mr. President, the sign of some dirty business."

"Why the hell did they put barbed wire up?" asked Victor.

"How should I know?" said Pavor. "There never used to be any."

"So you've been there before?"

"What makes you think so? I haven't. But I'm not the first sanitary inspector they've had here. And it's not a matter of barbed wire, the world is full of barbed wire. It's that nothing stops the kids from entering, nothing stops the slimies from leaving, and you and I can't get near the place. That's what's surprising."

"No, it's not the President," thought Victor. "The President just doesn't mix with reading Zurzmansor—or Banev for that matter. And this destructive ideology—if I wrote that they'd crucify me. I don't get it, there's something suspicious about it. Suppose I ask Irma," he thought. "I'll just ask and see how she reacts. In fact, Diana ought to know a few things herself."

"Aren't you listening?" asked Pavor.

"Sorry, I was thinking."

"I was saying that I wouldn't be surprised if the citizens took measures. Their usual type of measures—cruel ones."

"I wouldn't be surprised either," muttered Victor. "I wouldn't be surprised if I felt like taking a few measures myself."

Pavor stood up and walked to the window.

"Some weather," he sighed. "I can't wait to get out of here. Are you giving me the book or not?"

"I don't have any books," said Victor. "Everything I brought with me is at the health resort. Listen, what do the slimies need our children for?"

Pavor shrugged.

"They're sick people," he said. "How should we know? We're healthy."

There was a knock at the door, and Golem entered, bulky and wet.

"Let's ask Golem," said Pavor. "Golem, what do the slimies need our children for?"

"Our children?" said Golem, carefully studying the label on the gin bottle. "Do you have children, Pavor?"

"According to Pavor," said Victor, "your slimies seem to be inciting the local children against their parents. What do you know about it, Golem?"

"Hm," said Golem. "Where do you keep your clean glasses? Aha, . . . The slimies inciting the children? Well, what can you do? They're not the first and they won't be the last." Still in his raincoat, he sank onto the couch and started sniffing his gin. "And why not incite children against their parents in times like these? The whites are being incited against the blacks, the yellows are being incited against the whites, the stupid people against the smart ones. What's so surprising?"

"According to Pavor," repeated Victor, "your patients are hanging around town and teaching the children all sorts of strange things. I noticed something of this myself, although for the present I remain undecided. That being the case, I find nothing surprising. I'm simply asking you whether or not it's true."

"To the best of my knowledge," said Golem, attending to his gin, "the slimies have had free access to the city since time immemorial. I don't know what you have in mind when you talk about their teaching all sorts of strange things, but let me ask you one question as a native of this place: are you familiar with the toy they call a 'nasty top'?"

"Of course," said Victor.

"Did you have one?"

"I didn't, though I remember my friends did." Victor fell silent. "Of course," he said. "The kids said it was a present from a slimy. Is that what you meant?"

"Exactly. And the 'weatherwhiz,' and the 'wooden arm.'"

"Pardon me," said Pavor. "Would it be possible for a visitor from the capital to learn what the natives are talking about?"

"No," said Golem. "And to answer your next question, because I don't feel like it. Stop lying, you were trying to buy a weatherwhiz from Teddy, and you have a perfectly clear idea of what it is."

"Go to hell," snapped Pavor. "I'm not talking about the weatherwhiz."

"Hold it, Pavor," said Victor patiently. "Golem, you haven't answered my question."

"Really? I thought I did. In truth, Victor, the slimies are seriously and hopelessly ill. Genetic illnesses are no joke. But despite it they retain their kindness and intelligence, so there's no need to cast aspersions on them."

"Who's casting aspersions?"

"Aren't you?"

"At this point, no. At this point I'm still inclined to the contrary."

"Good," said Golem and stood up. "Then let's get going."

Victor started.

"Go where?"

"To the health resort. I'm going to the health resort; you, I see, are also heading for the health resort; and you, Pavor, should go to bed. Quit giving everyone the flu."

Victor looked at his watch.

"Isn't it early?" he said.

"Suit yourself. Only keep in mind that starting today the bus service has been canceled. It wasn't profitable."

"Maybe we could have some dinner first?"

"Suit yourself," Golem repeated. "Except I never have dinner, and I wouldn't advise you to either."

Victor felt his stomach.

"Right," he said. He looked at Pavor. "I think I'll go."

"What do I care?" said Pavor. He sounded offended. "Bring back some books for me."

"Sure," Victor promised and started getting dressed.

They got into the car. Beneath the damp canvas top the air was damp and smelled of tobacco, gas, and medicine.

"Can you take a hint?" asked Golem.

"Sometimes," said Victor. "When I know it's a hint. What of it?"

"Here's a hint. Stop shooting your mouth off."

"Hm," mumbled Victor. "And how would you like me to understand that?"

"As a hint. Stop talking so much."

"With pleasure," said Victor, and fell silent, thinking.

They crossed the town, past the cannery and the deserted city park, neglected, drooping, half-rotted from dampness.

They sped past the stadium, where the Brothers in Reason, splattered with mud, were busily whacking waterlogged balls with their waterlogged boots. Finally they drove out onto the road leading to the health resort. All around, beyond the shroud of rain, the wet steppe stretched out flat as a table— the dry, scorched, thorny steppe that was slowly turning into a swamp.

"Your hint," said Victor, "reminded me of a certain conversation I once had with his excellency the advisor to Mr. President on government ideology. His excellency called me to his modest office of five thousand square feet or so and put a question to me: 'Veektor, would you like to keep on getting your piece of bread and butter?' Naturally, I answered in the affirmative. 'Then shut your mouth,' barked his excellency and waved me out of the room."

Golem snorted, "And what did he want you to shut your mouth about?"

"His excellency was hinting about my experiments with a banjo in certain youth clubs."

Golem fixed his narrow eyes on Victor.

"What makes you so sure I'm not an agent?"

"I'm not sure," said Victor. "I simply don't give a shit. Incidentally, nobody says 'agent' any more. It's obsolete. Now everybody who is anybody says 'Fed.' "

"I don't get the difference," said Golem.

"In point of fact, neither do I," declared Victor. "So let's keep our mouths shut. Has your patient recovered?"

"My patients never recover."

"You have a great reputation. But I was asking about the poor guy who landed in a trap. How's his leg?"

Golem was silent for a moment.

"Which one of them did you have in mind?" he said.

"I don't understand," said Victor. "I mean, of course, the one who got caught in a trap."

"There were four of them," said Golem, staring at the rain-swept road. "The first got caught in a trap. The one you carried around on your back was the second one. The third one left with me in the car, and the disgraceful brawl you started in the restaurant not long ago concerned the fourth."

Victor, stunned, didn't say anything. Neither did Golem. He skillfully maneuvered the car around the innumerable potholes in the old asphalt.

"It's all right, don't think so hard," he said finally. "I was joking. There was only one of them. And his leg set the same night."

"Is that another joke?" Victor inquired. "Ha ha ha. Now I see why your patients never recover."

"My patients," said Golem, "never recover for different

reasons. First of all, like every decent physician, I cannot cure genetic diseases. Secondly, they don't want to be cured."

"Funny," muttered Victor. "I've already listened to so much talk about those slimies of yours that I'm ready to believe all of it: the rain, the cats, and the fact that a compound fracture can set in one night."

"What cats?" said Golem.

"You know what cats," said Victor. "How come there aren't any cats left in the city? Because of the slimies. Teddy can't keep up with the mice. You should have advised the slimies to remove the mice at the same time."

"A la the Pied Piper?" said Golem.

"Yes," said Victor lightheadedly. "Exactly." Then he remembered how the story about the Pied Piper ended. "There's nothing funny about it," he said. "Today I gave a talk at the middle school. I saw the children. And I saw them greeting one of the slimies. Now I won't be in the least surprised if one fine day some slimy appears on the town square with an accordion and lures the kids to kingdom come."

"You won't be surprised," said Golem. "But what will you do about it?"

"I don't know. Maybe I'll take his accordion away from him."

"And start playing yourself?"

Victor sighed. "It's true. I've got nothing to offer them, that much I understood. I wonder what they have. You must know, Golem."

"Veektor, shut your mouth," said Golem.

"Suit yourself," said Victor. "I see you're doing your best to get around my questions, and you're more or less succeeding at it. It's stupid. I'll find out anyway, and you'll have lost the opportunity to impart the information in its most advantageous emotional light."

"Privileged medical material," pronounced Golem. "Then again, I don't know anything. I can only guess."

He slowed down. Up ahead, beyond the veil of rain, some

figures were standing in the road. Three gray figures and a gray road marker with a sign: "Leprosarium—4 miles" and "Warm Springs Health Resort—1 1/2 miles." The figures stepped back onto the shoulder—a man and two children.

"Wait a minute, stop," said Victor, suddenly hoarse.

"What happened?" Golem braked.

Victor didn't answer. He was staring at the people standing by the road marker: a huge slimy in a black exercise suit saturated with water, a young boy, also raincoatless, in a sopping wet suit and sandals, and a barefoot little girl, dress clinging to her body. Then he threw open the door and jumped out onto the road.

The wind and rain whipped at his face, and he even gulped down a mouthful, unaware. He sensed the onslaught of a fit of unendurable rage, the rage that makes you want to destroy everything, the rage that comes when you know you're about to do something stupid and the knowledge only gladdens you. Stiff-legged, he walked straight up to the slimy.

"What's going on here?" he got out through his teeth. And then, to the little girl looking at him in astonishment, "Irma, into the car!" And again to the slimy, "What the hell are you up to?" And then to Irma, "Get into the car, I'm telling you!"

Irma didn't budge. The three of them stood as before. Above his black bandage, the slimy's eyes blinked calmly. "This is my father," said Irma in an almost indecipherable voice. And suddenly he realized, not with his brain, but with his spinal cord, that this was not the place for screaming and threatening, not the place for raising his hand to her and dragging her by the collar, and in general, not the place for carrying on.

"Irma," he said very quietly, "go to the car, you're soaking wet. Bol-Kunats, if I were you I'd also get into the car."

He was sure that Irma would obey him and she did. Not exactly the way he would have wanted. It wasn't that she looked up to the slimy for permission to leave, but he was left with the shadow of an impression that something had occurred, some exchange of opinion or short consultation, as a result of which the question had been decided in his favor. Irma made a face and set off for the car. Bol-Kunats looked at him politely. "Thank you, Mr. Banev, but I think I'd better stay."

"Whatever you want," said Victor. Bol-Kunats didn't worry him. Now he had to think up something to say to the slimy in parting. Victor knew beforehand that it would be something incredibly stupid, but what can you do? Simply picking himself up and leaving was beyond him. Purely from considerations of prestige.

"And you, sir," he said haughtily, "have not been invited. Apparently you're in your element here."

He turned around and, throwing an imaginary gauntlet, made his departure. "Having said these words," he thought with disgust, "the count proudly took his leave."

Irma scrambled into the front seat and wrung out her pigtails. Victor got into the back, groaning with shame. Golem started the motor.

"Having pronounced these words, the count took his leave. Let's have your legs, Irma, I'll give them a rubdown."

"What for?" said Irma with curiosity.

"You want to catch pneumonia? Give me your legs!"

"Go ahead," said Irma, and, twisting around on the seat, proffered him a leg.

Anticipating that now, at long last, he would be going something natural and useful, Victor took the thin, wet, touchingly girlish leg in both hands. He wanted to rub it till it turned red, he wanted to take this dirty, bony icicle, unending source of colds and flu, bronchitis and double pneumonia, into his kind, stern father's hands and rub it till it glowed. But then he discovered that his hand was colder than her leg. Out of inertia he made a few rubbing motions, and then carefully let it down. "Of course I knew it," he thought suddenly, "I knew it would be this way when I was still standing in front of them. I knew that there was some trick to it, that the children were safe and there wouldn't be any colds or pneumonia. Only I didn't want that, I wanted to save them, tear them from his claws, explode in just anger, fulfill my duty. And I came out of it looking like an ass again. I don't know how they do it, but I came out looking like an ass again, a real fool for the second time today."

"Take your leg back," he said, to Irma.

She took her leg back.

"Where are we going—to the health resort?" she asked.

"Yes," Victor answered. He looked at Golem, wondering if this latest disgrace had registered. Golem, his belly overflowing onto the seat, was calmly watching the road. He was graying, slovenly, hunched-over and all-knowing.

"Why?" asked Irma.

"You'll change into something dry and get into bed," said Victor.

"That's a good one!" said Irma. "What's the big idea?"

"All right, all right," muttered Victor. "I'll give you some books, you can read."

"Really, why in God's name am I taking her there," he thought. "Diana . . . well, we'll see about that. No drinking, and in general nothing of that sort, only how am I going to bring her back. Oh, hell, I'll grab somebody's car and take her home. I wish there was something to drink here."

"Golem . . ." he was about to start, but stopped himself. "Goddamn, I can't, not in front of her."

"Yes?" said Golem without turning around.

"Never mind," sighed Victor, fixing his gaze on the neck of a flask sticking out of the pocket of Golem's raincoat. "Irma," he said wearily, "what were you doing standing there at the crossroads?"

"We were thinking fog," answered Irma.

"What?"

"Thinking fog," Irma repeated.

"About fog," Victor corrected. "Or of fog."

"Why about fog?" said Irma.

"Think is an intransitive verb," Victor explained. "It takes a preposition. Didn't you have intransitive verbs in school?"

"It all depends," said Irma. "Thinking fog is one thing and thinking about fog is completely different. And I can't see who would want to think about fog."

Victor found a cigarette and lit it. "Hold on," he said. "You can't say 'think fog,' it's illiterate. There are such things as intransitive verbs: think, run, walk. They always take prepositions. Walk along the street. Think about . . . well, whatever."

"Think stupid thoughts," said Golem.

"Well, that's an exception," said Victor, slightly flustered.

"Walk quickly," said Golem.

"Quickly isn't a noun," snapped Victor. "Don't confuse the child, Golem."

"Would you mind not smoking, Daddy?" asked Irma.

Golem must have made some sound, or else it was the motor coughing as they started up the hill. Victor crushed his cigarette under his heel. They were climbing the hill to the health resort, and to the side, from the steppe, a thick whitish wall had moved to meet the rain.

"That's fog for you," said Victor. "You can think it. You can also smell it, run it, and walk it."

Irma was about to say something but Golem interrupted her.

"Incidentally," he said. "The verb 'think' can also be transitive with a clause as its direct object. For example, 'I think that,' etc."

"That's something else," objected Victor. He was sick of it. He needed to smoke and have a drink of something. He looked with longing at the neck of the flask. "You sure you're not cold, Irma?" he asked, hopefully but a bit uncertain.

"No. What about you?"

"I seem to have the chills," Victor confessed.

"You should have a drink of gin," said Golem.

"Not a bad idea. Do we have any?"

"We do," said Golem. "But we're almost there."

The jeep careened through the gates, and then there began something that Victor could have foreseen. The first streams of fog had barely begun to penetrate the garden railing and the visibility was perfect. Lying on the driveway, clothed in wet pajamas, was a body, and it looked as though it had already spent a good number of days and nights there. Golem carefully circumnavigated it. He continued on past the plaster vase with it's simpleminded drawings and corresponding inscriptions and ended up by the herd of cars huddled at the entrance to the right wing. Irma opened the door. An instant later, a seasoned face stuck itself out the window of the next car. "Want to have me, honey?" it squealed. Victor, mortified, climbed out. Irma looked around curiously. Victor grabbed her by the hand and led her to the entrance. Two whores in their underwear, arms around each other, were sitting on the steps in the rain, screeching out some ballad about a cruel druggist who wouldn't sell heroin. When they caught sight of Victor they shut up, but as he passed, one of them tried to catch hold of his pants. Victor pushed Irma into the lobby. Here it was dark, the shades were drawn, it smelled of tobacco smoke and something sour. A projector was sputtering, and pornographic pictures danced on the white wall. Grinding his teeth, Victor stepped on top of someone's feet, dragging the stumbling Irma behind him. After them came an angry burst of four-letter words. They made their way out of the lobby, and Victor started up the carpeted stairway three steps at a time. Irma still hadn't said anything, and he didn't dare look at her. On the landing, arms opened wide and poised for an embrace, stood the purple-faced, blowsy Member of Parliament, Rosheper Nant. "Veektor," he wheezed. "Friend!" Then he saw Irma and exploded with delight. "Veektor! You too! With the beauteous prepubertals!" Victor grimaced, stepped hard on his foot, and poked him in the chest. Rosheper fell backwards, knocking over a spittoon. Covered with sweat, Victor started down the corridor. Irma followed him with noiseless little leaps. He stumbled into Diana's door. It was locked; the key was missing. He started knocking wildly, and Diana responded at once. "Go to hell," she shrieked. "You stinking impotent, you dirty asshole, you piece of dogshit!"

"Diana!" barked Victor. "Open up!"

Diana fell silent, and the door opened. She stood at the threshold, French umbrella positioned for the attack. Victor shoved her back, dragged Irma into the room, and slammed the door.

"So it's you," said Diana. "I thought it was Rosheper again." She smelled of liquor. "Oh, God," she said. "Who is this?"

"This is my daughter," said Victor with effort. "Her name is Irma. Irma, this is Diana."

He looked fixedly at Diana with desperation and hope. It seemed, thank God, that she wasn't completely drunk. Or she had sobered up instantaneously.

"You must be out of your mind," she said softly.

"She's wet," he said. "Get her into something dry, put her to bed, and—"

"I won't," Irma announced.

"Irma," said Victor. "Kindly listen or I'll wallop you."

"Somebody here deserves to get walloped," said Diana hopelessly.

"Diana," said Victor. "I beg you."

"All right," said Diana. "Go to your room. We'll manage."

Victor, immensely relieved, walked out. He set off straight for his room, but even in his own room there wasn't any peace. As a preliminary step, he found it necessary to dispatch a pair of completely unknown lovers, followed by a quantity of stained bed linen. Then he locked the door, fell onto the bare mattress, lit up a damp cigarette, and started contemplating what he'd brought upon himself.

Chapter VII

THE NEXT DAY Victor woke up late, around lunchtime. He had a slight headache, but his mood was unexpectedly good.

The night before, after smoking a pack of cigarettes, he'd gone downstairs and forced open someone's car with a hairpin. Then he'd marched Irma out the service entrance and carted her home to mother. At first they'd driven in silence. Unpleasant memories had him writhing in his seat, and Irma sat beside him, neat and spanking clean. Her pigtails had given way to the latest hairstyle and it looked like she even had lipstick on. More than anything he wanted to get a conversation going, but to start with a confession of his own incredible stupidity—the only way—seemed pedagogically undesirable. In the end, Irma suddenly decided to let him smoke, on the condition that all the windows would be opened, and started telling him how interesting it had been for her. It was just like what she'd read but never really believed, and what a great guy he was for providing her with such an unexpected but to the highest degree instructive adventure. And he wasn't at all bad, he wasn't boring and he didn't talk a lot of nonsense, and Diana was "almost one of us" because she hated everyone. It was too bad that she didn't know very much and was rather too fond of drinking, but in the final analysis there's nothing so terrible about that, you're also rather fond of drinking. And the kids liked you because you were honest and didn't pretend to be some repository of higher knowledge which is good because you aren't. Even

Bol-Kunats said that you're the only worthwhile person in town, not counting Dr. Golem, of course, but "Golem, in fact, doesn't have anything to do with the town. And then he's not a writer, he doesn't express ideologies. And what do you think, is it necessary to have an ideology or is it better without one, recent opinion is leaning towards a future of deideologization."

It was a fine conversation, the speakers were full of respect for one another, and when he got back to the hotel (having left the car in some garbage-filled lot) Victor already felt that being a father was not such a thankless task. Especially if you know a thing or two about life and could use even its seamy sides for educational purposes. With this in mind, he took a drink with Teddy, who was also a father and also interested in education. Teddy's first-born was fourteen—"a bad thing, adolescence, and you've still got it to look forward to"—that is, his first-born grandchild was fourteen. He hadn't done anything about his son's education because his son had spent his childhood in a German concentration camp. "You must never beat your children," Teddy kept saying. "They'll be knocked around all their lives without your interference, and if you can't do without it, then better hit yourself instead, it'd be more useful."

After an indefinite number of drinks Victor remembered that Irma had not breathed a word about his dreadful behavior at the crossroads. He came to the conclusion that the child was shrewd and that, in general, running to the aid of your mistress every time you didn't know how to get yourself out of a tight spot—moreover a spot that you alone had gotten yourself into —was at best dishonorable. These thoughts distressed him. But then Dr. R. Quadriga came along and ordered his usual bottle of gin, and the two of them drank that bottle. Following which, Victor began to see everything in rainbow colors, because it had become clear that Irma simply hadn't wanted to hurt him, and that meant that she respected her father and maybe even loved him. Then someone else came and ordered something else. Then, most likely, Victor went off to bed.

Most likely. In all probability, he went. It's true that he retained one final memory: a tiled floor with water spilled all over it. But where the floor was and what the water was doing on it was impossible to reconstruct. And better not to try.

Victor pulled himself into shape. He went downstairs, got the morning papers from the desk clerk, and had a chat about the lousy weather.

"How'd I do last night?" he asked carelessly. "Not too bad?"

"Could be worse," said the desk clerk politely. "Teddy will give you the bill."

"Oh," said Victor, and, deciding not to pursue the matter just yet, went off to the restaurant.

It seemed to him that there was a slight decrease in the number of table lamps. "Christ!" he thought, frightened. Teddy hadn't come in yet. Victor bowed to the young man in glasses and his companion, took his usual seat, and unfolded the paper. The world was the same as ever. One country was detaining the merchant marine of another country, and this other country was sending sharply worded protests. Countries favored by Mr. President were waging just wars of liberation in the interests of real democracy. Countries which Mr. President for some reason did not favor were waging imperialist wars, or, more precisely, were not waging wars at all, but pursuing a policy of malicious, criminal aggression. Mr. President himself had delivered a two-hour speech on the necessity of stamping out corruption. Following that, he underwent a successful tonsillectomy. A critic Victor knew—a lousy son of a bitch—praised Rots-Tusov's latest book, and that was mysterious, because the book was good.

The waiter came, an unfamiliar one, probably new, and very friendly. He advised Victor to take the oysters, then wrote down his order, brushed the table with a napkin, and departed. Victor put down his newspaper. He lit up a cigarette and, making himself more comfortable, began to think about his work. After a good drinking bout he always found it pleasant to think about his work. It would be good to write a happy, optimistic story. About a certain man who likes what he does, and he's not stupid, he likes his friends and his friends value him. About how happy he is—a fine guy, on the eccentric side, a real wit. There's no story there. And if there's no story, it means it's boring. And anyway, if you're going to write a story like that then you have to figure out why he's happy, and the only conclusion you can come to is that he's happy only because he loves his work and doesn't give a shit about anything else. And how can he be a good person if he doesn't give a shit about anything except his beloved work? Of course you could always write about a man whose work consists of loving his neighbor, and who is happy because he loves his neighbor and he loves his work. But that was already done, a couple of thousand years ago, by Messrs. Luke, Matthew, John, and one other—four of them in all. Actually there were a lot more of them, but only those four were ideologically reliable, the others lacking various things, national self-awareness, for example, or mailing privileges. And the man they were writing about was, unfortunately, feebleminded. Although it would be interesting to write about Christ coming down to earth today, not like Dostoevsky did it, but like that Luke and company. Christ arrives at staff headquarters and makes his proposals about loving thy neighbor, etc. And naturally they've got some anti-Semite sitting there.

"Do you mind, Mr. Banev?" A pleasant masculine voice rumbled over him.

It was his honor the burgomaster himself. Not the apoplectically purple boor, grunting with sick satisfaction on Rosheper's oversized bed, but an elegantly rotund, ideally shaven, and impeccably dressed gentleman with a modest ribbon in his buttonhole and the Legion's shield on his left shoulder.

"Not at all," said Victor, far from overjoyed.

His honor the burgomaster sat down, glanced around the room, and folded his hands on the table.

"I will do my best not to burden you at length with my presence, Mr. Banev," he said, "as I have every intention of not disturbing your meal. However, the issue I would like to address you with today has ripened to the point that all of us, young and old alike, all those who value the honor and well-being of our city, must be prepared to put aside our private affairs in the interests of its expeditious and effective solution."

"What can I do for you?" said Victor.

"We are meeting here, Mr. Banev, in a setting that must be considered unofficial, since, taking your busy schedule into account, I would not risk disturbing you during your hours of work, particularly if one keeps in mind the specifics thereof. However, I am addressing you now as an official party—both personally, in my own name, and in the name of the town council as a whole."

The waiter brought the oysters and a bottle of white wine. The burgomaster stopped him with a raised finger.

"My friend," he said. "A half a portion of Kitchigan sturgeon and a glass of menthol vodka. The sturgeon without sauce. . . . So, allow me to continue," he said, again turning toward Victor. "In truth, I fear that our talk will hardly resemble the usual conversation over lunch, since we will be touching on various things and circumstances which are not only sorrowful, but, I would even say, unappetizing. It was my intention to talk with you about the so-called slimies, about that malignant tumor which has been eating away at our unhappy district lo these many years."

"Yes," said Victor. It was getting interesting.

The burgomaster delivered a low-key speech, well thought out and elegantly phrased. He spoke about the founding of the leprosarium in Horses' Hollow twenty years back, right after the occupation, as a quarantine camp for people suffering from the so-called yellow leprosy, or ocularis ringus. Of course, as Mr. Banev was well aware, the disease had been around since time immemorial, and in fact, historical studies show that for some reason it had always been particularly prevalent in this area. However, it was only thanks to the efforts of Mr. President that the most serious attention was paid to this disease, and only by his personal directive that these unhappy people, deprived of medical help and dispersed throughout the land, where they were persecuted by backward elements of the population (the occupiers had simply exterminated them), were at last united in a single place. Here they were provided with the opportunity for a tolerable existence befitting their pitiful state. None of this calls forth any objections, and the measures taken can only be welcomed. However, as occasionally happens in our country, the best intended beginnings turned against us. It is not our place here to seek out the guilty parties. We will not engage in an investigation of the activities of Mr. Golem, activities which may have been selfless, but which, as we later learned, were fraught with the most unpleasant consequences. Nor will we engage in premature backbiting, although the position of certain parties in high places who persist in ignoring our protests strikes us personally as enigmatic. Let us consider the facts. . . . The burgomaster polished off a glass of vodka and attended to his sturgeon. His voice became even more velvety—it was impossible to imagine him setting out traps for people. He wordily expressed his desire not to trouble Mr. Banev with certain rumors that had overtaken the city, rumors, which he must openly confess, were the result of the insufficiently precise and single-minded adherence to Mr. President's guidelines to be found on certain administrative levels. He had in mind the widespread belief concerning the fateful role of the so-called slimies in the sharp change in climate and their responsibility in, one, the increase in the number of miscarriages and sterile unions; two, the Homeric departure of certain domestic animals from the city; three, the appearance of a particular species of domestic bedbug, to be precise, the winged bedbug—

"Mr. Burgomaster," said Victor, letting out a sigh. "I must confess that I find it extremely difficult to follow your convoluted syntax. Let's talk simply, like good sons of the same nation. Let's not talk about what we're not going to talk about. Let's talk about what we're talking about."

The burgomaster threw a quick glance at him. Apparently he was calculating or weighing something, God knows what. Probably everything went into it. That Victor had boozed it up with Rosheper and that he'd boozed it up in general, noisily on a nationwide scale. That Irma was a prodigy, that there was such a woman as Diana, and, no doubt, much more of the same. So that the burgomaster perceptibly lost some of his polish and called for a glass of cognac. Victor also shouted for a glass of cognac. The burgomaster guffawed, and glanced around the hall, already grown empty. He slapped his fist lightly on the table.

"All right, why should we beat around the bush. It's impossible to live in this town, for which you can say thank you to your buddy Golem—incidentally, are you aware of his Communist leanings? Yes, I assure you, we have evidence; he's hanging by a thread, your Golem. So I'm saying, the children are being corrupted before our very eyes. The slimies have wormed their way into the school and completely ruined the kids. The voters are dissatisfied, some of them have left, there are rumblings, the next thing you know there'll be lynchings, and the district administration does nothing. That's the kind of situation we're in." He downed his glass. "I must admit I personally hate that scum. I'd rip them to shreds with my own teeth if the very thought didn't make me sick. You wouldn't believe it, Mr. Banev, but it's gotten so bad that I've been putting out traps for them. Well, so they've corrupted the children, well, all right. Children are children, you can corrupt them all you want and they'll still want more. But step into my shoes for a minute. No matter how you look at it, this rain is their doing. I don't know how they manage it, but that's the way it is. We built the health resort—healing waters, superb climate—go rake up the money, it's yours. People used to come here from the capital. And how did it all end? Rain, fog, the guests all have colds, and it only gets worse. This famous physicist comes—I forget his name but you probably know it. He stays two weeks and it's all over: ocularis ringus. Straight to the leprosarium. Some advertisement that is. Then another case, and then another one, and it's all over—they've cut off our livelihood with a knife. The restaurant is going bankrupt, the hotel is going bankrupt, the health resort is hardly holding its own. Thank God some crazy coach turned up and brought his Brothers in Reason, he's coaching a special team to play in wet climates. And of course Mr. Rosheper helps to a certain extent. Can you sympathize with me? I tried to come to an agreement with this Golem. It's like talking to a brick wall. Once a red, always a red. I sent a letter to my superiors; no results. I tried their superiors; still nothing. I went still higher, and they said they would take it into account, that they'd send the matter down through the ranks. I hate them, but I forced myself and went to the leprosarium. They let me in. I begged them, I showed them. Christ are they disgusting. They wink at you with those scaly eyes of theirs as if you were some sparrow, as if you didn't exist." He bent over toward Victor. "I'm afraid of a revolt," he whispered, "there'll be blood flowing. Can you sympathize with me?"

"Yes," said Victor. "But what do I have to do with it?"

The burgomaster leaned back in his chair, got a half-smoked cigar out of an aluminum case, and lit up.

"In my position," he said, "there's only one thing left to do: pull out all the stops. We need publicity. The city council put together a petition to the Department of Health. Mr. Rosheper will sign it, and you, I hope, will also sign it but that's no big deal. What I need is real publicity. I need a good exposé. I need it in an influential paper and I need it under a famous by-line. Your by-line, Mr. Banev. A hot issue like this demands an advocate of your caliber. I beg you. In my own name, in the name of the town council, in the name of the unhappy parents. Make them take their leprosarium and get it the hell out of here. I don't care where, as long as not a single slimy footprint remains. Scum! That's what I had to tell you."

"Yes, yes, I understand," said Victor slowly. "I understand you very well."

"You may be a boor," he thought, "you may be a dirty swine but there's no problem understanding you. But what's happened to the slimies? They used to be timid and hunched over, they kept to themselves. People never used to talk this way about them. They said they smelled, they said they could infect you, they said they made great toys and all sorts of things from wood. I remember Fred's mother saying that they had the evil eye, that they made milk go bad, and that they'd bring us war, pestilence, and famine. And now they've got themselves behind barbed wire, and what are they up to there? A whole lot of things. They're playing with the weather, they're winning over the children (why?), they've chased the cats away (another why), they've got their bedbugs airborne."

"No doubt you're thinking that we're sitting here with our hands folded," said the burgomaster. "In no way. But what can we do? I'm preparing a case against Golem. The sanitary inspector Mr. Pavor Summan has agreed to serve as consultant. We're basing it on the fact that the question of infectiousness is far from resolved, and that Golem, who has Communist leanings, is making use of this. That's one thing. Further, we are trying to fight terror with terror. The town Legion, our pride and joy, we've gotten a terrific bunch of kids together, real eagles. But that's not exactly what we need. The orders from above just haven't come, the police are in a false position, and in general. . . . So we set up whatever barriers we can. We hold back the freight that's being sent to them. Private things, of course, there's nothing industrial, and no sanitary necessities or anything like that. But they do get all sorts of books, they order them. Today we held up a truck, and I'm breathing just a little bit more freely. But all this is child's play; we're doing it from despair. What we need is something radical."

"So," said Victor. "Eagles, you say. What's his name— Flamenda? You know, the nephew?"

"Flamen Juventa," said the burgomaster. "Yes, sir. My right hand in the Legion, an eagle! You already know him?"

"Not well," said Victor. "Why would you want to hold up books?"

"What do you mean, why? It's silly, of course, but we're only people, we're only human beings, it mounts up. And then . . ." The burgomaster gave an embarrassed smile. "It's ridiculous, of course, but there are rumors that they can't live without books, like normal people can't live without food and so forth."

They fell silent. Victor, without appetite, poked at his steak.

"I don't know much about the slimies," he thought, "and what I do know doesn't arouse my sympathy toward them. Maybe it's because I never particularly liked them as a kid. But the burgomaster and his gang I know well. The Fat and Lard of the Nation. The President's lackeys, pogrom-makers. No, my friend, once you're against the slimies it means there's something to them. On the other hand, I can always write your exposé, even a really steamy one. Nobody's going to print me anyway. The burgomaster would be satisfied, I'd milk him for whatever it's worth, and I'd be in clover. Which of our real writers can boast that he lives in clover? I could set myself up here, get some sinecure as, for example, the town beach inspector, and write to my heart's content. About how good it is to be a good man who is absorbed in his beloved work. And then I could give a talk on the subject to the local prodigies. It's all a matter of learning how to wipe yourself off. You got spat at in the face and you wiped yourself off. The first time you were ashamed to do it, then you were puzzled, and here you go, wiping yourself off with grace and even getting a certain satisfaction out of it."

"Of course, we wouldn't presume to hurry you," said the burgomaster. "You are a busy man, and so forth. How about something, oh, say, in about a week? We'll give you all the material you need, we can even give you a bit of an outline, a little plan it would be most desirable for you to . . . All you have to do is touch your masterful hand to the paper, and we're in business. And the signatories would be three of the most outstanding sons of our town: Member of Parliament Rosheper Nant, the well-known writer Victor Banev, and the National Laureate Dr. Rem Quadriga."

"Nice work," thought Victor. "They've got it all over us liberals. We can't come near that sort of persuasiveness. We drag things out, beat around the bush, anything so as not to overdo the pressure and hurt someone's feelings; God forbid they might suspect us of acting in our own self-interest. Outstanding sons! And the bastard is completely convinced that he'll have my exposé and my signature; that the poor, disgraced Banev will hold up his hands and use the sweat of his soul to pay off a quiet stay in his native town. And that little outline of his. We know what kind of outline that is and what kind of outline that has to be to insure that our friend Banev, sprayed with presidential spit, gets published without delay. That's the way it goes, Mr. Banev. You like your cognac and your girls, you like your marinated eel with onions, now go pay for them."

"I've thought over your proposal," he said, smiling. "The project strikes me as sufficiently interesting, but its realization would require a certain straining of the conscience. As you of course know, we writers are not up for sale, we work exclusively according to the dictates of conscience." He gave the burgomaster an outrageous, obscene wink.

The burgomaster chuckled.

"But of course! The Conscience of the Nation, the True Mirror, and so on. How could I forget it?" He again leaned toward Victor with a conspiratorial air. "I invite you to my place tomorrow," he intoned. "A small circle of good friends. Only watch out—no wives. How about it?"

"Here," said Victor, rising, "I am obliged to make a decisive and straightforward refusal. I have some business to attend to." He gave another obscene wink. "In the health resort."

They parted almost friends. The writer Banev was admitted

to the ranks of the town elite, and, so as to calm his nerves which were quite shaken by the honor of it, he was obliged to empty a glass of cognac as soon as the burgomaster's back had disappeared behind the door.

"I could of course take off from here and head for the sticks," thought Victor. "They'd never let me out of the country, and I don't even want to get out of the country. What would I do there—it's the same story everywhere. But even here there are a good dozen places where you can hide and sit it out." He imagined some distant, sunny place: beech woods, intoxicating air, taciturn farmers, the scent of milk and honey, manure and mosquitoes, the stench of the privy, and the awful boredom, every night, ancient televisions and the local intelligentsia, the sharp priest with an eye for the ladies and the teacher hooked on moonshine. "Although what am I thinking about, there are places I could go. Except that's just what they need, for me to run off and hide, crawl into my burrow, and all by myself, too, without coercion. Because it's a pain in the neck to exile me, it would get around, people would start talking. And that's the whole problem: they'd be terribly pleased. The troublemaker's quieted down, he's stopped shooting his mouth off. Gone and forgotten."

Victor paid for his meal, went to his room, put on his raincoat, and walked out into the rain. He had a sudden desire to see Irma again. He wanted to talk to her about progress, explain why he drank so much (as a matter of fact, why did he drink so much?). Maybe Bol-Kunats would be there, and, in any event, Lola wouldn't. The streets were wet, gray, and empty; apple trees on the front lawns were quietly perishing from the damp. For the first time Victor noticed that some of the houses were boarded up. The town had really changed a lot. Fences were falling in, white mold was breaking out under the cornices, paints were fading, and on the streets the rain held sway over everything. Rain was falling simply, rain was spraying from the rooftops in a fine, watery dust, rain caught in the crosswinds was gathering into swirling columns of mist and whipping from wall to wall. Rain thundered out of rusty downspouts, rain poured down the gutters and streamed through the furrows between the well-washed cobblestones. Gray-black clouds moved slowly over the very roofs. A man on the streets was an uninvited guest, and the rain had no pity for him.

Victor emerged onto the town square and saw some people. They were standing under an awning on the porch of the police station—two policemen in regimental raincoats and a small, grubby-looking youth in oilcloth overalls. A huge truck with a canvas top loomed awkwardly in front of the porch, its left wheels on the side walk. One of the policemen was the chief himself. Having stuck out his powerful lower jaw, he looked off to the side. The kid, desperately waving his arms about, his voice breaking, was trying to prove something. The second policeman looked sour. He said nothing and dragged at his cigarette. Victor was walking toward them, and at about twenty paces from the roof he began to hear snatches of conversation.

"What do I have to do with it?" The kid was shouting. "Did I break any rules? No! Do I have all my papers? Yes! I've got the right load, here's the invoice. It's not like it's the first time I've come here."

The chief noticed Victor, and his face took on an extraordinarily hostile expression. He turned to his colleague, completely ignoring the young kid.

"All right, you stay here. Make sure everything's in order. Don't go climbing into the cab or everything'll get stolen. And don't let anyone near it. Got it?"

"Got it," said the policeman. He looked extremely hostile.

The police chief climbed down the porch stairs, got into his car, and took off. The grubby driver spit vindictively on the floor and called to Victor.

"Hey, mister, why don't you tell them if it's my fault or not." Victor stopped momentarily, and the driver took heart. "I'm driving along minding my own business, I've got a load of books for the restricted zone. This is the thousandth time I've done it. So what happens—I get stopped and I'm told to go to the police station. What for? Did I break any rules? No. Are my papers in order? They are, look at my invoice. They took my license so I wouldn't run away. And just where would I run to?"

"That's enough out of you," said the policeman.

The kid turned to him.

"But what did I do? Did I break the speed limit? No! They'll fine me for standing here. And now my license is gone."

"It'll work out," said the policeman. "What are you getting so upset over anyway? Go get yourself a drink, this doesn't concern you."

"Look at the big shots," groaned the kid, shoving his cap onto his tousled head. "There's no justice anywhere. You make a wrong move and they stop you, you make a right move and they still stop you." He turned to leave, then paused. "Maybe I can pay a fine or something?"

"Go get lost," said the policeman.

"But they promised me a bonus for a quick delivery! I was on the road all night."

"Get lost, I'm telling you," said the policeman.

The driver spat again, and walked over to his cab. He gave two kicks to the front tire, then suddenly hunched over and, sticking his hands in his pockets, sashayed across the square.

The policeman looked at Victor, then at the truck, then at the sky. His cigarette went out. He spit out the butt and, throwing off his hood, disappeared into the building.

Victor stood there for a while, then slowly circled the truck. It was a massive, powerful affair, the kind they used to transport troops in. He looked around. A few yards in front of the truck a police Harley stood soaking under the rain, its right wheel turned to the side. There were no other cars in sight. "They may catch up with me," thought Victor, "but there's no way they'll stop me." He started feeling happy. "What the hell," he thought. "The well-known writer Victor Banev, inebriated as usual, went for a joyride in a vehicle which did not belong to him; fortunately there were no casualties."

He understood that it wasn't that simple, that he wouldn't be the first person who, out of sheer restlessness, presented the authorities with a convenient pretext for hauling him off to jail. But he didn't feel like thinking; he wanted to give in to his impulse. "If worst comes to worst, the schmuck will have his exposé," flashed through his head.

He quickly opened the door and sat behind the wheel. There was no key; he had to find the wires leading to the starter and make a connection. When the motor had finally started, before slamming the door, Victor glanced back at the police station. The policeman was standing on the porch with his old dissatisfied expression, a cigarette hanging from his lip. It was obvious that he saw everything and couldn't understand it.

Victor slammed the door, carefully pulled off the sidewalk, shifted gears, and tore off into the nearest cross street. It was good to race along the empty, ever empty streets, your wheels raising waterfalls from the deep puddles. It was good to turn the heavy wheel, straining with your whole body: past the cannery, past the park, past the stadium where the Brothers in Reason like wet mechanical toys kept kicking at their soggy balls. And farther on, on the main road, how good it was to slam along the potholes, jumping in your seat and hearing from behind the heavy thump of the poorly secured load. The rearview mirror revealed no sign of a chase, and indeed how could you see it so quickly and in such rain. Victor felt very young, very needed, and even drunk. Paper beauties cut out from magazines winked at him from the roof of the cab. He found a pack of cigarettes in the glove compartment, and he felt so good that he almost missed the crossroads, but he managed to brake in time and turned in the direction of the road sign's arrow: "Leprosarium 4 miles." He felt like an explorer —he had never been on this road before. And the road turned out to be a good one, nothing like the road kept up by the city. It was asphalt, very smooth and well cared for. Then it turned into concrete, and when he saw the concrete he immediately remembered the barbed wire and the soldiers. Five minutes later he saw it all for himself.

The single row of barbed wire began at the road and stretched out on both sides, disappearing beyond the screen of rain. The entrance was blocked by a high gate with a guard booth. The door of the booth was already opened, and a soldier in a helmet and boots was standing on the threshold, the butt of his submachine gun sticking out from under his poncho. A second soldier, without a helmet, peered through the window. "I'd never seen the camps before," sang Victor, "but what the future had in store . . ." He took his foot off the gas and braked right before the gate. The soldier left the booth and went over to the car—a young, freckled kid, no older than eighteen.

"Howdy," he said. "Why the delay?"

"Well, uh, circumstances," said Victor, astonished at the liberal attitude.

The soldier took a closer look at him and straightened up.

"Your documents," he snapped.

"What documents?" said Victor gaily. "I've been telling you, there were circumstances."

The soldier pursed his lips.

"What are you bringing?" he asked.

"Books," said Victor.

"You have a pass?"

"Of course not."

"Aha," said the soldier and his face brightened. "So that's it. Then wait a minute. In that case I'm afraid you'll have to wait a minute."

"Keep in mind," said Victor, raising his finger. "It's possible that I'm being chased."

"Don't worry, I'll be quick," said the soldier and, pressing his submachine gun to his chest, raced over to the booth.

Victor climbed out of the cab and, standing on the running board, looked behind him. Nothing was visible in the rain. He got back behind the wheel and lit up a cigarette. It was terrific. There in front of him, beyond the gates and the barbed wire, rain was swirling in all directions. You could barely make out some dark structures, houses or maybe towers, but it was impossible to say anything definite about them. "Are they really not going to invite me in for a look?" thought Victor. "That would be dirty of them. Maybe I should try Golem, he must be somewhere around here. That's a good idea," he thought. "I'm not playing the hero for nothing."

The soldier once again emerged from the booth, followed by an old friend, the pimply-faced nihilist, naked except for his underwear. The boy looked very cheerful and free from all traces of universal anguish. Running ahead of the soldier, he jumped onto the running board, took a look into the cab, recognized Victor, and burst out laughing.

"Hello, Mr. Banev! Is it really you? Great! You brought the books, right? And we've been waiting for them."

"Well, is everything under control?" asked the soldier, who had come up to the truck.

"Yes, it's our truck."

"Then take it in," said the soldier. "And you, sir, will have to leave the cab and wait."

"I would like to see Mr. Golem," said Victor.

"You can see him out here," proposed the soldier.

"Hm," said Victor, fixing an expressive gaze on the boy. The boy threw up his hands guiltily.

"You don't have a pass," he explained. "And they don't let anybody in without one. Of course we'd be happy. . . ."

There was no way out of it, he'd have to climb out into the rain. Victor jumped down onto the road and, raising his hood, watched the gates swing open. The truck jerked forward and passed beyond the barrier. Then the gates closed. For some time, Victor could still hear the rumble of the motor and hissing of the brakes. Then all was silent save the splash and murmur of the rain.

"So that's that," thought Victor. "And what about me?" He

felt frustrated. Only now did he understand that his heroism had not been entirely disinterested, that he had counted on seeing and understanding a great deal, on penetrating, so to speak, into the epicenter. "Oh, the hell with it," he thought. He looked down the road. Four miles till the cross roads and thirteen miles from there to town. He could, of course, go right to the health resort—a little over a mile. The dirty ingrates . . . and in the rain. He suddenly noticed that the rain had died down. "Thanks for that, anyway," he thought.

"Should I call Mr. Golem for you?" asked the soldier.

"Golem?" Victor brightened. In fact, it wouldn't be such a bad idea to make the old boy take a walk in the rain. And then he had a car. And a flask. "Well, why not, call him."

"That's within the rules," said the soldier. "We'll call him. Only he'll never come, he'll say he's busy."

"It doesn't matter," said Victor. "Say that Banev is asking for him."

"Banev? All right, I will. Only he still won't come. But it's easy enough for me to tell him. Banev, you say." And the soldier left, such a friendly soldier, gentle, nothing but freckles under a helmet.

Victor lit up a cigarette, and then heard the roar of a motor-cycle engine. Out of the fog, traveling at a crazy speed, appeared the policeman's Harley, fixed up with a side carriage. It flew right up to the gate and stopped. Straddled in the seat was the policeman with the sour face; another officer, wrapped up to the eyes in canvas, sat in the side carriage. "Here goes," thought Victor, pulling his hood on tighter. It didn't help.

The policeman with the sour face got off the motorcycle and walked over to Victor.

"Where's the truck?" he barked.

"What truck?" asked Victor in a surprised voice, trying to win time.

"Don't go kidding me," hollered the policeman. "I saw you. I'll haul you into court for this. Making off with a detained vehicle."

"Don't shout at me, please," said Victor in a dignified voice. "You're being boorish. I'll file a complaint."

The second policeman, kicking off his canvas vestments, walked up to them.

"Is this the one?" he asked.

"It's him all right," said the policeman with the sour face, taking his handcuffs out of his pocket.

"Careful now," said Victor, taking a step backwards. "This is arbitrariness. How dare you?"

"Don't compound your guilt by resisting," advised the second policeman.

"I'm not guilty of anything," said Victor insolently, sticking his hands in his pockets. "You're mistaking me for someone else, friends."

"You made off with the truck," said the second policeman.

"What truck?" yelled Victor. "Why do you keep bringing up this truck? I came here to visit Mr. Golem, the head physician. Ask the guards. What are you bringing up some truck for?"

"Maybe he's the wrong one," said the second policeman doubtfully.

"What do you mean, the wrong one," objected the policeman with the sour face. Readying his handcuffs, he moved toward Victor. "All right, let's see your hands," he said in a businesslike way.

At that moment the door banged open. "Break it up!" said someone in a high, penetrating voice.

Victor and the policeman both jumped. By the door of the booth stood the freckled soldier. He had taken his submachine gun out from under his poncho.

"Away from the door!" he screamed.

"Who do you think you're talking to, buster?" said the policeman with the sour face. "This is the police."

"The congregation of more than one unauthorized person at the gates of the restricted zone is forbidden! Three warnings and I shoot! Clear the gates!"

"Go on, go on, move away," said Victor, full of concern, gently prodding both policemen in the chest. The policeman with the sour face gave him a nervous look, pushed away his hand, and stepped toward the soldier.

"Listen, pal, have you gone off your rocker or something?" he said. "This big-mouth here made off with a truck!"

"No trucks!" cried the friendly, gentle soldier in a high-pitched drawl. "My last warning! Both of you, a hundred yards back from the gates!"

"Listen, Roch," said the second policeman. "Let's move away, the hell with them. We'll get him later, there's nowhere for him to go."

Officer Roch, his sour face crimson with rage, was about to open his mouth, but at this point the doors opened to reveal a fat sergeant. In one hand he held a bitten-off sandwich and in the other a glass.

"Private Jura," he said, chewing. "Why aren't you firing?"

The freckled face under the helmet turned brutal. The two policemen threw themselves on the motorcycle, made a quick U-turn and sped off past Victor, who had assumed the pose of a traffic cop. The purple-faced policeman shouted something at him, but he couldn't hear it over the roar of the motor. About fifty paces away the motorcycle stopped.

"Too close," quibbled the sergeant. "What are you standing there for? They're too close."

"Get back!" shrieked the soldier, waving his submachine gun.

The two policemen drove some distance back and disappeared from view.

"A lot of unauthorized persons hanging around here lately," advised the sergeant, eyeing Victor. "Well, all right, return to your duties." He went back to the guard booth, and the freckled soldier, slowly cooling down, paced a couple of rounds in front of the gates.

Victor waited a few minutes, then made a tentative inquiry.

"Excuse me, but what's the story on Mr. Golem?"

"He's out," muttered the soldier.

"What a pity," said Victor. "Then I guess I'll be going." He looked into the rain and fog, where the two policemen were lying in wait.

"What do you mean you'll be going?" said the soldier nervously.

"Isn't it allowed?" asked Victor, also nervously.

"Why not?" said the soldier. "I mean the truck. You'll walk off, and what about the truck? Trucks cannot be left at the gate."

"What does that have to do with me?" asked Victor, getting even more nervous.

"With you? You drove it here, didn't you? That is, uh, that's the way it always is, what did you think?"

"Shit," thought Victor. "What'll I do with it?" From a hundred yards away he could hear the policemen revving up their engine.

"Did you really steal it?" asked the soldier, curious.

"Sure. The police were detaining the driver, so I, like an idiot, decided to help."

"So-o," sympathized the soldier. "I really don't know what to tell you."

"And what if, say, I were to walk off now?" asked Victor deviously. "You wouldn't shoot?"

"I don't know," confessed the soldier. "I don't think regulations require me to. You want me to go ask?"

"Ask," said Victor, trying to figure out how long it would take him to get beyond the limit of visibility.

At that moment a horn sounded behind the gates. The gates opened, and the unfortunate truck slowly rolled out of the zone. It stopped next to Victor, the door opened, and Victor saw that behind the wheel, in place of the expected boy, was a bald, bent-over slimy. The slimy stared at him. Victor didn't budge, whereupon the slimy removed a black-gloved hand from the wheel and tapped the seat next to him in a sign of welcome. "So Their Excellencies have deigned to notice me," thought Victor bitterly. The soldier was overjoyed. "There, you see, everything's worked out, have a nice trip."

The thought flashed through Victor's mind that if the slimy was intending to deposit the truck somewhere in town, if the slimy, that is, was intending to do the depositing himself and make his own peace with the police, then it would be best for Victor to say his good-byes now and head straight across the field to the health resort. The best maneuver to avoid the motorcycle ambush.

"The police are waiting up ahead," he said to the slimy.

"It doesn't matter, get in," said the slimy.

"The problem is that I stole the truck. It was being detained."

"I know," said the slimy patiently. "Get in."

The moment was lost. Victor said a polite and warm farewell to the soldier, clambered onto the seat, and slammed the door. The truck moved forward, and a minute later they saw the Harley. It was parked at right angles to the road. The two policemen were standing next to it, motioning for them to pull over. The slimy came to a stop, turned off the motor, and leaned out the window.

"Take away your motorcycle, you're blocking the road."

"Pull over!" ordered the policeman with the sour face. "And let me see your papers."

"I'm on my way to police headquarters," said the slimy. "Perhaps we could talk there."

The policeman made a couple of false starts, muttering something on the order of "we know your type." The slimy waited patiently.

"All right," said the policeman finally. "Only I'll drive the truck. Your friend there can go in the motorcycle."

"Certainly," said the slimy. "Only if it's possible I'll go in the motorcycle myself."

"So much the better," muttered the policeman with the sour face, which seemed to grow sweeter. "Climb out."

They changed places. The policeman, throwing Victor an

ominous sideways glance, started fidgeting and squirming in his seat, trying to straighten out his raincoat. Victor, one eye on the policeman, watched the slimy walk over to the motorcycle and climb into the sidecar. Pigeon-toed and even more bent over, he looked, from the back, like a huge, emaciated monkey. The rain grew more intense, pouring down as if from an over-turned bucket, and the policeman turned on the windshield wipers. The cortege started moving.

"I'd like to know how this is going to end," thought Victor with a certain feeling of oppression. He derived a vague hope from the slimy's intention to appear at police headquarters. "Your present-day slimy is a brazen one. Brazen and insolent. Of course they'll fine me, there's no getting out of it. The police would hardly lose the opportunity to collect a fine. Oh, I don't give a shit, no matter what I'll have to clear out of here. Everything's okay. At least I got it off my chest."

He got out a pack of cigarettes and offered it to the police-man. The policeman grunted indignantly but took one. His lighter wasn't working, and he was compelled to grunt once more when Victor offered him his own. In fact, it wasn't all that difficult to understand him. He wasn't so young anymore, probably about forty-five, and still a junior officer. Probably one of the former collaborators. Jailed the wrong people and licked the wrong asses, how could he have learned which ass was the right one? The policeman smoked, and his face already looked a little less sour: things were taking a turn for the bet-ter. "If only I had some booze," thought Victor. "First I'd give him a swig, then I'd tell him a few Irish jokes, then I'd curse out his superiors for only promoting their favorites, then I'd swear at the students and before you knew it the guy would melt."

"No way out of it, look how it's teeming," said Victor.

The policeman gave a rather neutral grunt, without ill feeling.

"But what a climate we had here before," continued Victor. Then it hit him. "Think about it—there's no rain at the leprosarium, but the moment you get near town it starts pouring."

"Sure," said the policeman. "They've got themselves a good spot in that leprosarium."

The connection took. They talked about the weather—what it used to be like and what the hell had happened to it. They found their common acquaintances in town. They talked about life in the capital, about miniskirts, about the blight of homosexuality, about French cognac and smuggled dope. They observed, naturally, that there had been a deterioration of law and order—things just weren't the way they'd been before the war or, say, right after it. That being a policeman was a lousy way to earn a living, even though the papers called them the Good Strict Guards of Law and Order, the Irreplaceable Cogs of the Government Machine. Retirement age kept going up, for injury in the line of duty they gave you peanuts, and now they were confiscating weapons. Who would stick his neck out under conditions like that? In short, their relationship had developed to the point that had they had a couple of drinks to top it off, the policeman would have said, "All right, pal, let's drop it. I didn't see you, and you didn't see me." Unfortunately they didn't have a couple of drinks to top it off, and the moment to slip him a ten-spot hadn't ripened. So when the truck rolled up to the station, the policeman resumed his churlish state and drily told Victor to follow him and make it snappy.

The slimy refused to give an explanation to the officer on duty and demanded to be taken to the chief at once. The officer on duty responded that the chief would probably be willing to see him, but only him. As for this citizen here, who is under suspicion of stealing a truck, he has no business seeing any chiefs. He's staying here for questioning, after which we will draw up the appropriate complaint.

"No," said the slimy in a firm and quiet voice, "none of this is going to happen. Mr. Banev is not going to have to answer any questions and he will not sign any complaints, for reasons which concern the chief alone."

The officer on duty, who didn't much care, shrugged his shoulders and went to make his report. While he was at it, the driver walked in, still in his oilcloth overalls. The driver, who knew nothing and was by now strongly under the influence, immediately began yelling about justice and innocence and other frightening things. The slimy carefully relieved the driver of the invoice which he was waving about in the air, leaned against the railing, and put his signature to it. The driver, taken aback, stopped yelling, and then the slimy and Victor were motioned toward the inner offices.

The police chief met them coldly. He looked at the slimy with evident displeasure, and avoided looking at Victor at all.

"What can I do for you?" he asked.

"May we sit down?" the slimy inquired.

"Yes, of course," said the chief with forced politeness, after a short pause.

They sat down.

"I have been instructed," said the slimy, "to register with you our second protest concerning the unlawful detainment of goods intended for the leprosarium."

"Yes, I've heard about this," said the police chief. "The driver was drunk and we were obliged to detain him. I believe that the matter will be resolved in the near future."

"You detained the goods, not the driver," objected the slimy. "However, that's no longer important. Thanks to the kindness of Mr. Banev, who is sitting before you here, the goods were delivered with only a short delay. You are in fact most indebted to him, as a significant delay in the delivery which could be traced to police interference or, more specifically, to the interference of the police chief, would bring about extremely unpleasant consequences for you."

"Funny," said the police chief. "I don't understand what you're talking about, and I have no desire to. As an office-holder I will not tolerate threats. As far as Mr. Banev is concerned, he will be treated in accordance with the criminal code which contains provisions for such incidents." He was clearly unwilling to look at Victor.

"I see that you really don't understand your position," said the slimy. "But I have instructions to bring to your attention that if our goods should be detained a third time you will be dealing directly with General Pferd."

There was a short silence. Victor didn't know who General Pferd was, but the police chief obviously did.

"In my opinion, that's a threat," he said hesitantly.

"It is," said the slimy. "And a very real one."

The police chief jerked to his feet, followed by Victor and the slimy.

"I will take everything into consideration," announced the police chief. "Your tone, sir, leaves much to be desired. However, I promise your superiors that I will look into the matter and that the guilty parties will be punished. This includes Mr. Banev as well."

"Mr. Banev," said the slimy. "If you have any trouble with the police on account of this incident, immediately inform Mr. Golem. Good-bye," he said to the police chief.

"Best regards," said the chief.

Chapter VIII

AT EIGHT in the evening, Victor went down to the restaurant. He was about to go right to his table, where the usual company had gathered, when Teddy called to him.

"Teddy!" said Victor, leaning against the bar. "How are things?" Then he remembered. "Of course. The bill. I had a bad night, didn't I?"

"It's not the bill," muttered Teddy. "The bill isn't so bad— you broke a mirror and twisted off a washstand. The problem, if you remember, is the police chief."

"What do you mean?" said Victor, surprised.

"I didn't think you'd remember," said Teddy. "Your eyes, brother, were like the eyes of a boiled piglet. You had no idea what you were doing. What happened"—he touched a finger to Victor's chest—"is that you backed him into the toilet. Then you barricaded the door with a broom and refused to let him out. And we didn't know who was in there. He'd just come in, and we thought it was Quadriga. So we thought, all right, let him sit there. And then you dragged him out, and started yelling 'you poor bastard, you got yourself all dirty in there.' Then you tried sticking his head into the washstand. The washstand twisted off, and we barely got you out of there."

"No kidding," said Victor. "How do you like that? No wonder he's been giving me dirty looks all day."

Teddy nodded sympathetically.

"Only it's one hell of a position to be in," said Victor. "I've got to excuse myself somehow. How'd he let me get away with it? The guy's still strong."

"I was afraid they'd make out a complaint against you," said Teddy. "This morning we even had a cop walking around taking evidence. They'll stick you with article sixty-three, insulting actions under aggravating circumstances. Or even worse—an act of terrorism. You see what that smacks of? If I were you. . . ." Teddy shook his head.

"Well?" asked Victor.

"I hear that the burgomaster came to see you today," said Teddy.

"He did."

"And?"

"A lot of crap. He wanted me to write an article. Against the slimies."

"So that's it!" said Teddy and livened up. "Then it's really only a lot of crap. Write him his article and everything'll be all right. If the burgomaster is satisfied, the police chief won't dare let out a peep, you can take him every day and stick his head down the toilet if you want. The burgomaster has him in his fist. Like this." Teddy made a gesture with his huge, bony fist. "So everything's all right. For that I'll give you a drink on the house. Vodka?"

"Vodka, if you want," said Victor, distracted.

He saw the burgomaster's visit in a completely new light. "They've really got me," thought Victor. "Either clear out, or do as you're told or we'll screw you. Unfortunately clearing out of here is not so easy. If it's really an act of terrorism, then they'll find me. Oh, brother, you old alcoholic, it's disgusting to look at you. You didn't pick just anyone, did you. The police chief. Well designed and well executed." He didn't remember anything except the tiled floor flooded with water, but he could easily imagine the whole scene. "Yes, Victor Banev, old friend. Yes, you boiled piglet and kitchen dissident, or rather toilet one. My dear favorite of Mr. President, the time has come for you to sell out. Rots-Tursov is an experienced man, and he says that selling out must be done lightly and for a good price. The more honest your pen, the more the powers that be will have to pay for it—so that in selling out, you cause your enemy to take a loss, and it is your duty to see that this loss is maximized." Victor finished off his vodka without the slightest sense of satisfaction.

"All right, Teddy," he said. "Thanks. Let's have the bill. How much am I out?"

"You can handle it," smirked Teddy. He took a piece of paper out of the cash register. "You owe as follows: seventy-seven for the bathroom mirror, and sixty-four for the large porcelain washstand, that makes, you can see for yourself, a total of one hundred forty-one. The lamp we wrote off on the last fight. There's only one thing I don't get," he continued, watching Victor count out the money. "How did you manage to smash the mirror? It was a heavy mirror, two fingers thick. What did you do, beat your head against it?"

"Not mine," said Victor sullenly.

"All right, don't take it to heart," said Teddy, taking the money. "You'll write your little article, you'll get rehabilitated, you'll take your payment, and all your accounts will be settled. Pour you some more?"

"No, later. I'll stop by after supper," said Victor and went to his place.

In the restaurant everything was as usual: the semidarkness, the smells, the clash of dishes in the kitchen. The young man in glasses with his attaché case, companion, and bottle of mineral water; Dr. R. Quadriga, all hunched over; and Pavor, straight-backed and elegant despite his cold. Golem sprawling in his chair, a drunken prophet with a cavernous nose. A waiter.

"The eel," said Victor. "A bottle of beer. And something with meat in it."

"You're done for," Pavor reproached him. "I told you to stop drinking."

"When did you tell me? I have no recollection."

"And how come you're done for?" inquired Dr. R. Quadriga. "What did you do, murder somebody?"

"So you don't remember either?" Victor asked him.

"You mean last night?"

"Yes, last night. I drank myself into a stupor," said Victor, turning to Golem, "and locked the police chief into the lavatory."

"Oh, that," said R. Quadriga. "That's all lies. Which is just what I told the investigator. The investigator came to see me this morning. There I was, I had this awful heartburn, my head was pounding, and I'm sitting staring out the window, and then this oaf appears and starts sewing up the case."

"What did you say?" asked Golem. "Sew?"

"Yes, sew," said R. Quadriga, drawing an imagined needle through an imagined piece of cloth. "Only not pants, but a case. I told him straight out: It's all lies. Yesterday I spent the whole evening in the restaurant and everything was quiet and civilized, as always. No scenes. Boring as could be. Don't worry," he said cheerfully. "No big deal. But why did you do it? Don't you like him?"

"Let's not talk about it," proposed Victor.

"Then what will we talk about?" asked an offended Quadriga. "These two can't stop arguing about who's keeping whom out of the leprosarium. Then at long last something interesting happens, and right away we can't talk about it."

Victor took a bite of eel, chewed it, and washed it down with beer.

"Who's General Pferd?" he asked.

"A horse," said R. Quadriga. "A stallion. *Der Pferd*. Or maybe *das*."

"Seriously," said Victor, "has anybody heard of him?"

"When I was in the army," said Dr. R. Quadriga, "our division was commanded by His Excellency General of the Infantry Arschmann."

"So what," said Victor.

"*Arsch* means ass in German," said Golem, breaking his silence. "The doctor is making a joke."

"And where did you hear about General Pferd?" Pavor asked.

"In the police chief's office," said Victor.

"Well?"

"That's it. So nobody knows who he is? Fine. I was just asking."

"And the general was called Battoks," announced Quadriga. "General Battoks."

"So you know English as well?" asked Golem.

"If we stick to certain fields," answered R. Quadriga.

"Let's have a drink," Victor proposed. "Waiter, a bottle of cognac!"

"Why a whole bottle?" asked Pavor.

"So there'll be enough for everybody."

"You'll make another scene."

"Drop it, Pavor," said Victor. "You're hardly a teetotaler."

"I never said I was," said Pavor. "I like a drink and I never pass up the chance to have one, like any real man. But I don't see why you have to get drunk. And I especially don't see why this has to happen every evening."

"Back again," sighed Quadriga. "Too soon."

"We won't get drunk," said Victor, giving everyone some cognac. "We will simply drink. Along with a good half of the nation. The other half is getting drunk, but the hell with them, we'll just drink."

"That's just the point," said Pavor. "When the entire country is drinking itself sick, and not just the country but the whole world, it's the duty of every decent man to retain his sense of balance."

"Do you really consider us decent men?" asked Golem.

"In any event, civilized."

"In my opinion," said Victor, "civilized people have far more reason to get drunk than uncivilized ones."

"Possibly," said Pavor. "Except that a civilized person is obliged to keep himself in certain bounds. Civilization obliges him to. Look at us, we sit here practically every night, talking, drinking, shooting dice. And during all this time has even one of us said something which if not intelligent is at least serious? Sneers and wisecracks, nothing but sneers and wisecracks."

"Why should we say anything serious?" Golem asked.

"Because the world is toppling into an abyss, and we're sneering and making wisecracks. We're feasting during a plague. In my opinion, it's disgraceful, gentlemen."

"All right, Pavor," said Victor peaceably. "Tell us something serious. If not intelligent, then at least serious."

"I don't want anything serious," said R. Quadriga. "Leeches. Hummocks. Ugh!"

"Shush," said Victor. "Go back to sleep. Really, Golem, let's at least once talk about something serious. Pavor, you begin. Tell us about the abyss."

"Is that another wisecrack?" said Pavor bitterly.

"No," said Victor. "I give you my word. Maybe I'm being ironic. But that's because all my life I've been hearing about the abyss. Everyone insists that humanity is falling into one, but nobody can prove it. And if you look more closely, all that philosophical pessimism turns out to be the result of family problems or insufficient income."

"No," said Pavor. "No. Humanity is falling into the abyss because humanity has become bankrupt."

"Insufficient income," muttered Golem.

Pavor didn't pay any attention to him. He was addressing Victor alone, and he spoke sullenly, with his head down.

"Humanity is bankrupt in the biological sense. The birthrate is falling, cancer is spreading along with feeblemindedness and neuroses of all sorts, people are turning into drug addicts. Every day they consume hundreds of tons of alcohol, nicotine, or simply narcotics, they started with hashish and cocaine and ended with LSD. We're degenerating. We've ruined the natural world and the man-made one is ruining us. And we've bank-rupted ourselves ideologically. We've gone through all phil-osophical systems and discredited every one, we've tried all possible ethical systems and we've stayed the same amoral louts we always were, no better than troglodytes. And that's the worst of it, that this whole ignorant human mass is not going to improve, it started out as trash and that's the way it's going to stay. It thirsts after gods and leaders, law and order, it demands them. And every time it gets its gods, its leaders, and its order, it becomes dissatisfied because in fact it doesn't need any of it. It doesn't need gods and it doesn't need order, what it needs is chaos and anarchy, bread and circuses. Right now the iron will of necessity has forced it into dependence on a weekly paycheck. But it's sick of this necessity, and it escapes from it every evening into alcohol and narcotics. But the hell with it, the hell with this rotting pile of shit, it's been stinking for ten thousand years and that's all it's good for. There's something more frightening—that this process of dis-integration has seized us as well, the real people, the individ-uals. We see this disintegration and we imagine that it doesn't affect us. But it's mastering us through hopelessness, it's eating away at our will, swallowing us up. And then this damned democratic upbringing: *égalité, fraternité*, all men are brothers, we're all made the same. We're constantly identifying with the common herd and we blame ourselves if we happen to find that we're smarter, that we have different needs and differ-ent goals in life. It's time we understood this and drew some conclusions from it. It's time to save ourselves."

"It's time to drink," said Victor. He was already regretting that he'd agreed to a serious talk with a sanitary inspector. It was unpleasant to look at Pavor. Pavor had become over-wrought; his eyes were even twitching. It was out of character for him. He was spewing forth the sheerest banalities, like all adepts of the abyss. You felt like saying to him: quit disgracing yourself, Pavor, we prefer you in profile with your usual ironic grin.

"Is that all you can say to me?" Pavor asked.

"One more piece of advice. More irony, Pavor. Don't get so heated up. You can't do anything about it anyway. And even if you could do something, you wouldn't know what."

Pavor grinned ironically.

"I do know what," he said.

"Well?"

"There's only one means of stopping disintegration."

"We know, we know," said Victor lightly. "Issue the fools their golden shirts and let them march. The whole of Europe under our feet. It's been tried."

"No," said Pavor. "That's just a delaying tactic. There's only one real way to do it: destroy the masses."

"You're in a fine mood today," Victor said.

"Destroy ninety percent of the population," continued Pavor. "Maybe even ninety-five. The masses have fulfilled their purpose—they have brought forth the flower of humanity, the creators of civilization. Now they are dead, like a rotten potato that has given life to a new plant. And when the corpse starts to rot, it's time to bury it."

"Christ," said Victor. "And all this just because you have a cold and they won't give you a pass to the leprosarium? Or maybe you're having family problems?"

"Don't play the fool," said Pavor. "Why don't you want to think about things that are utterly clear to you? What is it that has distorted our brightest ideas? The obtuseness of the ignorant masses. What is it that has caused war, chaos, every sort of outrage? The obtuseness of the ignorant masses, who choose a government which is worthy of them. Why is it that the Golden Age is as far from us now as it ever was? The stagnation and ignorance of the masses. In principle Hitler was right, subconsciously he was right, he sensed that much on this earth is superfluous. But he was a product of the masses and spoiled everything. It was stupid to start the destruction on racial grounds. And besides, he didn't have the real means for carrying it out."

"And what grounds do you intend to use?" asked Victor.

"Inconspicuousness," said Pavor. "If a person is dull, if he's inconspicuous, then he has to be destroyed."

"And who is going to determine whether a person is conspicuous or not?"

"Drop it, those are just details. I'm giving you the theory. Who, what, and how are nothing but details."

"Then why get involved with the burgomaster?" asked Victor, fed up with Pavor.

"You mean—"

"What the hell do you need this court case for? You're getting petty, Pavor. And that's the way it always is with you supermen. You're preparing to plow over the whole earth, you won't agree to less than three billion dead, and the whole time you're worrying about your rank or getting treatments for gonorrhea, or wasting your time helping doubtful people do their dirty little deeds."

"Take it easy," said Pavor. It was clear that he was furious. "Look at you, an indolent drunk—"

"In any case I don't go around manufacturing political lawsuits, and I'm not trying to remake the world."

"That's right," said Pavor. "Because you're not even capable of it, Banev. All you'll ever be is a bohemian, that is, in short, a lousy son of a bitch, a cheap dissident, and a piece of shit. You yourself don't know what you want, and you only do what other people want you to. You titillate some readers who are sons of bitches like yourself, and you think that makes you an earthshaker and a free artist. You're nothing but a producer of dirty rhymes, a graffiti artist of the public johns."

"That's all correct," said Victor. "It's only a pity that you never said this before. You had to be insulted before you'd say it. The result of it is that you're a dirty little individual, Pavor. Simply one of many. And if they're going to start destroying, then they'll destroy you too. On the grounds of inconspicuousness. A philosophizing sanitary inspector? Into the ovens!"

"It would be interesting to see what we look like from the outside," he thought. "Pavor is sickening. What a filthy smile. What's gotten into him? And Quadriga is fast asleep—what does he care about all these ignorant masses? And Golem is sprawled out like a spectator at a show—shot glass at his finger-tips, arm flung over the back of the chair. He's waiting for the outcome: who strikes who with what? For some reason Pavor isn't saying anything. What is he doing, putting together his arguments?"

"Well, all right," said Pavor finally. "We had our little talk and that's enough."

His smile disappeared, and once again his eyes hardened into the eyes of a *Sturmbannfuhrer*. He threw some money on the table, finished his cognac, and left without saying good-bye. Victor felt pleasantly disappointed.

"You know, for a writer you have absolutely no understanding of people," said Golem.

"That's not my business," said Victor lightly. "That's for psychologists and security police. My business is to isolate tendencies with the heightened sensitivity of an artist. But why are you telling me this? Another case of 'Veektor, shut your mouth'?"

"I told you: leave Pavor alone."

"For Christ's sake," said Victor. "First of all, I'm leaving him alone. He's the one that isn't leaving me alone. And second, he's a pig. You know that he's helping the burgomaster haul you into court?"

"I guessed as much."

"That doesn't bother you?"

"No. His reach is short. That is to say, the burgomaster's. Also the court's."

"And Pavor's?"

"And Pavor's is long. Therefore stop shooting your mouth off in front of him. You see that I don't."

"I wonder, who you do shoot your mouth off in front of?" muttered Victor.

"From time to time in front of you. I have a weakness for you. Pour me some cognac."

"My pleasure." Victor poured it. "Maybe we should wake Quadriga up? What's gotten into him, he didn't even defend me against Pavor."

"No, don't. Let's talk. Why are you getting yourself mixed up in this? Who asked you to steal the truck?"

"I felt like it," said Victor. "I don't believe in confiscating books, I think it's lousy. And then the burgomaster provoked me. He impinged on my freedom. Every time they impinge on my freedom I start misbehaving. Incidentally, Golem, maybe this General Pferd can put in a good word with the burgomaster?"

"He pisses on you and the burgomaster both," said Golem. "He's got enough problems of his own."

"You tell him, let him put in a word. If not, I'll write an exposé of your leprosarium, about how you use the blood of Christian infants for treating ocularis ringus. You think I don't know why the slimies are luring in the children? First of all, they suck their blood, and second of all, they defile them. I'll shame you before the whole world. A bloodsucker and defiler masquerading as a physician." Victor clinked glasses with Golem. "Actually, I'm being serious. The burgomaster is forcing me to write an exposé. Of course you're aware of this, too."

"No, I'm not," said Golem. "But it's insignificant."

"Everything is insignificant for you," said Victor. "The entire city is against you: insignificant. You're being hauled into court: insignificant. The sanitary inspector Pavor is disturbed by your conduct: insignificant. The fashionable writer Victor Banev is also annoyed and is readying his angry pen: once again, insignificant. Maybe General Pferd is a pseudonym for Mr. President? By the way, does the all-powerful general know you're a Communist?"

"And why is the writer Banev annoyed?" asked Golem tranquilly. "Only stop shouting, Teddy is looking at us."

"Teddy's on our side," objected Victor. "Besides, he's annoyed too: the mice have gotten to him." He frowned and lit a cigarette. "Wait a minute, what was it you were asking me? Oh. I'm annoyed because you didn't let me into the leprosarium. No matter how you look at it, I performed a noble deed for you. It might have been stupid, but they always are. And before that I carried a slimy on my back."

"And fought on his behalf," Golem added.

"Exactly."

"With the fascists," said Golem.

"Right again."

"Do you have a pass?" Golem asked.

"A pass. You don't let Pavor in either, and he's turning into a demophobe right before your eyes."

"Yes, Pavor just isn't having any luck here," said Golem. "He's a good operator, but nothing seems to be working out for him here. I keep on waiting for him to start putting his foot in it. I think he's started."

Dr. R. Quadriga raised his disheveled head.

"Hard. I'll walk in and then we'll see. Out of breath." His head thumped back onto the table.

"Still, Golem," said Victor, lowering his voice. "Is it true that you're a Communist?"

"I seem to recall that the Communist party is illegal here," observed Golem.

"Christ," said Victor. "What party is legal? I'm not asking about the party, I'm asking about you."

"As you see, I'm legal," said Golem.

"Have it your way," said Victor. "I don't care. But the burgomaster—although you don't give a shit about the burgomaster. But what if it gets to General Pferd?"

"We simply won't tell him," winked Golem. "And why should a general dip into these petty matters? He knows that there's such a thing as the leprosarium, that in the leprosarium there's someone named Golem and some sort of slimies; enough."

"An odd general," said Victor thoughtfully. "General of the

Leprosarium. Although he'll be having his troubles because of those slimies soon. I feel that with the heightened sensitivity of an artist. The town is dead set against them."

"If it were only the town," said Golem.

"But what's the problem? They're just sick people, apparently they're not even infectious."

"Don't get devious, Victor. You're perfectly well aware that they're more than just sick people. They're even infectious in a certain way."

"Meaning?"

"Meaning that Teddy, for example, can't be infected by them. And the burgomaster can't, to say nothing of the police chief. But somebody else can."

"You, for example."

Golem took the cognac, spent a moment admiring its color, and poured himself some.

"I can't either. Not anymore."

"What about me?"

"I don't know. In general, all this is only my hypothesis. Don't pay any attention to it."

"I won't," sighed Victor. "What makes them unusual?"

"What makes them unusual?" repeated Golem. "Perhaps you've noticed yourself, Victor, that all people can be divided into three big groups. More precisely, into two big groups and one little one. There are people who can't live without the past, more or less distant; they're completely immersed in it. They live by traditions, customs, and dogmas; the past is their model and their source of happiness. Take Mr. President, for example. Where would he be without our illustrious past? Where would he find his justification, and how could he even have come about? Then there are people who live for the present and don't wish to know either the future or the past. For example, you. All your ideas about the past have been ruined by Mr. President. No matter what past you looked into, Mr. President got there first. As for the future, in my opinion you don't have the slightest conception of it, and you're afraid to have one. And finally there are people who live for the future. They have appeared in noticeable quantity only recently. They don't expect anything good out of the past, in which expectation they're completely justified, and the present for them is just something to build the future with, raw material. You could say that they're already living in the future—on islands of the future, which have formed around them in the present." Golem, smiling strangely, raised his eyes to the ceiling. "They're intelligent," he said tenderly, "they're incredibly intelligent, as opposed to most people. Every single one of them is talented, Victor. They have strange desires and completely lack the normal ones."

"Normal desires—that would be, for example, women?"

"In a certain sense, yes."

"Vodka, circuses?"

"Absolutely."

"A terrible disease," said Victor. "I don't want to. . . . And no matter that I can't understand. I don't understand anything. I can understand why intelligent people are put behind barbed wire. But why they're allowed out, and we're not allowed in. . . ."

"Maybe they're not the ones behind the barbed wire, maybe you are."

Victor smirked.

"Wait a minute," he said. "That's not all I don't understand. Take Pavor. I can see why they don't let me in, I'm an outsider. But doesn't somebody have to inspect the bed linen and the toilets? Maybe it's unsanitary there."

"And what if that's not what interests him?"

Victor in confusion looked at Golem.

"You're joking again?" he asked.

"Again, I'm not joking," said Golem.

"So you think he's a spy?"

"Spy is too broad a concept," Golem objected.

"Hold on," said Victor. "Let's start over. Who put up barbed wire and ordered the guards?"

"Oh, that wire again," moaned Golem. "You can't imagine how many uniforms have gotten torn because of it, and the soldiers are constantly suffering from diarrhea. You know the best cure for diarrhea? Tobacco and cheap wine, or rather, cheap wine and tobacco."

"All right," said Victor. "So, General Pferd. Aha," he said. "And that young man with the attaché case. So that's it. You've got a military think tank going. It's all clear. And Pavor is a civilian. A different branch of the service. Or maybe he's not our spy, maybe he's a foreign one."

"God forbid!" said Golem, shuddering. "Just what we need."

"So. . . . And does he know who the guy with the attaché case is?"

"I think so," said Golem.

"And the attaché case knows who Pavor is?"

"I think not," said Golem.

"You didn't say anything to him?"

"Why should I?"

"And you didn't tell General Pferd?"

"I wouldn't think of it."

"That's unfair," said Victor. "He should be told."

"Listen, Victor," said Golem. "I've allowed you to shoot your mouth off on this topic only to get you scared, to stop you from sticking your nose into other people's business. This isn't doing you any good. They've got an eye on you as it is. They can stamp you out whenever they want, you won't have time to let out a squeak."

"It's not that hard to get me scared," said Victor, sighing. "I've been scared since childhood. But I still can't understand it—what do they all want from the slimies?"

"Who's 'they'?" said Golem, tired, reproachful.

"Pavor. Pferd. The one with the attaché case. All those reptiles."

"God," said Golem. "What do reptiles need intelligent and talented people for in our time? What I can't understand is what you need them for. Why are you getting involved in all this? Don't you have enough problems of your own? Isn't Mr. President enough for you?"

"More than enough," agreed Victor. "I've had it up to my ears."

"Well, then, fine. Go to the health resort, take some paper with you, if you want I can give you a typewriter."

"I work in the old style," said Victor. "Like Hemingway."

"Wonderful. I'll give you a pencil stub. Do your work, love Diana. Maybe you'd like a plot as well? Maybe you've written yourself out?"

"Plots grow out of themes," pronounced Victor. "I'm studying life."

"Go right ahead," said Golem. "Study life as much as you want. Only keep your nose out of lawsuits."

"That's impossible," objected Victor. "The instrument unavoidably affects the experimental picture. Don't you remember your physics? We don't observe the world as such, but the world plus the observer's effect on it."

"You've already had a taste of their brass knuckles, the next time they'll simply shoot you."

"Well," said Victor. "First of all, maybe it wasn't brass knuckles, maybe it was a brick. Second of all, this isn't the only place in the world where it could happen. They can get me at any moment—does that mean I can't leave my hotel room?"

Golem bit his lip. He had the yellow teeth of a horse.

"Listen, instrument," he said. "The first time you interfered in the experiment it was a matter of chance, and they wasted no time taking care of you. If, now, you do it consciously—"

"I didn't interfere in any experiments," said Victor. "I had just left Lola's and I was walking along minding my own business when I suddenly saw—"

"Idiot," said Golem. "Minding his own business and looking at the same time. You should have crossed the street, blockhead."

"Why in God's name should I have crossed the street?"

"Because a good acquaintance of yours was busy fulfilling his professional duties, and you marched in there like an ass."

Victor straightened up.

"What good acquaintance? There wasn't a single acquaintance there."

"Your acquaintance came from behind with the brass knuckles. Do you know anyone with brass knuckles?"

Victor gulped down his cognac. It came back to him with astonishing clarity: Pavor with his nose red from the flu taking a handkerchief out of his pocket, and the brass knuckles banging onto the floor—heavy, dull, custom-made.

"Drop it," said Victor, sputtering. "Nonsense. Pavor couldn't."

"I haven't named any names," objected Golem.

Victor put his hands on the table and stared at his clenched fists.

"What do you mean by his duties?" he asked.

"Somebody needed a living slimy, apparently. A kidnapping."

"And I prevented it?"

"You tried to."

"In other words, they got him anyway?"

"And carried him away. You can say thank you that they didn't seize you as well to avoid leaving any witnesses. The future of literature is not one of their concerns."

"So it was Pavor," said Victor slowly.

"No names," Golem reminded him. He was severe.

"Fucking bastard," said Victor. "All right, we'll see. But what did they need a slimy for?"

"What do you mean, what for? Information. Where can they get information? You know it yourself—barbed wire, soldiers, General Pferd."

"So they're questioning him there now?" Victor continued.

Golem was silent for a long time.

"He died," he said finally.

"Did they beat him?"

"No. On the contrary." Golem was silent again. "They're idiots. They didn't give him anything to read, and he died of starvation."

Victor threw a quick glance at him. Golem was smiling sadly. Or crying from grief. Victor felt overcome by horror and despair, a suffocating despair. The lamp grew suddenly dim. It was like a heart attack. Victor, choking, managed to undo the knot of his tie. "My God," he thought, "he's a snake, a criminal, a murderer in cold blood. Right after that, an hour after that, he washed his hands, sprinkled himself with cologne, weighed up what his superiors owed him for it, and sat down next to me. And he was clinking glasses with me, and smiling at me, and talking to me as a friend, the bastard. And he was lying, smiling and lying, lying with the greatest enjoyment. He was laughing at me, giggling up his sleeve whenever I turned around and winking at himself, and then inquiring sympathetically about my head." Through a black fog Victor saw Dr. R. Quadriga slowly raise his head, open his caked-up mouth in a silent scream, and start jerking his shaking hands over the tablecloth like a blind man. And his eyes were like a blind man's when he twisted his head and kept screaming and screaming, and Victor didn't hear a sound. "And that's right, I'm also shit, a shabby, useless mediocrity, kick him in the face and grab his arms, don't let him wipe the spit away. Why should anybody need me, they should have hit harder, so that I couldn't get up, and I was like a sleepwalker beating my fists in the air. And my God, why am I living, why is anybody living? Because it's so simple, you come up from behind with a piece of iron and land a blow on the head, and nothing changes, nothing in the world changes, at the same instant a thousand miles away another little bastard is being born." Golem's puffy face grew ever more flaccid, darkening suddenly from the stubble on his chin. His eyes seemed to sink into his fleshy cheeks. He was sprawled motionless in his chair like a wineskin full of rancid oil. Only his fingers were moving, as he slowly took a wine glass from the table, soundlessly broke off the stem and dropped it on the floor, and then took another glass, and broke off the stem and dropped it on the floor. "And I don't love anybody, I can't love Diana. It doesn't matter who I sleep with, anybody can do that, but is it really possible to love a woman who doesn't love you, and a woman can't love when you don't love her! And everything is spinning in a damned inhuman ring, spinning like a serpent chasing its tail, like animals coupling and uncoupling—only animals don't think up words and don't create poetry, they just couple and uncouple." Teddy was weeping with his elbows on the bar, with his bony chin resting in his bony fist. His bald forehead shone saffron-bright under the lamp, and tears were flowing endlessly along his sunken cheeks, and they were also shining under the lamp. "And all because I'm shit, in no way am I a writer, what kind of writer can I be if I can't stand writing, if writing is torture for me, a painful unpleasant activity, like a disease of the bodily functions, like diarrhea, like pus squeezing out of boils? It's horrifying to think that I'll have to do this for the rest of my life, that I'm condemned to it, they won't let me free, they'll keep on demanding let's have it, let's have it, and I'll give it to them, but I can't now, I can't even think about it now, oh God, don't let me think about it or I'll throw up." Bol-Kunats was standing behind R. Quadriga and looking at his watch. He was thin and wet, with a wet, fresh face and wonderful dark eyes. A fresh smell was coming from him, cutting through the thick hot closeness of the room: a smell of grass and spring water, a smell of lilies, sun and dragonflies above a lake. The world came back to him. There remained only a troubled remembrance or sensation, or the remembrance of a sensation flashing like a shadow in a corner; somebody's desperate, broken-off scream, an incomprehensible screeching and ringing, the crunch of glass.

Victor licked his lips and stretched out his hand for the bottle. Dr. R. Quadriga, head on the tablecloth, was muttering hoarsely: "Don't need anything. Hide me. The hell with . . ."

Golem was concentrating on clearing bits of glass from the table.

"Please excuse me, Mr. Golem," said Bol-Kunats. "I have a letter for you." He put an envelope before Golem and once again glanced at his watch. "Good evening, Mr. Banev," he said.

"Good evening," said Victor, pouring himself some cognac.

Golem read the letter attentively. Behind the bar, Teddy was loudly blowing his nose into a checkered handkerchief.

"Listen, Bol-Kunats," said Victor. "Did you see who hit me that time?"

"No," said Bol-Kunats, looking him straight in the eye.

"How could that be?" asked Victor, frowning.

"He had his back to me," explained Bol-Kunats.

"You know him," said Victor. "Who was it?"

Golem made an indefinable noise. Victor threw a quick look at him. Golem, not paying anybody any attention, was thoughtfully tearing the note into little shreds. He hid the pieces in his pocket.

"You're mistaken," said Bol-Kunats. "I don't know him."

"Banev," muttered R. Quadriga. "I beg you. . . . I can't be there by myself. . . . Come with me. . . . It's terrifying. . . ."

Golem rose and rummaged through his vest pocket.

"Teddy!" he shouted. "Write me up a bill. And keep in mind that I broke four glasses. Well, I'm off," he said to Victor. "Think hard and make a wise decision. Maybe it would even be best for you to leave."

"Good-bye, Mr. Banev," said Bol-Kunats politely. Victor thought he saw the boy ever so lightly shaking his head.

"Good-bye, Bol-Kunats," he said. "Good-bye."

They left. Victor, lost in thought, finished the cognac. The waiter came. His face was swollen and covered with red spots. He started to clear the table, and his movements were unusually awkward and hesitant.

"You haven't been here long, have you?" asked Victor.

"No, Mr. Banev. Starting this morning."

"What happened to Peter? Is he sick?"

"No, Mr. Banev. He left. He couldn't stand it. Probably I'll leave too."

Victor looked at R. Quadriga.

"Take him up to his room," he said.

"Yes, of course, Mr. Banev," answered the waiter in an unsteady voice.

Victor paid up, waved good-bye to Teddy, and went out into the lobby. He went up to the second floor, walked over to Pavor's room, and raised his hand as if to knock. He stood there for some time. Then, not having done anything, he went downstairs. The desk clerk was sitting and staring at his hands in astonishment. His hands were wet, and clumps of hair were stuck to them. Hairs were strewn all over his tuxedo and there were fresh scratches on his face, over both cheeks. He looked at Victor and his eyes were crazed. But now was not the time to notice odd details, it would have been tactless and cruel, and even worse would have been to say something about it. It was imperative to pretend that nothing had happened, everything had to be put off until tomorrow or maybe even the day after. Victor spoke.

"Could you tell me the room number of that, uh, you know, the young man in glasses, he always carries an attaché case."

The desk clerk wavered. Seeking a way out, he looked at the numbered board with the keys on it, then answered anyway.

"Number three twelve, Mr. Banev."

"Thank you," said Victor, putting a coin on the desk.

"Only they don't like to be disturbed," warned the desk clerk halfheartedly.

"I know," said Victor. "I wasn't intending to disturb them. I was just asking. A little prophesying: if it's an even number, then everything will be all right."

The desk clerk gave him a weak smile.

"What kind of problems could you have, Mr. Banev?" he said politely.

"All sorts," sighed Victor. "Big ones and little ones. Good night."

He went up to the third floor, moving slowly, intentionally slowly, as if to give himself time to think it all over and weigh the possible consequences, and consider everything for three years in advance. But in fact he was thinking that it was really time for them to change the carpet on the staircase; it was worn thin. And only just as he was about to knock at the door of number three twelve (deluxe class: two bedrooms and a sitting room, a television, a good radio, a refrigerator, and a bar), he almost said aloud: "You are reptiles, gentlemen. My pleasure. I'll have you feeding on one another."

He had to knock for a long time; at first a few light taps with his knuckles, and then, when there wasn't any response, a more decisive rap with his fist, and when even that brought no reaction, just a squeaking of floorboards and someone's breath at the keyhole, he turned around and banged with his heels, having lost all pretense at politeness.

"Who's there?" asked, at long last, a voice behind the door.

"A neighbor," answered Victor. "Open up for a minute."

"What do you want?"

"I have to say a few words to you."

"Come in the morning," said the voice behind the door. "We're already sleeping."

"You goddamned fools," said Victor, furious. "Do you want me to be seen here? Open up, what are you afraid of?"

The key clicked, and the door opened slightly. In the crack appeared the dull eye of the lanky professional. Victor spread open his hands.

"A few words," he said.

"Come in," said the professional. "Only no funny business."

Victor walked into the foyer, and the professional closed the door behind him and lit the light. The foyer was small, the two of them barely fitting into it.

"Well, speak," said the professional. He was wearing stained pajamas. Victor sniffed in astonishment. The professional had liquor on his breath. His right hand was, according to form, hidden in his pocket.

"Are we going to talk here?" inquired Victor.

"Yes."

"No," said Victor. "I don't care for the surroundings."

"As you wish," said the professional.

"As you wish," said Victor. "It's your loss."

They fell silent. The professional, no longer trying to hide it, scrutinized Victor carefully.

"It seems your name is Banev?" he said.

"So it seems."

"Aha," glowered the professional. "Then what kind of neighbor are you? You live on the second floor."

"It's the same hotel," explained Victor.

"Aha. And what you want from us, I can't understand."

"I have something to tell you," said Victor. " A certain piece of information. But I'm already starting to change my mind, I'm not sure it's worth it."

"Well, all right," said the professional. "Let's move to the bathroom."

"You know," said Victor, "I think I'll go."

"What do you have against the bathroom? Why so choosy?"

"You know," said Victor, "I changed my mind. I think I'll go. In the final analysis, it's not my problem."

The professional grunted, perplexed by contradictory feelings.

"If I'm not mistaken, you're a writer," he said. "Or maybe I'm taking you for someone else."

"A writer," said Victor. "Good-bye."

"No, wait a minute. You should have said so right away. Let's go. This way."

They entered the sitting room which was hung over with curtains, curtains to the right, curtains to the left, curtains straight ahead and over the large window. A huge color television flickered in the corner, but the sound was turned off. In the other corner, the young man in glasses, dressed in pajamas and slippers, sat in a soft chair by a lamp and stared at Victor from over the top of his opened newspaper. On the table next to him was a four-sided decanter and a seltzer bottle. The attaché case was out of sight.

"Good evening," said Victor.

The young man silently inclined his head.

"He came to see me," said the professional. "Pay no attention."

The young man nodded again and disappeared behind his paper.

"This way, please," said the professional. They went into the bedroom on the right, and the professional sat down on the bed. "There's a chair," he said. "Sit down and let's have it."

Victor sat down. The bedroom smelled heavily of tobacco smoke and officers' eau de cologne. The professional sat on the bed and stared at Victor, his hand still in his pocket. A newspaper rustled in the sitting room.

"All right," said Victor. It wasn't as though he had completely overcome his disgust, but now that he was here, he had to start. "I have some idea of who you are. I may, of course, be mistaken, in which case everything is all right. But if that's not so, then you might find it useful to know that you are being followed and your work may be interfered with."

"Let us suppose," said the professional. "And who is following us?"

"Your activities have attracted the interest of a certain Pavor Summan."

"What?" said the professional. "The sanitary inspector?"

"He is not the sanitary inspector. That's all I wanted to tell you." Victor stood up, but the professional didn't move a muscle.

"Let us suppose," he repeated. "How, if I might ask, do you know this?"

"Does it matter?" asked Victor.

The professional thought for some time.

"Let us suppose that it doesn't," he announced.

"Verifying it is your problem," said Victor. "That's all I know. Good-bye."

"Wait a minute, where are you going?" said the professional. He bent over to the night table and pulled out a bottle and a glass. "You wanted to see us so badly and now you're leaving so soon. Is it all right if we share a glass?"

"It depends on what's in it," answered Victor and sat down again.

"Scotch," said the professional. "Does that suit you?"

"Real Scotch?"

"The real thing. Allow me." He held out the glass to Victor.

"Some people have it good," said Victor and drank.

"We've got nothing against you writers," said the professional and also drank. "But if you could tell us in more detail."

"Forget it," said Victor. "You get paid for that. I told you the name and the address, it's your business, go get busy. The more so that I really don't know anything. Except for—" Victor stopped and pretended that something had just dawned on him. The professional took the bait.

"Well?" he said. "Well?"

"I know that he kidnapped a slimy and that he was working in collusion with the town legionnaires. What's his name—Flamenta, Juventa. . . ."

"Flamen Juventa," the professional helped him.

"That's it."

"About the slimy. You're sure that's right?" asked the professional.

"I'm sure. I tried to step in, but his honor the sanitary inspector knocked me on the back of the head with his brass knuckles. And then when I was sprawled out on the street they drove him away."

"Interesting," said the professional. "So it was Summan. Listen, you're really all right, Banev. Want some more whisky?"

"Please," said Victor. No matter what he told himself, no matter how much he steeled himself or tried to overcome it, he was still disgusted. "Well, all right," he thought. "At least now I know that I wouldn't make a good informer. No satisfaction there at all, even though now they really will start feeding on each other. Golem was right—it was stupid of me to get involved in this. Or maybe Golem was cleverer than I thought?"

"Your turn," said the professional, holding out a full glass to him.

Chapter IX

"What time is it?" asked Diana sleepily.

Victor, razor in hand, made a neat sweep through the lather on his left cheek. Then he looked at himself in the mirror.

"Sleep, little one, sleep. It's still early."

"You're right," said Diana. The bed creaked. "It's nine o'clock. What are you doing?"

"I'm shaving," answered Victor, removing some more lather. "I got this sudden urge to shave. You know—I said to myself— I think I'll have a shave."

"You're crazy," said Diana, yawning. "You should have shaved last night. You scratched me all over with your bristles. Cactus."

Through the mirror, he watched her stumble over to the armchair, curl up in it, and start looking at him. Victor winked at her. This was yet another Diana, tender, soft, and gentle, tucked into a ball like a contented cat, petted and blessed. It was completely different from the Diana who had torn into his room the night before.

"Today you look like a cat," he announced to her. "And not even a cat—a kitten, a soft, silky. What are you smiling for?"

"Not because of you. I just remembered."

She yawned and stretched out luxuriously. She was drowning in his pajamas—out of the formless pile of silk on the armchair you could see only her wonderful face and thin arms. As out of a wave. Victor started to shave faster.

"Don't hurry," she said. "You'll cut yourself. I have to leave soon anyway."

"That's why I'm hurrying," said Victor.

"No, don't, I don't like it that way. Only cats do it that way. How are my clothes doing?"

Victor stretched out a hand and felt her dress and stockings, draped over the radiator. Everything was dry.

"Where are you rushing to?" he asked.

"I told you. To Rosheper."

"There's something here I don't remember. What's the matter with Rosheper?"

"I told you, he hurt himself," said Diana.

"Oh, right," said Victor. "Right, you were saying something. He took a fall from somewhere. So he really got banged up, did he?"

"That idiot," said Diana, "suddenly decided that he wanted to kill himself and dove into the window. He charged it like a bull, headfirst, and broke the glass, but he forgot that his room was on the first floor. He hurt his knee, started howling, and now he's in bed."

"What got into him?" asked Victor. "Hallucinations?"

"Something like that."

"Wait," said Victor. "So it's because of him that you didn't come to see me for two days? Because of that lummox?"

"Why else? The head doctor ordered me to sit with him because he, that is, Rosheper, couldn't manage without me. He couldn't, and that's that. He couldn't do anything. Even urinate. I had to pretend I was a bubbling brook and tell him about pissoirs."

"What do you know about that?" muttered Victor. "There you were expounding about pissoirs, and I was in agony here all by myself. I couldn't do anything either, I didn't write a single line. You know, I never did like to write, but recently. . . . In general, my life. . . ." He stopped. "What does she care," he thought. "Coupling and uncoupling." "Yes, listen," he said. "When were you saying Rosheper took this nose dive?"

"Two days ago," answered Diana.

"In the evening?"

"Uhuh," said Diana nibbling at a cookie.

"At ten o'clock," said Victor. "Between ten and eleven."

Diana stopped chewing.

"That's right," she said. "How did you know? Did you pick up his necrobiotic waves?"

"Wait," said Victor. "I'm going to tell you something interesting. But first tell me. What were you doing at that moment?"

"What was I doing? Oh, I know. That was the evening that I broke down. I'd been rolling bandages, and then this incredible despair came over me, like a headache, I could have killed myself. So I buried my head in the bandages and started bawling. I hadn't bawled that way since I was a child. Whole rivers of tears were—"

"And suddenly it was all over," said Victor.

Diana thought.

"Yes. No. Then Rosheper started howling outside and I got scared and jumped up."

She was about to say something else when there was a knock at the door. Someone was turning the doorknob. Then Teddy's hoarse cry came through from the corridor. "Victor! Victor, wake up! Open the door, Victor!" Victor, razor in hand, stood stock still. "Victor!" sputtered Teddy. "Open up!" The doorknob rattled madly. Diana jumped up and turned the key. The door flew open and Teddy burst in, wet and lacerated, with a sawed-off shotgun in his hands.

"Where's Victor?"

Victor emerged from the bathroom.

"What's going on?" he asked. His heart was pounding. An arrest . . . war. . . .

"The children are gone," said Teddy, breathing heavily. "Get your things together, the children are gone."

"Hold it," said Victor. "What children?"

Teddy flung his weapon onto the table on top of a pile of scribbled-on, crossed-out, crumpled paper.

"They've lured the children away, the bastards!" he yelled. "They've lured them away, the sons of bitches! Well, that's the end! That's enough, we've been patient long enough. That's the end!"

Victor still didn't understand anything, he only saw that Teddy was beside himself. He had seen Teddy that way only once before, when someone broke his cash register in a restaurant brawl. Victor, in confusion, stared blankly at him. Diana grabbed her underwear from the back of the chair, slipped into the bathroom, and closed the door. At that moment, the telephone started ringing, shrilly, nervously. Victor grabbed the receiver. It was Lola.

"Victor," she whined. "I don't understand anything, Irma's gone off somewhere, she left a note that she's never coming back, and everyone's saying that the children have left town. I'm frightened! Do something!" She was almost crying.

"All right, all right, right away," said Victor. "Let me put my pants on." He threw down the receiver and looked at Teddy. The barman was sitting on the unmade bed, muttering terrible words to himself. He had gotten hold of Victor's liquor bottles and was pouring what remained into a single glass. "Hold on," said Victor. "No panicking. I'll be ready in a minute."

He went back to the bathroom and started shaving the rest of his lathered chin. He kept cutting himself, but there was no time to sharpen the blade. Diana, in the meantime, had jumped out of the shower; he could hear her clothes rustling behind his back. Her face looked cold and decisive, as though she were preparing for a fight, but she was completely calm.

. . . And the children walked in an endless gray column along the gray washed-out roads. They walked, stumbling and slipping, falling under the pouring rain. They walked bent over, soaked through and through, clutching their pitiful bundles in their small blue fists. The littlest ones, helpless, uncomprehending, walked in tears, walked in silence, walked looking behind them, holding on to their elders' hands or grasping at the belts of their coats. And all along the sides of the roads marched the somber black figures without faces. Where there should have been faces there were only black bandages, and above the bandages inhuman eyes stared out coldly and without pity. The black-gloved hands held submachine guns, and the rain poured down on the burnished steel, and the droplets trembled and rolled along the metal. . . . "Nonsense," thought Victor. "Nonsense, that's not it, that's not the way it's happening, that's something else I saw a long time ago, now it's quite different."

. . . They left joyfully, and the rain was a friend to them. They splashed happily through the puddles with their warm bare feet, they chattered and sang and didn't look back because everything was already forgotten, because they had only the future before them, their native town, snoring and sniffling in the predawn hours, was already lost to the past. Their native town, a treasury of bedbug nests, a cradle of petty passions and petty desires, pregnant with monstrous crimes, constantly exuding crimes and criminal intentions the way a queen ant exudes eggs. They left, twittering and chattering, and vanished into the fog. And we kept drinking, choking on the stagnant air and poisoned by nightmares which they never saw and never would see. . . .

He was getting into his pants, hopping around on one leg, when there was a sudden rattling of glass. A deep, mechanical roar penetrated the room. Teddy shot to the window, and Victor also rushed over, but there was nothing to see but the rain and the empty, wet street. Someone rode past on a bicycle —a wet, canvas sack, arduously pumping its legs. The glass continued to rattle and shake, and the low, anguished roar went on, followed in a minute's time by a plaintive intermittent whistle.

"Let's go," said Diana. She was already in her raincoat.

"No, wait," said Teddy. "Victor, do you have some weapon? A pistol, a submachine gun? Do you have anything?"

Victor didn't answer him. He grabbed his raincoat, and the three of them ran downstairs into the lobby. The lobby was already empty; the doorman and desk clerk were gone. It seemed that there was no one left in the hotel. Only R. Quadriga sat in the restaurant in his usual place, shaking his head in astonishment; apparently he was still waiting for his breakfast. They rushed out to the street and climbed into Diana's truck, all three in the cab. Diana sat down behind the wheel, and they started driving around the city. Diana was silent; Victor was smoking, trying to collect his thoughts, and Teddy, muttering under his breath, regaled them with a stream of the most incredible curses, half of which even Victor didn't understand. To understand them you would have had to have been Teddy: an orphanage rat raised in the shipyard slums, then a drug dealer, then a bouncer in a whorehouse, then a corpse hauler in the army, then a gangster, then a barman, then again a barman, and again a barman.

There were almost no signs of life in the city. Only on the corner of Sunrise did Diana stop to pick up a distracted-looking couple. The low roar of the antiaircraft sirens and the shriek of the factory whistle went on, and there was something apocalyptic in this moan of mechanical voices over the deserted town. All nerves were tensed; you felt like running somewhere and either hiding or shooting. Even the Brothers in Reason were chasing their ball around the stadium with less than their usual enthusiasm, and some of them were standing with their mouths opened, vaguely trying to reason it all out.

Farther down along the main road they came across more and more people. Some of them were walking, gulping in the rain—pitiful, scared, unable to understand what they were doing and why. Others were riding bicycles and they were also exhausted, because they'd had to ride against the wind. Several times the truck passed abandoned cars, broken down or out of

gas, because there'd been no time to get any; one car had
gone into a ditch. Diana stopped and picked up everyone,
and soon there was no more room in the back of the truck.
Victor and Teddy also climbed to the back, leaving their seats
to a woman with an infant and a half-crazed old lady. Then
there was no room left at all, and Diana didn't stop any more.
The truck sped forward, spraying dirty water on hundreds of
people dragging themselves to the leprosarium. A few times it
was passed by motorcyclists and cars filled to bursting with
people; another truck drove up and followed them from behind. Diana was used to making the cognac run for Rosheper
or driving the empty truck around the countryside for her own
enjoyment, and the ride, as a result, was terrifying. Not everyone could sit, there was no room, and those who were standing
were hanging onto each other and onto the heads of the sitters;
everyone was trying to keep clear of the sides, and no one was
saying a word. People were panting and cursing, a woman was
crying incessantly, and the rain came pouring down. Victor had
never seen a rain like that in his life, he had never even imagined
that such rains existed. It was a real tropical shower, but an icy
one, half mixed with hail, and a heavy wind lashed it across the
faces of the crowd. The visibility was terrible, fifty feet in front
and fifty in back, and Victor was very much afraid that Diana,
in addition to everything else, would run somebody over or
crash into the car ahead of her. But everything worked out, and
Victor suffered nothing more than a stamped-on foot, when
everyone fell in a heap for the last time and the truck skidded to
a stop before the huge collection of cars at the gate of the
leprosarium.

Probably the whole town had gathered there. Around the
leprosarium there was no rain, and it seemed that the whole
town had come to seek a refuge from the flood. To the right
and left of the road, along the barbed wire fence, a crowd of
thousands stretched as far as the eye could see. Here and
there, lost in the crowd, abandoned cars stood every which

way: elegant limousines, battered jeeps with canvas tops, trucks, buses, and even a crane with several people perched on the arm. A muffled din hung over the crowd, occasionally punctuated by piercing shrieks.

Everyone jumped out of the truck, and Victor immediately lost sight of Diana and Teddy. Around him were nothing but unknown faces—grim, hardened, and uncomprehending, weeping, screaming, with teeth bared and eyes rolling as if they were about to faint. Victor tried to push his way to the gates, but after a few steps was hopelessly entangled. People were pressed into a thick wall, and none of them wanted to give up their places. You could have pushed them, kicked them, beat them, and they wouldn't have even turned around, they would have sunk their heads into their shoulders and tried to push ahead. Ahead, ahead, closer to the gates, closer to their children. They stood on tiptoe, they craned their necks, and nothing could be seen beyond the swaying mass of hoods and rain hats.

"Why, oh Lord? Wherefore have we sinned, oh Lord?"

"Sons of bitches! We should have wiped them out a long time ago. People who knew were saying. . . ."

"And where's the burgomaster? What the hell is he up to? Where's the police? Where are all of those fat slobs?"

"Sim, they're crushing me! Sim, I can't breathe! Oh, Sim."

"What did we deny them? What didn't we do for them? We tore the bread from our own mouths, we went barefoot so they could have clothes and shoes."

"Let's give it one good shove, and that'll be the end of the gate."

"But I never lifted a finger to him. You liked to strap yours, I saw it, but in our house there was never nothing like that."

"Did you see those machine guns? What are they going to do, shoot at their own people? Because we want our own children?"

"Munny! Munny! Munny! Munny, my little sweetheart! Munny!"

"What is this, Lord? It's madness. When has anything like this ever happened?"

"Don't worry, the legionnaires'll show 'em. They're coming from the rear, get it? The gates'll open, and then we'll push. . . ."

"Have you seen the machine guns? It's no joke."

"Let me in! Let me in, I tell you! I've got a daughter in there!"

"They were getting ready for a long time, I saw it, only I was afraid to ask."

"Maybe there's nothing so bad about it. What are they, beasts or something? They're not the occupation, they haven't taken them there to shoot them or throw them in the ovens."

"I want to see their blood, I'll tear them to pieces."

"So, that's that, we're nothing but shit if our own children have left us for this filth." "Drop it, they left of their own will, nobody forced them."

"Hey, who's got a weapon? Step out? Whoever's got a weapon, I'm saying. Come over here, let's see you over here!"

"Those are my kids in there, mister. I gave birth to them and I'll do as I goddamn please with them."

"Where are the police, oh Lord?"

"We've got to send a telegram to Mr. President! Five thousand signatures, that's no joke!"

"A woman's been crushed! Move away, I'm telling you, you bastard! Can't you see?"

"Munny, sweetheart! Munny, Munny!"

"Those petitions won't get you anywhere. They don't give a shit about petitions here. They'll take those petitions of yours and shove them."

"Open the gate, you mother. You filthy slimies, you. Bastards."

"The gates!"

"Open the gates!"

Victor started back. It wasn't easy, a few times he even got hit, but still he made it, fighting his way out of the crowd. He scrambled over to the truck and once again climbed in the back.

A fog hung over the leprosarium; ten yards in from the fence you couldn't see a thing. The gates were shut tight. In front of them was an empty space, and in this empty space stood ten soldiers of the Security Corps: legs planted far apart, helmets pulled down over the eyes, submachine guns pointed into the crowd. On the guard-booth porch, an officer had pulled himself up to his full height. Visibly straining, he shouted something at the crowd, but you couldn't hear him. Above the guard booth, a wooden tower loomed in the fog like an enormous bookcase; gray-clad figures swarmed around a machine gun on its upper level. From down below, beyond the barbed wire, came a barely audible metallic hum: a half-track armored car was patrolling the border. It bounced a few times over the uneven ground and disappeared into the fog. When the crowd caught sight of the armored car it grew quiet, and for a moment you could even hear the strained cries of the officer (". . . Calm . . . I have orders . . . to your homes . . ."). Then the clamor started up again.

There was a movement in front of the gates. Copper helmets and golden shirts, familiar to the point of nausea, began to flash in the blue-gray mob of raincoats and ponchos. They arose in the crowd like points of light, migrated over to the empty space, and merged into a single golden mass: a mass of musclemen in knee-length golden shirts, buckled in army officers' belts and wielding sturdy nightsticks. Each one boasted a polished copper helmet, the source of their nickname, "firemen." And each one was plastered over with Legion emblems: an emblem on the buckle, an emblem on the left sleeve, on the breast, on the nightstick, on the helmet, on the fifth-rate beefy faces with their wolfish eyes. And then their badges, constellations of badges: Sharpshooter's, Parachutist's, Diver's; badges with the portrait of Mr. President, badges with the portrait of his Legion Founder son-in-law, badges with the portrait of his Legion

Oberchef son. And in each one's pocket was a tear-gas bomb, and if one of those monsters in a burst of hoodlum enthusiasm should throw such a bomb, then it would all go off: the gun on the tower, the guns on the armored car, and the guns in the hands of the soldiers. And all of them firing right at the crowd—at the crowd, and not at the golden shirts. The Legionnaires fell into ranks before the soldiers, and along the ranks, waving his nightstick, marched Flamen Juventa, the nephew. Victor was looking around in desperation, not knowing what to do, but then someone emerged from the guard booth with a megaphone for the officer. The officer was terribly pleased; he even cracked a smile, and his voice began to bellow over the crowd. But he managed only "I ask for your attention! I ask those gathered here—" when the megaphone apparently gave out. The officer, turning pale, was about to listen to Juventa. Then he started running around the platform and waving his megaphone with redoubled strength. And suddenly the crowd let out a roar. It seemed as though everyone was shouting at once, those who had been shouting before as well as those who had been silent, or talking among themselves, or crying, or praying. Victor also started to shout, forgetting himself in horrified awareness of what was about to happen. "Get those idiots away!" he shouted. "Get those firemen away! It's death! Diana, don't!" It was unclear who was shouting and what was being shouted, but the crowd, till then immobile, began swaying evenly like an enormous dish of pudding. The officer dropped the megaphone. Pale, his face splotched with red, he backed his way to the doors of the guard booth. The soldiers beneath their helmets grew frenzied and wild-eyed. Above them, on the tower, no one was stirring; silently, they took aim. And then the Voice rang out.

It was like thunder, it came from all sides at once and instantly drowned out all other sounds. It was calm, even melancholy, and it exuded boundless boredom and boundless tolerance. It was the voice of someone huge, arrogant, and scornful, standing with his back to the crowd and addressing it over his shoulder; the voice of someone engaged in important work and irritated, finally, by some trifle.

"Stop your shouting," said the Voice. "Stop waving your hands and making threats. Is it really so difficult for you to drop this nonsense and think calmly for a few minutes? You are perfectly well aware that your children left you of their own will, nobody forced them and nobody dragged them by the collar. They left because you had become totally disagreeable to them. They no longer wish to live the way you live and the way your forebears lived. You love to imitate your forebears and consider this a human virtue, and they don't. They don't want to turn into drunkards and debauchers, into petty slaves and conformists. They don't want you to turn them into criminals; they don't want your families and they don't want your government."

For a minute the voice fell silent. And for a whole minute not a sound was to be heard, only a vague rustling, like a fog sweeping over the earth. Then the Voice spoke again.

"You may feel totally at peace about your children. They will live well—better than with you and much better than you yourselves. Today they cannot receive you, but beginning tomorrow you may see them here. A meeting house will be set up in Horse's Hollow, and you may come every day if you like, after one o'clock. Every day three big buses will leave from the town square. Tomorrow this may prove insufficient; let your burgomaster worry about additional transport."

The Voice fell silent again. The crowd stood like a stone wall. People seemed afraid to make a move.

"Keep one thing in mind," continued the Voice. "Whether or not the children will want to see you depends on you. For the first few days, we will still be able to make them go to meetings. What happens after that is up to you. And now go home. You are disturbing us, and the children, and yourselves. And I urge you: think, try to think of what you could do for the children. Look at yourselves. You gave them life, and you are deforming them in your own image. Think about that, and now go home."

The crowd didn't move; maybe it was trying to think. Victor tried. His thoughts were all confused. Not even thoughts, really, just fragments of memories, bits of conversations, Lola's stupid made-up face. . . . "Maybe I should have an abortion, why should we burden ourselves now . . . father with his lips quivering in anger . . . I'll make an honest man out of you, you lousy puppy, I'll tear the skin off of you . . . I've got this twelve-year-old daughter on my hands, do you think you could set her up somewhere decent? . . . Irma looking curiously at the salivating Rosheper . . . not at Rosheper, at me . . . maybe I'm ashamed, but what does she understand, the little squirt? Scat! Here's a doll for you, a nice doll . . . you're still too young, when you grow up, you'll find out. . . ."

"Well, what are you standing here for?" said the thunderous Voice. "Go home!"

A gust of cold wind whipped them in the faces and died down.

"Go!" said the Voice.

A second gust, this time a really solid one, pressed their face like a cold, wet palm, then shoved them and blew off. Victor rubbed his cheeks and saw the crowd starting to step backwards. Someone's shriek was followed by uncertain cries; small whirlpools formed around the cars and buses. From all sides people were climbing into the truck, hurrying, shoving. They crawled into their cars, they disengaged their bicycles from the tangle of handlebars, they started up their motors. Many of them left on foot, constantly glancing behind them. But they weren't looking at the submachine guns, nor at the machine gun on the tower or the armored car which drove up with a metallic clang for all to see, its apertures opened. Victor knew why they were looking back and why they were hurrying; his cheeks were burning, and if there was one thing he feared it was that the Voice would once again say "Go!" and the heavy, wet palm would give him a squeamish shove in the face. A bunch of golden-shirted fools continued to mill around uncertainly before the gates, but there were already fewer of them. The officer, self-assured and imposing, fulfilling a pleasant duty, barked at those who remained. These also took a few steps backwards, then turned and got the hell out of there, grabbing on the run their blue and gray raincoats that lay strewn along the ground. Already not a single point of light remained. Buses and cars were driving past, and the people in the truck, looking around impatiently, were asking one another, "Where's the driver?"

Then Diana, Diana the Fierce, emerged from somewhere, climbed up the steps to the cab and took a look in the back of the truck. "Only up to the crossroads!" she snapped. "The truck is going to the health resort." Nobody dared to object; they were singularly quiet and submissive. Teddy never showed up; he must have gotten into a different car. Diana made a U-turn and they started down the familiar concrete road, passing groups of pedestrians and bicyclists and getting passed by crowded cars which bore down heavily on overburdened shocks. There was no rain, only fog and a light drizzle. The rain didn't start until Diana had brought the truck to the crossroads, the people had gotten out, and Victor had moved up to the cab.

They were silent all the way to the resort.

Diana went immediately to Rosheper, or so she said. Victor, throwing off his raincoat, flopped into his bed, lit up a cigarette, and started staring at the ceiling. For an hour or maybe two he smoked incessantly, tossing and turning, getting up and walking around the room, staring midlessly out the window. Then he would open and close the curtains, take a drink right from the faucet because he was tormented by thirst, and flop back onto the bed.

"Humiliation," he thought. "Of course. They slapped me on the cheek, called me names, chased me away as though I were some beggar making a nuisance out of myself. But there were real mothers and fathers there, and they loved their children. They may have beaten them, but they were ready to give their lives up for them; they may have corrupted them by their own example, but it wasn't on purpose, it was out of ignorance. Their mothers brought them forth in pain, and their fathers fed them and clothed them, and they were proud of their children and boasted to one another. Sometimes they cursed them, but they couldn't imagine life without them. And now their lives have become empty, there's nothing at all left. So can you really be so cruel to them, so arrogant and cold and rational, and then slap them on the face by way of good-bye.

"And goddamnit, is it really true that all the animal in man is bad? Even motherhood, the smile of madonnas, their tender, soft hands giving the breast to the child? Of course it's instinct, a whole religion built on instinct. The problem comes later, in trying to use instinct to bring them up, where no instincts work anymore, and if they do work, then they only cause harm. Because a mother wolf can say to her cubs, 'Bite, the way I do,' and that's enough, and the mother rabbit teaches her bunnies, 'Run for your lives the way I do,' and that's also enough, but if a man teaches children, 'Think as I do,' it's criminal. And how do they go about it, those slimies, those bastards, those whatever you want, only not men but at the very least supermen. How do they go about it? First: Look at what people thought before you came along, and look what happened as a result of it, that's bad because it resulted in *a* and *b* and what we need is *c* and *d*. Do you understand? And now start thinking for yourself, think about what to do so that there's no *a* and *b* but rather *c* and *d*. Only I don't know what the letters stand for, and anyway we've been through it before, it's all been tried before. And a few good people came out of it, but the vast majority kept right on going, treading down the old paths, it's our way, the simple way. And how could he bring up his own child when his father didn't bring him up right but merely trained him: 'Bite the way I do and hide the way I do.'

That's how his father had been trained and his father's father, and so on to the depths of the caves, to the hairy mammoth-eaters, carriers of spears. I feel sorry for them, for the hairless descendents, because I feel sorry for myself. But those other ones could give a shit, they have no use for us. They have no plans to reeducate us and they don't even want to blow up the old world, they don't want to have anything to do with it. They have their own business to take care of, and all they want from the old world is for it to leave them in peace. And now that's become possible, now it's possible to deal in ideas. There are powerful purchasers of ideas, and they will guard you, they'll herd the rest of the world behind barbed wire for you, so the old world doesn't cause you any problems. They'll feed you, they'll cherish you. In the most thoughtful possible way they'll sharpen your ax for you, and you'll take that ax and chop off the very branch they're planning to sit on, flashing their em-broidery and their medals.

"But goddamnit, in its own way it's grandiose. Everything's already been tried, sure, except for this: to bring up children coldly, without rosy kisses and without tears. Although what kind of crap is this, how should I know how they're doing it. Still, some of it is obvious—the cruelty, the scorn. And they won't get anywhere either, because reason is only one thing. Think, study, do your analyses, but what about the hands of a mother, the tender hands which take away the hurt and make the world warm? And the bristly face of a father, who knows how to play war and how to play tiger, who teaches boxing, and is the strongest person in the world and knows more than anybody else? Because that was part of the truth, too. It wasn't only parental fights, with or without shrieking. It wasn't only the belt and the drunken muttering, not only the unjustified box on the ears followed suddenly and incomprehensibly by a session of compulsive gift-giving—chocolates and a buck for the movies. Anyway, how should I know—maybe they have the equivalent of all that's good in motherhood and fatherhood. The way Irma was looking at that slimy! What kind of person would you have to be for her to look at you like that? And at any rate, neither Bol-Kunats, nor Irma, nor the pimply-faced nihilist will ever put on a golden shirt, and that's saying something. Goddamnit, what more can you ask of somebody?

"Wait," he said to himself. "Get down to what's most important. Are you for them or against them? There's another out, of course: not to give a shit. Except you do. How good it would be to be a cynic, how simple, how luxurious. Just think. All my life they've been conspiring to make a cynic out of me. They've spent a fortune on it, wasted bullets, flowery speeches, and paper. And they haven't spared their fists, either, and they haven't spared people, they haven't spared anything, just as long as I'll turn into a cynic. Except I haven't. Well, all right, that's enough. The question remains: am I for or against? Of course I'm against, because I can't stand contemptuousness, I hate every elite, I hate every sort of impatience, and I don't like, oh, how I don't like to get slapped on the face and chased away. And then I'm for them, too, because I like people who are intelligent and talented and I hate fools, I hate dimwits, I hate golden shirts, and I hate fascists. It's obvious that this way I won't decide anything. I don't know enough about them, and of the little that I do know, that I saw with my own eyes, what stands out is the bad part: cruelty, arrogance, inhumanity, physical deformity. And it adds up as follows. For them we have Diana, whom I love; Golem, whom I love; Irma, whom I love; and Bol-Kunats; and the pimply-faced nihilist. And who is against them? The burgomaster, the old son of a bitch, a fascist and a demagogue. The whore of a police chief, and Rosheper Nant, and that fool Lola, and the gang of golden shirts, and Pavor. Of course, on the other hand, the lanky professional is for them, along with a certain General Pferd; I can't stand generals. And Teddy is against them, and there must be a lot more like him. But you can't decide anything by looking at who's in the majority. It's like an election in a free society—the majority is always for a pig."

At about two o'clock, Diana came, Diana the Usual and

Cheerful, with her hair brushed and her lipstick in place, in a white lab coat belted tightly at the waist.

"How's your work?" she asked.

"I'm burning," he answered. "I'm burning out, lighting a path for others."

"No doubt—there's a lot of smoke in here. You could have at least opened a window. Want to grab a bite?"

"Hell, yes," said Victor. He remembered that he hadn't had breakfast.

"Then let's get the hell going!"

They went to the dining room. The Brothers in Reason, silent and submissive, faces dark from physical exhaustion, sat behind a long table and slurped their dietetic soup. Their fat coach, bulging out of his blue sweatshirt, made the rounds behind their backs, clapping them on the shoulders, ruffling their hair, and peering attentively into their plates.

"I'm going to introduce you to someone," said Diana. "He's going to eat with us."

"Who?" asked Victor, dissatisfied. He didn't feel like making conversation.

"My husband," said Diana. "My former husband."

"Oh," said Victor. "Oh. Well, I'd be delighted."

"Where'd she get that idea?" he thought wearily. "Who needs it?" He gave her a complaining look, but she was already leading him over to a service table in a far corner. The husband rose to meet them, sallow-faced with a hooked nose, in a dark suit and black gloves. He didn't hold out his hand to Victor, but simply bowed.

"Good afternoon. I'm glad to see you," he said quietly.

"Banev." Victor introduced himself with the false warmth that generally came over him in the presence of husbands.

"In fact, we're already acquainted," said the husband. "I am Zurzmansor."

"Of course!" exclaimed Victor. "Certainly! I have to admit, my memory. . . ." He fell silent. "Wait a minute," he said. "Which Zurzmansor?"

"Pavel Zurzmansor. Probably you've read me, and recently you defended me most energetically in the restaurant. There was another meeting as well, also in unhappy circumstances. Let's be seated."

Victor sat down. "Well, all right," he thought. "Let it be. So without the bandages they're the same. I never would have guessed. But excuse me, where are the rings around his eyes?" Zurzmansor—alias Diana's husband, alias the hook-nosed dancer playing the role of a dancer playing a dancer who is in fact a slimy, or maybe four slimies, or maybe five, counting the one in the restaurant—this Zurzmansor did not have any rings around his eyes. It was as if they had melted into his face, imparting to the skin a yellowish, Latin-American hue. Diana, her face lit up with a strange, almost maternal smile, was looking first at him, then at her husband. Her former husband. This was unpleasant. Victor felt something akin to jealousy, which he had never experienced before in his dealings with husbands. The waitress brought soup.

"Irma sends her greetings," said Zurzmansor, breaking a piece of bread. "She asks you not to worry."

"Thank you," said Victor mechanically. He took his spoon and started to eat, not tasting anything. Zurzmansor also ate, looking at Victor from under his brow. He wasn't smiling, but there was something amused in his expression. He didn't remove his gloves, but the way he used his spoon and napkin, the elegant way he broke his bread, betrayed a good up-bringing.

"So you really are that Zurzmansor," said Victor. "The philosopher...."

"I'm afraid not," said Zurzmansor, patting his lips with a napkin. "I am afraid that my relations with the famous philosopher are at the present time most distant."

Victor couldn't think of what to say, and decided to hold off on the discussion. "In the final analysis, I didn't initiate the meeting, I had nothing to do with it. He wanted to see me, let him start."

They brought the main course. Watching himself carefully, Victor started cutting his meat. At the long table, the Brothers in Reason chomped in a simple, friendly way, clanging their knives and forks. "I'm the real fool here," thought Victor. "A little brother in reason. She probably still loves him. He got sick, they had to part, and she didn't want to—otherwise why would she have gotten stuck in this hole, carrying bedpans for Rosheper? And they see each other often, he sneaks into the sanatorium, takes off his bandage, and dances with her." Victor remembered how they danced. . . .

"All the same. She loves him. And what difference does it make to me? It makes a difference. Despite everything. Only what kind of difference? He took my daughter away, but I'm not jealous of him as a father. He took my woman away, but I'm not jealous of him as a man. Christ, look at the words I'm using. Took away my woman, took away my daughter. My daughter who saw me for the first time in her twelve-year-old life—or maybe she's already thirteen? And I could count on my fingers the number of days I've known the woman. However, take note: I'm jealous, although not as a father and not as a man. It would be a lot simpler if he just said, 'Sir, I know everything, you have stained my honor. How about a duel?' "

"How is your work on the article going?" asked Zurzmansor.

Victor gave him a mournful look. No, he wasn't making fun of him. And he wasn't simply trying to get the conversation going. This slimy, it seemed, was really interested in finding out how his work on the article was going.

"Not at all," he said.

"It would be interesting to have a look at it," Zurzmansor informed him.

"Do you know what kind of article this is supposed to be?"

"We have some idea. But that's not the sort of article you'll write."

"And if I'm forced? General Pferd is not going to rush to my defense."

"The point," said Zurzmansor, "is that the article ordered

by his honor the burgomaster just won't come off. Even if you make every effort. There are people who automatically, independent of their own desires, transform in their own way any task that's set before them. You are one of those people."

"Is that good or bad?" asked Victor.

"From our point of view it's good. Very little is known about the human personality, if you don't count that part of it that's made up of reflexes. It's true that the mass personality contains little else. For that reason, the so-called creative personalities, those who recast information about reality in a personal light, are so valuable. By comparing a familiar and well-studied phenomenon with its reflection in the work of the creative personality, we can learn a great deal about the psychic mechanism which transforms information."

"And you don't see anything insulting in what you're saying?" said Victor.

Zurzmansor, screwing up his face in an odd way, looked at him.

"Oh, I see," he said. "A creator, not a laboratory rabbit. In fact, I was pointing out just a single circumstance which makes you valuable for us. The others are well known—true information about objective reality, a generator of emotions, a means of awakening fantasy and satisfying demands for empathy. The truth is, I wanted to flatter you."

"In that case I'm flattered," said Victor. "Except that all this has no relationship at all to writing defamations. You simply take the latest speech of Mr. President and recopy it from beginning to end, replacing the words 'enemies of freedom' with 'the so-called slimies' or 'the patients of the bloodstained doctor' or 'the vampires from the leprosarium.' So that my psychic mechanism won't play any part in it at all."

"It just seems that way to you," objected Zurzmansor. "But you'll look through the speech, and first of all you'll discover that it's repulsive. I mean stylistically repulsive. So you'll start correcting the style, searching for more precise expressions. Your imagination will start working, and the stagnant words will make you sick. And you'll want to make them into living words, you'll want to replace the official lies with disturbing facts, and you yourself won't notice when you start writing the truth."

"Maybe," said Victor. "In any event, I don't feel like writing it now."

"Do you feel like writing anything else?"

"Yes," said Victor, looking Zurzmansor in the eyes. "It would be a pleasure to write about how the children left town. A new Pied Piper."

Zurzmansor gave a satisfied nod.

"A wonderful idea. Write it."

"Write it," Victor thought bitterly. "And who the fuck is going to publish it? Not you."

"Diana," he said. "Can't we get something to drink here?"

Diana silently got up and went off.

"And it would be a pleasure to write about the doomed city," said Victor. "And about the strange commotion at the leprosarium. And about the wicked sorcerers."

"Are you out of money?" asked Zurzmansor.

"Not yet."

"Keep in mind that you will probably become the laureate of the leprosarium literary prize for the past year. You got into the last round together with Tusov, but Tusov's chances aren't as good, that's obvious. So you'll have money."

"Well," said Victor. "This is a first for me. Is there a lot of money?"

"Around three thousand. I don't remember exactly."

Diana returned and, still silent, placed a bottle and a single glass on the table.

"Another glass," said Victor.

"I'm not having any," said Zurzmansor.

"In fact, I . . . uh. . . ."

"I'm not having any either," said Diana.

"Is it for *Misfortune?*" asked Victor, filling his glass.

"Yes. And for *Cat*. So for three months or so you're taken care of. Or less?"

"Two months," said Victor. "But that's not the problem. Look—I'd like to visit you in the leprosarium."

"Absolutely," said Zurzmansor. "That's where you'll be given the prize. Only you'll be disappointed. No magic. An ordinary day off. A dozen cottages and the treatment complex."

"The treatment complex," repeated Victor. "Who gets treated there?"

"People," said Zurzmansor with a strange intonation.

He gave a short laugh and suddenly something terrible happened to his face. His right eye left its socket and rolled down toward the chin, his mouth became triangular, and his left cheek together with the ear separated from the skull and hung there. It lasted for an instant. Diana dropped her plate, Victor turned away automatically, and when he once again looked at Zurzmansor, the latter was already back to normal—sallow-faced and polite. "Jesus Christ!" said Victor in his thoughts. "Avaunt, impure spirit! Or was I imagining things?"

He hurriedly got out a pack of cigarettes, lit up, and started staring into his glass. The Brothers in Reason noisily stood up and made their way to the exit, calling loudly to one another.

"We want you to feel tranquil," said Zurzmansor. "You don't have to be afraid of anything. No doubt you've guessed that our organization occupies a special position which gives it certain privileges. There is a lot that we do, and because of it a lot of things are permitted to us. Climatic experiments, the training of replacements, and so on. There's no sense in spreading it around. Certain parties imagine that we are working on their behalf, and we aren't dissuading them." For a moment he was silent. "Write about whatever you want in whatever way you want to, Banev. Don't pay attention to barking dogs. If you run into difficulties with publishers, or if you have financial difficulties, we will support you. If worst comes to worst, we will publish you ourselves. For our own consumption, of course. So your marinated eel is provided for."

Victor took a drink and shook his head.

"So," he said. "I'm being bought off again."

"If you wish," said Zurzmansor. "But the most important thing is this. There exists a contingent of readers, maybe not a very numerous one yet, but nonetheless one that is extremely interested in your work. We need you, Banev. And we need you exactly as you are. We don't need a Banev who is our supporter and our bard, so don't break your head trying to figure out whose side you're on. Be on your own side, the same as any creative personality. That's all that we want from you."

"Very, very advantageous conditions," said Victor. "Carte blanche and piles of marinated eel in prospect. In prospect and in mustard sauce. And what widow would whisper to him, 'No'? Listen, Zurzmansor, did you ever have to sell your soul and pen?"

"Yes, of course," said Zurzmansor. "And you know, the pay was outrageously low. But that was a thousand years ago on a different planet." He fell silent again. "You're wrong, Banev," he said. "We're not buying you. We simply want you to remain yourself, and we're afraid that you'll be crushed. A lot of people have gotten crushed. Moral values can't be sold, Banev. You can destroy them, but you can't buy them. A given moral value can be used only in one side of an argument, so stealing it or buying it doesn't make any sense. Mr. President thinks that he bought the artist R. Quadriga. He is mistaken. He bought the hack R. Quadriga, and the artist slipped through his fingers and died. And we don't want the writer Banev to slip through anyone's fingers, even our own, and die. We need artists, not propagandists."

He stood up. Victor also stood up, feeling awkward and proud and mistrustful and humiliated and disappointed and responsible and something else as well that he couldn't yet make out.

"It was very nice to talk with you," said Zurzmansor. "I wish you success in your work."

"Good-bye," said Victor.

Zurzmansor made a quick bow and walked off with a wide, firm step, throwing his head back. Victor watched him go.

"That's what I love you for," said Diana.

Victor collapsed onto his chair and reached for the bottle.

"For what?" he asked absentmindedly.

"Because they need you. Because somebody like you, a slovenly drunken cur, a bastard and a scandalmonger, is needed by people like them."

She bent over the table and kissed his cheek. This was yet another Diana, Diana in Love, a Mary Magdalene with great dry eyes, Diana Looking Up at Him.

"Big deal," muttered Victor. "Intellectuals. Another caliph for an hour."

But these were only words. In reality nothing was that simple.

Chapter X

VICTOR RETURNED to the hotel the next day, after breakfast. On his way out, Diana handed him a birchbark basket. The capital hothouses had presented Rosheper with eighteen pounds of strawberries and she wisely decided that, his monstrous gluttony notwithstanding, there was no way he could cope with them alone.

The sullen doorman opened the door for Victor. Victor offered him some strawberries, and the doorman took a few, putting them into his mouth and chewing them like bread.

"That little puppy of mine was one of their troublemakers," he said.

"Come on," said Victor. "He's a fine kid. Smart, and well brought up."

"I beat the living daylights out of him," said the doorman, getting animated. "I did my damnedest." He turned sullen again. "The neighbors are after me," he offered. "So what could I do? I didn't know nothing."

"Screw your neighbors," Victor advised him. "They're jealous. You've got a terrific kid. I, for one, am very pleased that my daughter is friends with him."

"Ha!" said the doorman, returning to normal. "Maybe we'll be relatives."

"Why not?" said Victor. "It well may be." He thought about Bol-Kunats. "Why not?"

Seizing the occasion, they joked around for a while.

"You didn't hear the shooting last night?" asked the door-man, finally.

"No," said Victor, on guard. "What happened?"

"Well," said the doorman, "when we all got out of there, well, there were a couple of hotheads who didn't get out, and they got together and cut the wire and went through. And they started machine-gunning them."

"Jesus," said Victor.

"I didn't see it myself," said the doorman. "But people talk." He looked carefully around him, then beckoned Victor closer and whispered in his ear. "Teddy was there, he got hurt. Not too bad, though, he was lucky. He's home sleeping it off."

"Unfair," muttered Victor, upset.

He gave some strawberries to the desk clerk, took his key, and went upstairs. Without undressing, he dialed Teddy's number. Teddy's sister-in-law said that everything was all right, that they'd only hit the soft parts and that Teddy was lying on his stomach, cursing them out and guzzling vodka. She herself was planning to go to the meeting house today to see her son. Victor asked her to give Teddy his greetings, promised to stop by, and hung up. He should have called Lola too, but he could imagine the conversation, the reproaches and the yelling, and decided not to. He took off his raincoat, looked at the strawberries, then went down to the kitchen and got some cream. When he returned, Pavor was sitting in his room.

"Good afternoon," said Pavor with a blinding smile.

Victor went over to the table and emptied the strawberries into a bowl. He added cream and sugar and sat down.

"Greetings," he snapped. "What's doing?"

He didn't feel like looking at Pavor. In the first place, Pavor was a son of a bitch, and in the second place, looking at the person you'd informed on proved to be unpleasant. Even if he really was a son of a bitch and you'd informed on him for the most irreproachable reasons.

"Listen, Victor," said Pavor. "I'm willing to apologize. We

both acted stupidly, especially me. I'm having my troubles at work. I sincerely ask your forgiveness. It would bother the hell out of me if some nonsense like this broke up our friendship."

Victor stirred his strawberries and cream and started eating.

"God knows, I've been terribly unlucky lately," Pavor went on. "I've had it with everything. And nobody gives you any sympathy and nobody supports you. And that burgomaster, the pig, got me involved in a dirty business."

"Mr. Summan," said Victor, "stop playing the fool. You know how I put it on, but fortunately I've seen through you, and I get no enjoyment from watching your performance. Kindly do not spoil my appetite. You may go now."

"Victor," said Pavor reproachfully. "We are adults. You shouldn't attach such significance to table chatter. Do you really think that I believed in the crap I was dishing out? A migraine, troubles, a cold. What's a person to do?"

"A person could avoid hitting me from behind with brass knuckles," explained Victor. "And if he does hit me—there are circumstances—then I would rather he didn't buddy up to me afterwards."

"So that's it," said Pavor thoughtfully. His face seemed to sink. "Listen, Victor, I'll explain the whole thing to you. It was pure chance. I had no idea it was you. And then . . . you yourself just said that there are circumstances."

"Mr. Summan," said Victor, licking the spoon. "I have never been overly fond of people in your profession. One of them I even shot—he was very brave at headquarters when he accused officers of disloyalty, but when they sent him to the front lines. . . . In short, get out."

But Pavor didn't get out. He lit up a cigarette, crossed his legs, and leaned back in his chair.

He thought "Well, it figures—a big bruiser like that, probably knows judo too, and he has his brass knuckles on him. It would help if I could get really mad now. What's he doing ruining my dessert?"

"I see that you know a lot," said Pavor. "That's unfortunate. I mean, for you. Well, all right. In any case, you don't know that I respect and love you in the sincerest possible way. Don't shudder and pretend you're sick. I'm serious. I will be happy to express my regret for the brass knuckles. I'll even admit that I knew who I was hitting, but there was nothing I could do about it. We'd already knocked out one witness, and then you turned up. My only way out was to give it to you as delicately as possible, which I did. My sincerest apologies."

Pavor made an aristocratic gesture. Victor looked at him with some curiosity. Something in this situation was novel and hard to understand.

"However," continued Pavor, "I cannot offer any apologies for being a member of a certain department. And anyway, I don't really want to. Don't think that we're a bunch of lousy careerists who do nothing but smother free thought. I admit, I'm a counteragent. I do dirty work. Only work is always dirty, there's no such thing as clean work. In your novels you give vent to your subconscious and that notorious libido of yours. Well, I do it another way. I can't tell you all the details, but you've probably figured out most of it. You're right, I keep an eye on the leprosarium. I hate those slimy animals, I'm afraid of them. And not only for myself, I'm afraid for everyone who's worth anything at all. For example, you. You don't understand a thing. You're a free spirit, an artist. You're impressionable— you shed a few tears and that's the end of it. But we're talking about the future of the system, if you want, about the fate of all mankind. You pick at Mr. President—a dictator, a tyrant, an idiot. But what's coming is a dictatorship of the sort you free-spirited artists never dreamed of. Last night in the restaurant I laid it on thick, but the main idea is valid. Man is an anarchistic animal, and anarchy will tear him to pieces if the system isn't rigid enough. Well, your slimy friends are promising something so cruel that there won't be any place left for simple human beings. You don't understand this. You think that if a person cites Zurzmansor or Hegel, then, oh, boy. But a person like that looks at you and sees a pile of shit, and he doesn't feel sorry for you, because Hegel says that you're shit, and so does Zurzmansor. Shit by definition. And what lies beyond that definition doesn't interest him. Mr. President, by the very nature of his limitations, may bark at you; if worst comes to worst, he'll even stick you in prison. And then when some holiday comes around he'll get emotional and grant you amnesty; he'll even invite you for dinner. But Zurzmansor will look at you through a magnifying glass and classify you: dogshit, good for nothing. And thoughtfully, on the grounds of his great intelligence and general philosophical principles, he'll wipe you away with a dirty rag, throw you into the garbage can, and forget that you ever existed."

Victor had stopped eating. It was a strange spectacle, an unexpected one. Pavor was nervous, his lips were twitching, blood had drained from his face and he was even breathing hard. It was clear that he believed in what he was saying: the vision of that frightening world had petrified in his eyes. "Hold on," Victor warned himself. "This is the enemy. He's a son of a bitch, an actor, he's buying you off for a wooden nickel." He suddenly realized that he was forcibly pushing himself away from Pavor. "Don't forget he's part of a machine. By definition he can't have any ideas—his superiors gave him orders and there he is working for his stewed prunes. If they order him to defend the slimies, he'll defend them. I know the type, I've seen enough of them."

Pavor pulled himself together and smiled. "I know what you're thinking," he said. "It's clear from your expression what you're trying to figure out: just what is this guy pestering me for, what does he want from me? Get this: I don't want anything from you. I sincerely want to warn you, I sincerely want you to understand what's going on so that you'll choose the right side." He gave a sickly grin. "I don't want you to become a traitor to humanity. Later you'll see why, but it'll be too late.

I'm not only saying you ought to leave this place, I've come to you to insist on it. Hard times are coming, the authorities are having an attack of official zeal. The hint's been given, 'You're working badly, gentlemen, there's no law and order.' But that's all right, that's nonsense, we'll talk about that some other time. I want you to understand the most important thing. And the most important thing is not what's going to be tomorrow. Tomorrow they'll still be sitting behind their barbed wire, under the guard of those cretins." He grinned again. "But ten years from now . . ."

Victor never did find out what would happen ten years from now. The door of his room opened without a knock and the pair in identical gray raincoats walked in. Victor realized instantly who they were. As always, his heart skipped a beat. He rose obediently, feeling nauseous and impotent. But they told him to sit down, and to Pavor they said, "Stand up."

"Pavor Summan, you're under arrest."

Pavor, all white, even a sort of bluish-white, like skimmed milk, stood up and said hoarsely, "Your warrant."

They gave him a paper to look at, and while he stared at it with unseeing eyes, they grabbed him by the elbows, led him out, and closed the door behind them. Victor, completely limp, remained in his seat, staring at his bowl and muttering, "Let them devour each other, let them devour each other. . . ." He waited for car doors to slam and an engine to start. But it never happened. He lit a cigarette and went out into the corridor. He felt that he couldn't sit there any longer, that he had to talk to someone, get his mind off it. If nothing else, he had to find someone to drink with. "I wonder how they knew he was with me. No, I don't wonder at all. Nothing to wonder at there." The lanky professional loomed up at him from the staircase landing. It was so unusual to see him alone that Victor took a quick look around. And sure enough, the young man with the briefcase was sitting on a couch in the corner, unfolding a newspaper.

"Oh, just the man we're looking for," said the tall one. The young man looked at Victor, rose, and started to fold his paper. "We were just on our way to see you," said the tall one. "But since it's worked out this way, why don't you come to our room, it's even quieter there."

Victor didn't care where he went, and obediently dragged himself up to the third floor. The professional spent a long time opening up the door to three twelve. He had a whole key chain on him, and it seemed that he tried every one. In the meantime, Victor and the young man in glasses stood waiting. The young man had a bored expression on his face, and Victor thought about what would happen if he were to smash in his face, grab the attaché case, and run down the corridor. Then they went into the room. The young man went immediately to the bedroom on the left, and the professional told Victor "One moment, please," and retired to the bedroom on the right. Victor sat down gingerly at a mahogany table and drew his fingers over the rough circles left on the polished surface by innumerable wine and vodka glasses. They hadn't stood on ceremony with the table, they hadn't noticed what it was made of, and it bore the marks of burning cigarettes and at least one leaky ballpoint. Then the young man emerged from his bedroom, this time in slippers, minus his attaché case and without his jacket. He had a newspaper in one hand and a full glass in the other. He sat down in his armchair by the lamp. Instantly the professional appeared at the door of his room with a tray, which he lost no time in putting on the table. The tray held an opened bottle of Scotch, a glass, and a large square box covered in Morocco leather.

"First the formalities," said the professional. "Although no, wait a minute, first let's have the second glass." He looked around and grabbed a glass pencil container off a small desk. He peered into it, blew, and put it on the table. "So, the formalities," he said.

He stood at attention, his face assuming a rigid stare. The

young man put aside his paper and also stood up, staring dully at the wall. Victor stood as well.

"Victor Banev," pronounced the professional in an officially elevated voice. "In the name of Mr. President and by his special directive, I hereby grant you the Silver Trefoil of the Second Rank as an award for services rendered by you to the department which I have the honor to represent here!"

He opened the blue box, solemnly removed the medal with its white silk ribbon, and started pinning it on Victor's chest. The young man burst out in polite applause. Then the professional handed Victor the certificate and the box, shook his hand, stepped back, admired him for a minute, and also started clapping. Victor, feeling like an idiot, joined in.

"And now let's drink to it," said the professional.

They sat down. The professional poured the whisky, taking the pencil container for himself.

"To the Knight of the Trefoil!" he pronounced.

They stood up, exchanged smiles, drank, and sat down again. The young man in glasses grabbed his paper and disappeared behind it.

"It seems that you already had the Third Rank," said the professional. "Now all you need is the First, and you'll be a full Knight. Free transportation and all that. How'd you get your Third?"

"I don't remember," said Victor. "Something or other, probably I killed somebody. Oh, yeah. For the Kitchigan bridgehead."

"Oh," said the professional, pouring some more whisky. "I didn't get to fight. It ended too soon."

"You were lucky," said Victor. They drank. "Between you and me, I don't understand what I got this for."

"I told you, for special services."

"You mean for Summan?" said Victor with a bitter laugh.

"Drop it," said the professional. "You are an important person. We know who you associate with." He made a vague gesture somewhere in the vicinity of his ear.

"What do you mean, who I associate with," said Victor.

"We know, we know," said the professional slyly. "We know everything. General Pferd, General Pukki, Colonel Bambrach. Good for you."

"It's news to me," said Victor nervously.

"The colonel started it all. Of course, you yourself understand, no one objected, how could they? Well, then General Pferd was at the president's for a meeting, and he stuck a report about you under the president's nose." The professional chortled. "They say it was really something. The old man blew up. 'Which Banev? The scribbler? I won't have it.' But the general stuck to his guns. 'You have to, your excellency.' Anyway, it all worked out. The old man was touched. 'All right,' he says, 'I forgive him.' What was it he had against you?"

"Nothing much." Victor didn't feel like talking. "We argued about literature."

"So you really write books?" asked the professional.

"I do. Like Colonel Lawrence."

"And you get paid pretty well for it?"

"Pretty well."

"I should really try my hand at it," said the professional. "Only I never have any free time. First it's one thing, then another."

"You're right, there's no time," agreed Victor. Every time he moved the medal swayed and knocked him in the ribs. It felt like a mustard plaster. If he could only take it off, he'd immediately feel better.

"You know, I think I'd better be going," he said, getting to his feet. "Don't have much time."

The professional sprang to his feet.

"Of course," he said.

"Good-bye."

"My pleasure," said the professional. The young man in glasses lowered the paper and bowed.

Victor went out into the corridor and tore off the medal. He had a strong desire to toss it into a spittoon, but he held back and stuck it in his pocket. He went down to the bar and got a bottle of gin. As he was walking back, the desk clerk called over to him.

"Mr. Banev, his honor the burgomaster has been calling you. Twice already. You weren't in your room, and I—"

"What does he want?" muttered Victor.

"He asked you to return his call immediately. Are you going to your room? If he calls again—"

"Kick him in the ass," said Victor. "I'm pulling out my phone, and if he calls you, then tell him, quote, that Mr. Banev, Knight of the Trefoil Second Rank, kicks his honor the burgomaster in the ass."

He locked himself in his room, and disconnected his phone, for some reason covering it with a pillow. Then he sat down at the table, poured himself some gin, and drank down an entire glass, straight. The gin burned his throat and his insides. Then he took a spoon and started wolfing down the strawberries and cream, not noticing the taste, not realizing what he was doing. "I've had it, I've had it," he thought. "I don't need anything, I don't need your medals or your royalties or any crumbs from you. I don't need your attention, or your anger, or your love. Leave me alone, I'm fed up to the teeth with myself, and don't get me involved in your dirty business." He covered his head with his arms to block out Pavor's blue-white face and those colorless, pitiless mugs in their identical raincoats. You've got General Pferd and General Battocks, you've got General Arschmann by your decorated breast and Zurzmansor with his discombobulating face. He kept trying to understand how he felt. He gulped down another half glass and understood that he was crouching at the bottom of a trench, and above him the earth was heaving. Whole geological strata, gigantic masses of granite, basalt, and lava were bending and breaking, groaning from strain, distending, protruding, and, in passing, pressing him up to the surface, pressing higher and higher, squeezing him out of the trench and suspending him over the defenses. And the times were hard, the authorities were having an attack of official zeal, the hint's been given, you aren't doing your work, gentlemen, and there he was, above the defenses, naked, covering his eyes with his fists and utterly exposed.

"To lie on the bottom of the sea," he thought. "To lie on the very bottom so they can't hear me or see me. To lie like a submarine on the sea floor," he thought, and something supplied the rest, "so the enemy can't get my bearing. That's right, to lie on the bottom of the sea like a submarine, so they can't get my bearing. And not to let anyone find out about me. I don't exist. I'm not saying a word. You figure it out. Oh God, why can't I be a cynic? To lie like a submarine on the sea floor, so the enemy can't get my bearing. To lie like a submarine down in the deep and refuse to transmit my location." He could already feel the beat, and the rest came quickly: "I'm fed up to my teeth, down to my core. I don't want to drink or write." He poured himself some gin and drank it. "I don't want to sing or write, I've had it with singing and writing. Where's the banjo? Where'd I put the banjo?" He crawled under the bed and dragged out the banjo. "I don't give a shit about you," he thought. "If only you knew how much I don't give a shit about you! To lie like a submarine down in the deep and refuse to transmit my location."

He started hitting the strings rhythmically, and in this rhythm at first the table, and then the whole room, and then the whole world started stomping its feet and swinging its shoulders. All the generals and colonels, all the slimy people with their disconnected faces, all the government security departments, all the presidents and Pavor Summan, whose arms were being twisted, who was getting beaten in the face.

"I'm fed up to my teeth and down to my core, I've even got tired of singing. I'm more than tired of it, I'm sick of it, but tired of it, that's good, so that's how it'll be. To lie like a submarine on the sea floor so the enemy can't get my bearing. Submarine, can't be seen, booze, a broad, the camp's no fraud. That's it, that's it."

The knocking at his door had been going on for a long time,

getting louder and louder. Victor finally heard it but didn't panic. It wasn't that sort of knock, only the ordinary, comforting knock of a peaceful man, furious because he wasn't being let in. Victor opened the door. It was Golem.

"Having fun, eh?" he said. "Pavor's been arrested."

"I know, I know," said Victor cheerfully. "Sit down, listen."

Golem didn't sit down, but Victor, unperturbed, banged on the strings and started singing.

> I'm fed up to my teeth and down to my core,
> I've even got tired of singing.
> Oh, to lie like a submarine on the sea floor
> So the enemy can't get my bearing.

"I haven't written any more yet," he shouted. "Later there'll be booze, a broad, the camp's no fraud. And then—listen:

> Vodka's no help now and girls you can keep,
> For women I've no admiration.
> Oh, to lie like a submarine down in the deep
> And refuse to transmit my location.
> I'm fed up to my teeth and down to my core,
> I've had it with playing and drinking.
> Oh, to lie like a submarine on the sea floor
> So the enemy can't get my bearing.

"That's it!" he shouted and threw the banjo on the bed. He felt tremendously relieved. As if something had changed, as if he had suddenly become very necessary out there, beyond the trenches, exposed to everyone. He tore his hand away from his scrunched-up eyes and looked over the dirty gray field, the rusty barbed wire, the gray sacks that had once been people, the boring, dishonest game that had once been life. From all sides people were emerging from the trenches and looking around . . . somebody's finger dropped off the trigger. . . .

"I'm envious," said Golem. "But isn't it time to sit down with that article?"

"I wouldn't think of it," said Victor. "You don't know me,

Golem. I don't give a shit about anyone. Sit down, will you, goddamnit. I'm drunk, and you've got to drink too! Take off your raincoat. Take it off, I tell you," he shouted. "And sit down. Here's a glass, drink! You don't understand a thing, Golem, for all you're a prophet. And I won't let you. Not to understand is my prerogative. In this world everyone is much too clear on the way things ought to be, the way they are and how they'll turn out. There's a great shortage of people who don't understand. You know why I'm valuable? Only because I don't understand. They unfold new vistas before me and I say, 'No, I don't get it.' They try to dupe me with their theories, incredibly simplistic ones, and I say, 'No, I don't understand anything.' That's why I'm necessary. Want some strawberries? Except I ate them all. Then let's have a smoke."

He got up and paced around the room. Golem, holding a glass, watched him without turning his head.

"It's an astonishing paradox, Golem. There was a time when I understood everything. I was sixteen, I was a senior knight in the Legion. I understood absolutely everything, and nobody needed me. Then my head got cracked up in a fight, I spent a month in the hospital, and things went on in their own way. The Legion moved victoriously forward, without me; Mr. President continued his inexorable transformation into Mr. President, again without me. The same thing happened during the war. I was an officer, I snapped up medals, and naturally I understood everything. Then I got shot in the chest and spent a year in the hospital, and do you think anybody got worried, do you think anybody wondered where Banev was, what had happened to their brave, omniscient Banev? Nothing of the sort! And then when I stopped understanding whatever it was—oh, then everything changed. All the newspapers noticed me. A whole bunch of government departments noticed me. Mr. President himself was so kind as to take a personal . . . You see? Do you realize what a rarity it is—a person who doesn't understand. People know him, corpse . . . uh, corporals and generals fuss over him, he's terribly necessary to the slimies, he's considered a personality. Awful. And what's the reason? The reason is, gentlemen, that he doesn't understand anything." Victor sat down. "I'm really plowed, huh?" he asked.

"Can't deny it," said Golem. "But never mind, go on."

Victor threw up his hands.

"That's all," he said guiltily. "I've played myself out. Maybe I should sing something for you?"

"Go ahead," said Golem.

Victor took the banjo and started to sing. He sang "We Are Brave Guys," then "Uranium Men," then "About a Shepherd, Who Had One Eye Butted Out by a Bull and Because of That Violated the International Border," then "I'm Fed Up to My Teeth," then "Indifferent City," then something about truth and falsehood, then another round of "I'm Fed Up to My Teeth." After that he led into the national anthem to the tune of "Oh, What Little Tootsies She Has," but he forgot the words, mixed up the verses, and put the banjo aside.

"I'm played out again," he said despondently. "So, you say Pavor's been arrested? I know it. He was sitting here, right where you are. And you know what he wanted to say but didn't get a chance to? That in ten years the slimies will be in control of the whole globe and they'll crush all of us. What do you think?"

"Unlikely," said Golem. "Why should they crush us? We'll do it by ourselves."

"What about the slimies?"

"Maybe they won't let us crush one another. It's hard to say."

"And maybe they'll help?" said Victor with a drunken laugh. "Because we don't even know how to do it properly. We've been trying for ten thousand years and can't finish each other off. Listen, Golem, why did you lie to me? You're not curing them there. What kind of patients are they anyway? They're all healthy, just like us, only a little yellow for some reason."

"Hm," said Golem. "Where did you get your information? I wasn't aware of it."

"Oh, come on, you're not going to take me in any more. I had a talk with Zurz . . . with Zu . . . with Zurzmansor. He told me everything: a high-security think tank . . . they wear the bandages for the purpose of maintaining . . . You know, Golem, your friends over there imagine that they can manipulate General Pferd forever. And in fact it's a case of king for a day. He'll devour them together with their bandages and their gloves as soon as he gets hungry. Oh, damn, how drunk I am, everything's swimming."

But he was cheating a little. Before him, he could clearly see the heavy, gray face with its beady, unusually attentive eyes.

"And Zurzmansor told you he was well?"

"Yes," said Victor. "Although I don't remember. Most likely he didn't. But you could see."

Golem scratched his chin with the tip of his glass.

"A pity you're drunk," he said. "Although maybe that's good. Today I'm in the mood. Do you want me to tell you everything I know and can guess about the slimies?"

"Shoot," said Victor. "Only don't lie anymore."

"This four-eye disease," said Golem, "is a very curious thing. You know who comes down with it?" He stopped. "No, I'm not going to tell you anything."

"Drop it," said Victor. "You already started."

"My fault for starting," said Golem. He looked at Victor and smirked. "Ask me questions," he said. "If the questions are stupid, I'll answer them with pleasure. Go on, go on, or I'll change my mind again."

There was a knock at the door.

"Go to hell," barked Victor. "I'm busy."

"Excuse me, Mr. Banev," came the timid voice of the desk clerk. "Your spouse is calling."

"Lies! I don't have any spouse. Wait a minute, I forgot. All right, I'll call her back, thank you." He grabbed a glass, filled it to the brim, and pushed it toward Golem. "Drink and don't think about anything. I'll be right back."

He connected the phone and dialed Lola. Lola spoke very drily.

"Excuse me for bothering you, but I'm getting ready to visit Irma and I was wondering if you would deign to join me."

"No," said Victor. "I won't deign. I'm busy."

"She's still your daughter! Have you really let yourself go to such an extent—"

"I'm busy!" barked Victor.

"You don't care about what happens to your daughter?"

"Stop being a fool," said Victor. "You wanted Irma off your hands. You've got it. What else do you want?"

Lola started crying.

"Cut it out," said Victor, frowning. "Irma's fine there. Better than in the best boarding school. Go and see for yourself."

"Dirty, selfish, egotistical pig," declared Lola and hung up.

Victor cursed under his breath, disconnected the telephone, and went back to the table.

"Listen, Golem," he said. "What are you doing there with my children? If you're preparing replacements for yourselves, then I don't agree."

"What kind of replacements?"

"What kind. That's what I'm asking you, what kind?"

"To the best of my knowledge," said Golem, "the children are very satisfied."

"That's not the point. I know that without you. What do they do there?"

"Didn't they tell you?"

"Who?"

"The children."

"How could they tell me if I'm here and they're there?"

"They're building a new world," said Golem.

"Oh, yes. That they told me. But that's just talk, philosophy. Why are you lying to me again, Golem? What kind of new world can there be behind barbed wire? A new world under the command of General Pferd? And what if they come down with it?"

"With what?"

"With ocularis ringus, naturally!"

"For the sixth time I repeat that genetic illnesses are not infectious."

"The sixth, the sixth," muttered Victor, losing the thread. "And what is it, anyway, this ocularis ringus? What does it affect? Or maybe that's classified information?"

"No, it's available everywhere."

"Well, tell me," said Victor. "Only no jargon."

"First there are changes in the skin. Blisters and eruptions, particularly on the hands and feet. Sometimes, festering ulcers."

"Listen, Golem, is this what's important?"

"For what?"

"For the essence."

"For the essence—no. I thought you were interested."

"I want to understand the essence," declared Victor.

"The essence is just what you won't understand," said Golem, slightly raising his voice.

"Why not?"

"First of all, because you're drunk."

"That's not a reason," said Victor.

"And secondly, because it's impossible to explain."

"That can't be," announced Victor. "You simply don't want to talk. But I'm not offended. An oath of secrecy, unauthorized disclosure, a military tribunal, Pavor's just been arrested. So do what you want. But I still can't understand why a child has to build a new world in a leprosarium. Wasn't there anyplace else?"

"No," said Golem. "There are architects living in the leprosarium. And builders."

"With automatics," said Victor. "I saw. I don't understand anything. One of you is lying. Either you or Zurzmansor."

"Zurzmansor, of course," said Golem coolly.

"And maybe both of you are lying. And I believe both of you, because there's something to you. Just tell me one thing, Golem, what is it they want? Only tell me honestly."

"Happiness," said Golem.

"For whom? For themselves?"

"Not only."

"And at whose expense?"

"For them that question has no meaning. At the expense of the grass, at the expense of the clouds, at the expense of the flowing water. At the expense of the stars."

"Just like us," said Victor.

"No," objected Golem. "Not that way at all."

"Why not? We also—"

"No, because we trample the grass, disperse the clouds, dam the water. You took me too literally, I meant it as an analogy."

"I don't understand," said Victor.

"I warned you. I don't understand a lot myself, but I can make conjectures."

"And is there anyone who does understand?"

"I don't know. I doubt it. Maybe the children. But even if they understand it, it's in their own way. Very much in their own way."

Victor took the banjo and touched the strings. His fingers refused to obey him. He put it back on the table.

"Golem," he said. "You're a Communist. What the hell are you doing in the leprosarium? Why aren't you at the barricades? Why weren't you at a meeting? Moscow won't thank you for it."

"I am an architect," said Golem quietly.

"What kind of architect can you be if you don't understand anything? And anyway why are you leading me around by the nose? We've been at this for an hour, and what have you told me? You've been swilling gin and pulling the wool over my eyes. It's shameful, Golem. And you're lying nonstop."

"Nonstop is on the strong side," said Golem. "Although there's been some. They don't have festering ulcers."

"Give me your glass," said Victor. "Oh, are you drunk." He splashed some gin out of the bottle and drank. "God knows what you're up to, Golem. What do you need all this for? What kind of game is it? If you can tell me, then tell me; if it's a secret, then you shouldn't have started."

"That's very easy to explain," said Golem good-humoredly, stretching out his legs. "I'm a prophet, you called me that yourself. And prophets are all caught in the same trap: they know a lot, and they want to talk about it, share it with a good listener, praise themselves to give some weight to their position. And when they start to talk, they feel incredibly uncomfortable and awkward. Then they get evasive, like the Lord God when he was asked about the stone."

"However you like," said Victor. "I'll go to the leprosarium and find it all out without you. Well, go ahead, prophesy something."

He followed with interest the growing paralysis in his arms and legs, and thought it would be good to drink one more glass to round it off and then fall into bed, and then wake up and go to Diana. It wasn't working out that badly. And anyway nothing was that bad. He imagined singing to Diana about the submarine, and it made him feel just fine. He took the wet oar which was lying in the stern and pushed away from the shore, and the boat responded at once, rocking. There wasn't any rain, there weren't even any clouds, only a blazing sunset. And he sailed right into the sunset and the oar splashed out of the waves. To lie in the deep. . . . And he would have done it, but it was awkward for him because Golem's voice was buzzing lazily in his ear.

". . . They're very young, they have everything before them, and we have only them. Of course, man will possess the universe, but there won't be a red-cheeked hero with big muscles, and, of course, man will cope with himself, but first he'll have to transform himself. Nature doesn't deceive, it fulfills its promises, only not the way we thought and often not the way we would have liked."

Zurzmansor, sitting in the bow of the boat, turned his head, and it became clear that he didn't have a face, that he was holding his face in his hands and the face was looking at Victor—a good face, an honest one, but it made him sick, and Golem didn't lay off, he kept buzzing. . . .

"Go to sleep," muttered Victor, stretching out on the bottom of the boat. The ribs of the boat dug into his sides and it was very uncomfortable, but he felt so sleepy. "Go to sleep, Golem."

Chapter XI

When he woke up, he found himself lying in bed. It was dark; rain drummed and lashed at the window. He raised his arm with difficulty and stretched it toward the night table, but his fingers banged into a cold, smooth wall. "Funny," he thought. "Where's Diana? Or maybe this isn't the resort?"

He tried licking his lips, but his thick, rough tongue refused to obey him. And he really wanted a smoke, but he knew he shouldn't, not for anything.

"What I really want is some water." "Diana!" he called. "No, this isn't the sanatorium. In the sanatorium the night table is on the right, and here there's a wall. . . . So it's my room in the hotel!" he thought, triumphant. "How'd I get here?" He was covered with a blanket, with nothing on but underwear. "I can't remember getting undressed," he thought. "Somebody undressed me. Although maybe I got undressed myself. If I have my shoes on, then I did it myself." He rubbed one bare foot against the other. "So, no shoes. Goddamnit, my arms are itching, some sort of blisters, they must have bedbugs here. I'll move out. Where was it I was going in the boat? Oh, it was Pavor who put the bedbugs here." He suddenly remembered about Pavor and sat up, but he felt nauseous and he once again stretched out. "I haven't gotten stewed like this in a while. Pavor . . . the Silver Trefoil . . . when was that? Yesterday?" He made a face and started dragging his fingernails along his left arm. "What time is it now—morning or night?

Probably morning. But maybe it's night. Golem!" he remembered. "Golem and I did in a whole bottle. And we didn't mix it. And before that I had half a bottle with the professional. And before that I had something else, somewhere or other. Or maybe that was yesterday. Wait a minute, what is it now—today or yesterday? Gotta get up, get a drink, this, that. No," he thought, obstinate. "First I'll figure things out.

"Golem was saying something interesting, he thought I was drunk and couldn't understand anything, and maybe that's why he was speaking frankly with me. Of course I really was drunk, but I remember understanding it. What did I understand?" He furiously rubbed the back of his left hand against the wool blanket. "Hard times are coming. No, that's Pavor. What was Golem saying? They have everything in front of them, and we have only them. And genetic illness. Well, why not, completely possible. It's got to happen some time. Maybe it's been going on for a long time now. A new species arising out of an old one, and we call it a genetic illness. The old species is adapted to one set of conditions, and the new one is adapted to another. Before we needed strong muscles, fertility, resistance to cold, aggressiveness, and, so to speak, managerial talents. Maybe we still need all that, but it's probably just inertia. You can use your managerial talents to knock off a whole population, and nothing really changes. That's for sure—it's been tried many times. Who was it said that if we removed a few dozen people from the history of the human race—well, maybe a few hundred—we'd be right back in the stone age. Well, maybe a few thousand. What kind of people? A completely different kind, old pal.

"And it's not impossible. Maybe Newton, Einstein, and Aristotle were all mutants. The environment was not too favorable, of course, and it's not impossible that whole bunches of them died without revealing themselves, like the boy in Capek's story. Of course they were all special: they didn't have any managerial talents and they didn't have normal human needs. Or maybe that's just the way it seems. Maybe their spiritual side is so hypertrophic that you can't see anything else." "Here you're wrong," he said aloud. "Einstein used to say that the best possible job was a lighthouse keeper's, which sounds human enough to me. But it would be interesting to imagine *homo super* in our times. A good theme. Damn it, this itch is unbearable. I should really make it into a utopia, in the spirit of Orwell or Bernard Wolfe. Although it would be hard to picture a superman like that: a huge, bald skull, emaciated arms and legs, impotent. Banalities. But anyway it's got to be something on that order. In any event, a displacement of human needs. No need for vodka, no need for fancy food, no luxury, not even women—or just occasionally, to insure tranquility and concentration. A perfect object for exploitation: give him an office, a desk, paper, and a pile of books, a shaded path for peripatetic musing, and in return he'll give you ideas. No utopia will come of it; the military will grab him, and that's your utopia. They'll set up a think tank, bring all the supermen there, put up a guard, and that's the end of it."

Victor, grunting, picked himself up and, slapping his bare feet against the cold floor, made his way to the bathroom. He turned on the faucet and took a long, satisfied drink. He didn't even bother to turn on the light. The very thought horrified him —turn on the light. Then he got back into bed and spent some time scratching and cursing the bedbugs. "In fact, for a plot it's even better that way: a think tank, guards, spies . . . the patriotism of the patriotic cleaning woman Clara . . . all sorts of cheap tricks. The difficulty is that it's hard to imagine their work, their ideas, their potential. And how could I? It's impossible. A chimpanzee can't write a book about humans. How could I write a book about someone who doesn't have any needs except for spiritual ones? Of course you can picture some of it. The atmosphere. A state of continuous creative ecstasy. A sense of one's own omnipotence and independence, the absence of complexes, complete fearlessness. To write something like that you'd have to stuff yourself with LSD. In general, from the point of view of a normal person, the emotional makeup of a superman has to seem pathological. A disease. Life is a disease of matter, thought is a disease of life. Ocularis ringus," he thought.

And suddenly everything fell into place. "So that's what he had in mind!" Victor thought, remembering Golem. "Intelligent and talented, every single one of them. And what does it lead to? That they're not human anymore. Zurzmansor was just pulling the wool over my eyes. So it's begun. It's impossible to hide anything," he thought with satisfaction. "Especially something like this. I'll go see Golem, no use in him playing the prophet any more. No doubt they've told him a lot. Hell, this is it, the future, that very future that was extending its feelers into the heart of the present. We have only them before us!"

A feverish excitement seized him. Every second was historic. What a pity he didn't know that yesterday, because yesterday and the day before yesterday and a week ago every second was also historic.

He jumped up, turned on the light, and, squinting from the sharp pain in his eyes, started groping for his clothes. They weren't there. Then his eyes got accustomed to the light, he grabbed the pants that were hanging over the footboard of the bed, and suddenly he saw his arm. His arm was covered up to the elbow with a red rash and deathly white goose bumps. Some of them were bleeding from the scratching. His other hand was the same. "What the hell is this," he thought, growing cold, because in fact he already knew. He remembered it all: changes in the skin, a rash, blisters, sometimes festering ulcers. So far there weren't any of those, but all the same he broke out in a cold sweat, and, letting his pants drop, sat down on the bed. "It can't be," he thought. "So it's got me, too. Could it really have gotten me too?"

He carefully stroked the gooseflesh on one arm, then closed

his eyes, and, holding his breath, focused his attention inward. His heart was beating slowly, resonantly, blood whined faintly in his ears. His head seemed huge and empty but nothing hurt, and the cottony thickness in his brain was gone. "Idiot," he thought grinning. "What did you expect? It has to be like death: a second before you were a man, then a quantum of time flashes past and you're already a god, only you don't know it. And you'll never know it, either, like a fool doesn't know that he's a fool, like someone who's intelligent—providing he really is—doesn't know that he's intelligent. It must have happened while I was sleeping. In any event, before I fell alseep, I had only the foggiest understanding of the slimies, and now I see everything with absolute clarity, and I got there through naked logic, I didn't even notice it."

He laughed happily, stepped onto the floor, and, flexing his muscles, walked over to the window.

"My world," he thought, looking through the water-splattered glass, and the glass disappeared. Way below, the city, paralyzed in horror, drowned in the rain, and the huge, wet country drowned with it. Then everything shifted, floated away, and there remained only the small blue sphere with its long blue tail, and he saw the giant lens of the galaxy, hanging sideways and deathlike in the glimmering abyss. A tuft of shining matter, twisted by fields of force, and bottomless funnels where there wasn't any light. He stretched out his hand and dipped it into the puffy white nucleus. He felt a light warmth, and when he made a fist, matter slipped between his fingers like soapsuds. He laughed again, giving his reflection in the glass a tap on the nose, and tenderly stroked the bumps on his swollen skin.

"This is something to drink to!" he said out loud.

There was still a little gin in the bottle, poor old Golem couldn't finish it, the poor old false prophet. Not false because his prophecies were untrue, but because he was no more than a talking puppet. "I will always love you, Golem," thought

Victor, "you're a good man, you're a wise man, but that's all you are—a man."

He poured what was left of the gin into a glass, and with a swift, practiced movement tipped the glass and took a mouthful. Then, not even managing to swallow, he made for the bathroom. He threw up.

"Christ," he thought. "Disgusting." He saw his face in the mirror: worn and slightly flaccid, with unnaturally big and unnaturally black eyes. "Well, that's it," he thought. "That's it, Victor Banev, drunkard and loudmouth. No more drinking and no more raucous singing, and no more laughing at stupid jokes and no more lighthearted bullshitting. No fights, no brawls, and no disorderly conduct. No more terrorizing pedestrians, no more trading insults with policemen, no more falling out with Mr. President, and no more nighttime pub crawls with a noisy company of young admirers."

He got back into bed. He didn't feel like smoking. He didn't feel like doing anything, everything was making him nauseous and he felt sad. The sense of loss, at first barely noticeable, light as the touch of a spider's web, began to grow. Gloomy rows of barbed wire cut him off from the world he loved so much. "Everything has its price," he thought, "you don't get anything for free, and the more you get, the more you have to pay for it. If you get a new life, you have to pay for it with your old one." He scratched furiously, breaking the skin, but he didn't notice it.

Diana came in without knocking. She threw off her raincoat and stood in front of him, smiling and seductive. She raised her arms, fixing her hair.

"I'm frozen," she said. "Will the gentleman allow me to warm up?"

"Yes," he said, only dimly understanding what she was saying.

She turned off the light. Now he could no longer see her, he only heard the key turning in the lock, the snap of clothing unfastened, and the rustle of its fall. Then he heard her shoes hitting the floor, and she was next to him, warm, smooth, fragrant. And he kept thinking that the end was at hand. The end of everything: the eternal rain, the gloomy houses with their roofs like sieves, the impassive strangers with their wet, black clothing, with the black bandages on their faces. Now they would take off their bandages, take off their gloves, take off their faces and put them into special little cubbyholes, and their hands would be covered with festering ulcers. Anguish, terror, loneliness. Diana pressed against him, and he embraced her with his habitual motion. She was the same as ever, but he was not, and he couldn't do anything anymore, because he didn't need any of it.

"What's the matter, sweetheart?" she asked gently. "Drink too much?"

He carefully removed her arms from around his neck. Now he was really scared.

"Wait a minute," he said. "Just wait."

He got up, felt for the switch, turned on the light, and stood for a few seconds with his back to her. He couldn't bring himself to turn around. Finally he did. No, she was still beautiful. She was probably even more beautiful than usual, she was always more beautiful than usual, but this time she was like a picture. It stirred his pride in humankind, it stirred his delight in human perfection, but that was all it stirred. She looked at him, raising her brows in surprise. Then she must have gotten scared, because she suddenly sat down, and he saw her lips moving. She said something, but he didn't hear.

"Wait," he repeated. "It can't be. Wait."

He dressed himself with feverish haste, continually repeating, "Wait, wait," but he was no longer thinking about her, she was only a small part of it. He dashed out into the corridor and tried Golem's door. The door was locked. He didn't immediately understand where he should go next, but then he tore off and ran downstairs, to the restaurant. "I don't need it," he insisted, "I don't need it, I didn't ask for it."

Thank God, Golem was in his usual place. He was sitting with his arm stretched over the back of his chair, looking at the light reflected through his glass of cognac. Dr. R. Quadriga was red-faced and aggressive. Seeing Victor, he shouted at the top of his voice:

"Those slimies. Carrion. Away."

Victor fell into his chair. Golem, without saying a word, poured him some cognac.

"Golem," said Victor. "Golem, I came down with it."

"Next time be more careful," pronounced R. Quadriga. "Me too."

"Have some cognac, Victor," said Golem. "Don't get so upset."

"Go to hell," said Victor, looking at him in horror. "I've got ocularis ringus. What can I do?"

"All right, all right," said Golem. "But have a drink anyway." He raised a finger and shouted to the waiter. "Club soda! And some more cognac."

"Golem," said Victor, desperate. "You don't understand. I can't. I've come down with it, I'm telling you. I caught it! It's not fair. I didn't want. You told me it wasn't infectious."

He was terrified at the thought that he was speaking too disconnectedly, that Golem didn't understand him and thought that he was simply drunk. He thrust his hands in front of Golem's nose. The glass tipped over, rolled along the table, and fell off.

At first Golem recoiled. Then he looked more closely. He leaned forward, taking Victor's hand by the tips of his fingers, and started examining the scratched-up bumps on his skin. Golem's fingers were cold and hard. "Well, that's it," thought Victor, "the first medical examination. Then there will be more examinations, and more false promises that there's still hope, and tranquilizers. And then he'd get used to it, and there wouldn't be any more examinations. They'd take him off to the leprosarium, cover his mouth with a black bandage, and it would all be over."

"Did you have any strawberries?" asked Golem.

"Yes," said Victor submissively. "Hothouse ones."

"I suppose you put away five pounds or so," said Golem.

"What do strawberries have to do with it?" shouted Victor, freeing his hand. "Do something! It can't be too late! It only just started. . . ."

"Stop yelling. You have a rash. An allergy. It is contraindicated for you to wolf down strawberries in such quantity."

Victor still didn't understand. Staring at his hands, he muttered, "You were the one who told me . . . blisters . . . a rash."

"You can get blisters from bedbugs," said Golem in a didactic tone. "It so happens that you have an allergy to certain compounds. And more imagination than intelligence. Like most writers. Some slimy!"

Victor felt himself coming back to life. "I made it!" sounded in his head. "It looks like I made it. If I really did make it, I don't know what I'll do. I'll stop smoking."

"You're not lying?" he said in a pitiful voice.

Golem snorted.

"Have some cognac," he proposed. "You shouldn't drink cognac during an allergic reaction, but you go ahead and drink. You look pitiful."

Victor took his glass, made a face, and drank. "It's all right! A little nausea, but that's probably from the hangover. It'll go away." And it did.

"My dear writer," said Golem. "To become an architect, you have to have more than blisters."

The waiter came and put some cognac and club soda on the table. Victor sighed deeply and freely. He drank in the familiar restaurant air and smelled the beautiful odor of tobacco smoke, marinated onions, burnt oil, and fried meat. Life returned.

"Friend," he said to the waiter. "A bottle of gin, lemon juice, ice, and four portions of eel to two sixteen. And make it snappy! Alcoholics," he said to Golem and R. Quadriga. "Lousy restaurant rats. You can rot here by yourselves, I'm going to Diana!" He was ready to kiss them.

"Poor lovely duckling," said Golem, not addressing anyone.

For a second Victor felt a twinge of regret. The remembrance of lost possibilities floated off and disappeared. But he only laughed, kicked the chair out of his way, and strode toward the exit.

Chapter XII

A YEAR AFTER THE WAR Lieutenant B. is discharged because of wounds. They give him a Victoria medal and fork over a month's severance pay and a cardboard box full of presents from Mr. President: a bottle of liberated schnapps, two tins of Strasbourg pâté, two loops of horse sausage, and a pair of liberated silk shorts to facilitate his transition to family life. Back in the capital, the lieutenant doesn't mope around. He's a good mechanic, and he knows that the university garage where he worked before he enlisted will take him back at a moment's notice. But he isn't in any hurry. He renews old friendships, makes new ones, and spends the remainder of his time getting drunk on the proceeds of the junk seized from the enemy as war reparations. At a party he meets a woman named Nora, a lot like Diana. A description of the party: scratched-up records from before the war, kitchen-distilled wood alcohol, American Spam, silk blouses on naked bodies, and carrots in every possible guise. The lieutenant, medals jingling, disperses with ease the small crowd of civilians busily engaged in filling Nora's plate with boiled carrots, and begins his siege. Nora acts strangely. On the one hand, she's clearly willing, but on the other, she lets him understand that associating with her is dangerous. But the ex-lieutenant, fired up with kitchen-distilled alcohol, doesn't want to hear. They leave the party and go to Nora's. The postwar capital at night: occasional street lamps, the road pitted with holes, ruins everywhere. The new circus, not even finished, where six thousand prisoners of war are rotting under the guard of two invalids. In the narrow street, by now completely dark, someone's getting mugged. Nora lives in an old-style three-story house. The staircase is covered with filth, one of the doors boasts a chalk inscription: "The German shepherd lives here." In the long corridor, filled with all sorts of trash, moldy figures recoil into the shadows. Nora, jangling innumerable keys, unlocks her door, a door covered with shining leather, preserved there by some miracle. In the foyer she gives him another warning, but B., figuring that it's nothing more than some criminal affair, answers only that he used to attack tanks on horseback. The apartment is spotless and comfortable, a relic from another era. There's a huge sofa. Nora looks at the lieutenant with something like pity. She leaves for a short time and returns, dressed to kill, with an opened bottle of cognac. It turns out that they have only a half hour at their disposal. In a half hour's time, the satisfied lieutenant leaves with the hope of a second meeting. At the end of the corridor, the two moldy figures from the shadows are lying in wait for him. Snickering unpleasantly, they bar his path and propose a little chat. Without wasting his breath, the lieutenant starts beating them up. His victory is unexpectedly easy. Knocked off their feet, weeping and giggling, the moldy figures explain B.'s position to him. The ex-lieutenant had beaten up his own brothers. Now they are all brothers. Nora is more than a seductive woman, Nora is the queen of the capital bedbugs. "You're finished now, officer. We'll be meeting you in the 'Atakerama,' that's where we all meet, every night. Go home, and when you can't stand it any more, come to see us, we stay open till morning."

On the western outskirts of the city, in a rented house next to a chemical plant, lives the titular councillor B. with his large family. An intentionally detailed, intentionally dull description of the hero's surroundings: three rooms, a kitchen, a foyer, a worn-out wife, five greenish kids, and a hardy old mother-in-law, brought in from the country. The chemical plant stinks; day and night columns of colored smoke hang over it. The trees are dying from the poisonous fog, the grass is turning yellow, and the flies are mutating wildly. For the past few years, the titular councillor has waged a campaign to tame the plant: angry demands addressed to the administration, tearful petitions up the ranks, thunderous editorials in all the papers, fruitless attempts to organize a picket at the gates. But the plant still stands like a bastion. Poisoned sentries keel over on the opposite embankment; pets die; whole families leave their apartments and become vagrants; the newspapers print an obituary mourning the premature death of the plant director. The titular councillor's wife is dying; one by one his children fall victim to bronchial asthma. Then one evening, searching for firewood in the cellar, he comes across a mortar and a huge quantity of shells left over from the time of the Resistance. That very night, he drags it all up to the attic and opens a dormer window. The plant is stretched out before him, as in the palm of his hand. In the glare of searchlights, workers are scurrying, trolleys are moving, yellow and green clouds of poisonous vapors float in the air. "I'll kill you," whispers the titular councillor and opens fire. That day he stays home from work; the next day as well. He doesn't sleep and he doesn't eat, he squats under the dormer window and shoots. From time to time he takes breaks, to let the mortar cool down. He goes deaf from the firing and blind from the smoke. Sometimes he thinks that the chemical haze is breaking, and then he smiles, licks his lips, and whispers, "I'll kill you." Then, his strength gone, he falls asleep. When he wakes up, he sees that he's running out of shells; there are only three left. He fires the last round and leans out the window. The wide yard of the plant is riddled with craters. There are gaping holes in place of windows, and the sides of the huge gas tanks are covered with dents. The yard is crisscrossed by a complicated network of trenches, and workers are running along them in short bursts. Trolleys are moving faster than before, the drivers of autocars are protected by metal plates, and when the wind blows the poisonous vapor off to the side, a new white sign appears on the brick wall of the administration building: "Attention! During Shooting This Side Is Particularly Dangerous!"

Victor reread the last page, lit a cigarette, and looked at the sheet of paper in the typewriter. It contained all of a line and a half: "Leaving the editorial board, journalist B. wanted to take a taxi, but he thought the better of it and headed for the subway." Victor knew precisely what was going to happen to journalist B. But he couldn't write any more. His watch showed a quarter to three. He got up and threw open the window. It was pitch black outside, and the rain glistened darkly. Standing at the window, he finished his cigarette, cast the butt into the wet night, and called the desk clerk. An unfamiliar voice answered. Victor asked what day of the week it was. After a pause, the unfamiliar voice informed him that it was the early hours of Saturday. Victor blinked, put down the receiver, and with a decisive gesture removed the paper from his typewriter. Enough is enough. Two days and two nights without stretching, without talking to anyone, without plugging in the phone or responding to knocks at the door. Without Diana, without booze, and, it seemed, without food either, only tumbling into bed from time to time to see the Queen of the Bedbugs in his dreams, to watch her sitting on the door frame and twitching her black mustache. Enough. Journalist B. will remain on the platform until the train comes with the sign "No Passengers." Nothing's going to happen to him. "And in the meantime we'll have a bite to eat, we certainly earned it."

Victor put the typewriter away. He hid the manuscript in his desk and rummaged in the empty bar. Then he chewed a stale roll with jam, bitterly mourning the fact that yesterday he'd poured a half bottle of brandy down the sink to avoid temptation. But he was glad that the series "Backstage in the Big City" was at least started, and not badly, either. In fact, it was a fine start, satisfactory in all respects. Although he would probably have to rewrite the whole thing.

"Still," he thought, "it's odd that I got going with these stories now. Why not a year ago, why not two years ago, when they first came to me. Now I should be writing about some schlepp who thinks he's a superman, that's what. That's what I started with. But it isn't the first time this has happened to me. And if I think hard and really press my memory, it turns out that it always works that way. And that's just the reason it's impossible to write on demand. You set out to write a novel about the early years of Mr. President, and you end up with an island inhabited by a strange race of monkeys who feed on thoughts of shipwrecks instead of bananas. Well, in this case, at least, there's an obvious link. Although, what the hell, there always is. All you have to do is dig for it, only who feels like it, after two days of abstinence I feel like a drink. How about a trip downstairs, the desk clerk always has something on him. Let me finish this roll and I'll go down."

Victor shuddered and stopped chewing. From the black abyss beyond the window, through the splash of the rain there came a loud sound, as if a hammer were pounding a board. "They're shooting," thought Victor with astonishment. For some time he listened intently.

Well, all right. But what did the author mean to say in these works? Why did he have to resurrect the difficult postwar period, when here and there you could still come across a bed-bug or a frivolous woman? Perhaps the author wished to show the heroism and steadfastness of the capital, which under the leadership of His High Excellency. . . . It won't do, Mr. Banev! We won't allow it! The whole world knows that by the specific directive of Mr. President, chemical industries responsible for air pollution in the capital alone have been fined to the tune of . . . that thanks to the indefatigable personal attention of Mr. President, each year more than 100,000 children living in the capital are sent to suburban camps . . . that according to the Table of Ranks, persons in positions below that of Court Counselor do not have the right to collect signatures for a petition.

The lights went out.

"Hey," said Victor out loud, and the lamp went on again, but at half power. "What's this—what the hell," he muttered, but it didn't get any lighter. Victor waited a while, then called the desk clerk. Nobody answered. He could always call the power plant, but for that he needed a phone book, and where was he to look for one, and anyway it was time to go to bed. Only first he had to have a drink. Victor got up and suddenly heard some sort of rustling. Someone was groping along the door. Then whoever it was began to knock.

"Who's there?" asked Victor. Nobody answered; all he could hear was somebody knocking and sniffling.

Victor got the creeps. The walls, cast in a reddish half-light, seemed alien and strange. There were too many shadows in the corners, and whatever was beyond the door was big, dumb, and irrational. "What'll I stop him with," thought Victor, looking around, but at that moment a hoarse whisper came from behind the door. "Banev, hey, Banev, are you there?"

Muttering "Idiot," Victor went to the door and turned the key. In staggered R. Quadriga. He was wearing a robe, his hair was rumpled, his eyes were rolling wildly.

"Thank God, at least you're here," he began immediately. "Or I'd go completely crazy from fright. Listen, Banev, we've got to get out of here. Let's go, huh? Let's get out of here, Banev." He grabbed Victor by the shirt and dragged him into the corridor. "Let's go, I can't take it anymore."

"You've gone off the deep end," said Victor, tearing himself free. "Go to bed, you rum addict. It's three o'clock in the morning."

But Quadriga once again deftly seized him by the shirt and Victor discovered to his astonishment that the doctor *honoris causae* was completely sober. There wasn't even the smell of liquor.

"This is no time for sleep," said Quadriga. "We've got to get out of this damned building. You see what's going on with the light? We'll die here. And anyway we've got to get out of this town. I have a car at the villa. Let's go. I'd go by myself, but I'm afraid to walk out—"

"Wait, don't grab at me," said Victor. "Calm down first."

He pulled Quadriga into the room, sat him down in the armchair, and himself went into the bathroom for a glass of water. Quadriga jumped up and ran after him.

"You and I are alone here, nobody else is left," he said. "Golem's gone, the doorman's gone, the director's gone."

Victor turned on the faucet. There was a gurgling in the pipes, and a few drops dribbled out.

"You want water?" said Quadriga. "Let's go, I've got a whole bottle. Only fast. And together."

"What's going on?" asked Victor, turning cold. "War?"

Quadriga waved his hand.

"What do you mean, war? We've got to get out of here before it's too late, and he's talking about war."

"In what way, get out?"

"The roadway," said Quadriga, giggling stupidly.

Victor shoved him away, left the room, and went downstairs. Quadriga scurried after him.

"Listen," he muttered. "Let's go out the back stairway. Let's just get out of here and then we'll have my car. I already put gas in it, it's packed up. I had a feeling, God knows. We'll have a drop of vodka and take off, because there isn't any vodka left here."

In the corridor, the overhead lamps shone dimly, like red dwarf stars. There was no light at all in the stairwell and none in the vestibule either. The only weak light came from a bulb above the main desk. Someone was sitting there, but it wasn't the desk clerk.

"Let's go, let's go," said Quadriga and pulled Victor toward the exit. "You don't have to go there, it's no good over there."

Victor freed himself and walked over to the desk.

"Just what kind of nonsense is going on?" he said and stopped.

Behind the desk sat Zurzmansor, writing hurriedly in a thick notebook.

"Banev," he said without looking up. "This is it, Banev. Good-bye. And don't forget our conversation."

"I'm not going anywhere," objected Victor. His voice cracked. "I intend to find out what's happened to the electricity and the water. Is that your work?"

Zurzmansor raised his yellow face.

"No," he said. "We aren't working anymore. Good-bye, Banev." He held out his gloved hand over the desk. Victor took it mechanically, felt the pressure, and responded to it. "Such is life," said Zurzmansor. "The future is created by you, but not for you. No doubt you already realized this. Or you will shortly. This concerns you more than it does us. Good-bye."

He nodded and went back to his writing.

"Let's go," Quadriga hissed in Victor's ear.

"I don't understand anything," said Victor loudly, his voice carrying over the entire vestibule. "What's happening here?"

He didn't want it to be quiet in the vestibule. He didn't want to feel like an outsider here. He wasn't the outsider here, and Zurzmansor had no business sitting at the main desk at three in the morning.

"And don't try to scare me off, I'm no Quadriga."

But Zurzmansor either didn't hear or chose not to. Victor shrugged his shoulders conspicuously, turned, and set off for the restaurant. He stopped short at the door.

Everything in the hall shone dimly: the lamps, the chandeliers, the clarions on the wall. The hall was full. Slimies were sitting around the little tables. They were all identical, only they sat in different poses. Some were reading, others slept, and many, as if frozen to the spot, stared motionless into space. Their bare skulls glowed; it smelled of dampness and medications. The windows were wide open, and there was water on the floor. Not a sound was to be heard beyond the splash of rain that carried in from the street.

Golem appeared in front of Victor. He looked strained and burdened, an old man.

"Why are you still here?" he said in a low voice. "Go, you're not allowed here."

"What do you mean, not allowed," said Victor, flaring up again. "I want a drink."

"Shh," said Golem. "I thought you had already gone. I knocked at your door. Where are you off to now?"

"Back to my room. I'm getting a bottle and going back to my room."

"There's no liquor here," said Golem.

Victor silently pointed to the bar, where the rows of bottles gleamed dully. Golem took a look.

"No," he said. "Alas."

"I want a drink!" repeated Victor in a stubborn voice.

But he felt no stubbornness within himself. It was a false front. The slimies were looking at him. The ones who were reading had dropped their books, the ones who were frozen to the spot had turned their skulls, only the sleepers continued to sleep. Dozens of shining eyes, as if suspended in a reddish twilight, stared at him.

"Don't go back to your room," said Golem. "Leave the hotel. Go to Lola's. Or to Quadriga's villa. Only so I know where you are. I'll come for you. Listen, Victor, don't bristle, do as I'm telling you. There's no time for explanations, and it wouldn't be right. Too bad Diana isn't here, she'd support me."

"And where's Diana?"

Golem looked around again and glanced at the clock.

"At four o'clock, or at five, she'll be at the Sunrise Gates Bus Terminal."

"Where is she now?"

"Now she's busy."

"So," said Victor, also glancing at the clock. "At four or five at the Sunrise Gates." He wanted very badly to get out of there. It was unbearable to stand there, the center of attention of that whole silent congregation.

"Maybe at six," said Golem. "Go to the villa and wait there."

"In my opinion, you're just trying to get rid of me," said Victor.

"Yes," said Golem. Suddenly, with interest, he looked Victor straight in the eye. "Veektor, you are absolutely sure you don't want to make yourself scarce?"

"I want to go to sleep," said Victor carelessly. "I haven't slept for two nights." He took Golem by a shirt button and led him out into the lobby. "All right, I'll go," he said. "Only what's the reason for the pandemonium. What are you having here, a convention?"

"Yes," said Golem.

"Or is it a rebellion?"

"Yes," said Golem.

"Or maybe it's war."

"Yes," said Golem. "Yes, yes, yes. Get out of here."

"All right," said Victor. He turned to go, but then stopped. "What about Diana?" he asked.

"There's nothing threatening her. At least until six. Maybe until seven."

"You'll answer to me for Diana," said Victor softly.

Golem took out a handkerchief and wiped his neck.

"I answer for everything," he said.

"Really? I would prefer it if you only answered for Diana."

"I'm sick of you," said Golem. "Oh, how I'm sick of you, you beautiful duckling. Diana is with the children. Diana is absolutely safe. Now go. I have work to do."

Victor turned and walked toward the staircase. Zurzmansor was no longer sitting at the main desk, there was only the small lamp smoldering above the thick oilcloth-bound notebook.

"Banev," called R. Quadriga from a dark corner. "Where are you going? Let's get out of here!"

"I'm not going to march around in the rain in my slippers," snapped Victor without turning around. "They kicked us out," he thought. "They kicked us out of the hotel. And maybe they've kicked us out of the town hall, too. And maybe they've kicked us out of town. And then what?" Back in his room, he quickly changed his clothes and threw on a raincoat. Quadriga was constantly underfoot.

"Is that how you're going, in your robe?" asked Victor.

"It's warm," said Quadriga. "And I have another one at home."

"Idiot. Go get dressed."

"I'm not going," said Quadriga firmly.

"We'll go together," Victor proposed.

"No. Not together either. Don't worry, I'll go this way. I'm used to it."

Quadriga was like a poodle eager for a walk. He jumped up and down, looking Victor in the eye; he panted, grabbed at Victor's clothing, ran to the door and ran back. It was useless to try to stop him. Victor tossed him his old raincoat and concentrated for a moment. He took his documents and money out of his desk drawer, stuffed them into his pockets, shut the window, and turned off the light. Then he gave himself up to Quadriga.

The doctor honoris causae, head thrust forward, pulled Victor through the corridor, down the back staircase, and past the dark, cold kitchen. Then he kicked him out the door, into the pouring rain and the pitch blackness. An instant later they were together.

"Thank God we made it," he said. "Let's run!"

But he couldn't. He got out of breath, and then it was so dark that they almost had to feel their way forward, grasping at the sides of buildings. The streetlights, burning at half power, and the reddish glow emerging here and there through half-closed curtains, could show only the general direction. The rain lashed down relentlessly, but the streets were not completely deserted. Somewhere there was a muffled conversation; a baby squealed; a few times they were passed by heavy trucks, and a wagon clanged its iron wheels on the asphalt.

"Everybody's running," Quadriga muttered. "Everybody's

getting out of here. We're the only ones dragging ourselves along."

Victor was silent. Their shoes, soaked through and through, squelched underfoot; warm rain dripped down their faces. Quadriga was adhering to him like a tick, and it was all stupid and hackneyed. They still had the whole city to cross, and there was no end in sight. He walked into a downspout, something crunched, and Quadriga, tearing himself loose, shouted tearfully for the whole city to hear: "Banev! Where are you?"

While they fumbled around in the wet darkness, searching for each other, a window banged open above their heads.

"Well, what's up?"

"It's fucking dark out here," said Victor.

"Right you are!" the voice shot back with spirit. "No water either. It's good we got the tub in quick enough."

"What's next?" asked Victor, trying to keep a rein on Quadriga. After a short silence, the voice spoke up.

"There'll be an evacuation, I'll bet you anything. Some life!"

And the window slammed shut.

They pressed on ahead. Quadriga, hanging on to Victor with both arms, began a meandering narration about how he'd awakened in a state of terror, gone downstairs, and walked right into their black mass. In the pitch darkness they collided with a parked truck, felt their way around it, and collided with a person. The person was carrying something. Quadriga shrieked.

"What's the matter?" snarled Victor.

"He hurt me," complained Quadriga. "Right in the liver. With a carton."

The sidewalks were blocked with cars, refrigerators, and cupboards, with groves of potted plants. Quadriga landed in an opened mirrored wardrobe and then got tangled in a bicycle. Victor was seething with rage. At a street corner, a flashlight was thrust into their faces; they were stopped. Wet helmets glittered in the rain, and a rough voice with a southern drawl barked out orders.

"This is a military patrol. Show us your documents."

Quadriga, needless to say, didn't have any documents. He immediately began shouting that he was a doctor, that he was a laureate, and a personal friend of. . . . The voice, rough and disdainful, cut him off.

"Locals. Let 'em go."

They crossed the town square. In front of police headquarters there was a pileup of cars with their lights on. Golden shirts were swarming around helplessly, their fire helmets flashing copper. Someone was booming out orders, but you couldn't make them out. It was obvious that the epicenter of panic was here. For a time the road was lit up by reflected light, then it once again grew dark.

Quadriga wasn't muttering anymore, he merely puffed and moaned. Every so often he would fall, dragging Victor with him. They'd gotten themselves filthy as pigs. Victor had grown completely numb, he'd even stopped cursing. Apathy and resignation shrouded his brain. He would have to keep on walking, walking today and walking tomorrow, bumping into unseen figures and pushing them aside, lifting up Quadriga again and again by the collar of his sodden robe. He couldn't stop, and he couldn't under any circumstances turn back. He remembered something long forgotten, something shameful, bitter, and unreal. Only then the sky was flaming and the streets were crammed with people. In the distance there was thundering and shooting; behind them was horror, and all around were empty houses with boarded-up windows. Ashes flew into their faces, there was a smell of burning paper. A tall colonel in an elegant hussar's uniform emerged onto the porch of a beautiful mansion, removed his cap, and shot himself. And we, ragged and bloody, sold and betrayed, also in hussars' uniforms but no longer hussars, all but deserters, started kissing, laughing, and booing, and somebody hurled his broken saber at the colonel's corpse.

"Stop, don't move," whispered a voice in the darkness, poking something familiar into his chest. Mechanically, Victor put up his hands.

"How dare you!" squealed R. Quadriga from behind his back.

"Quiet," said the voice.

"Help!" yelled Quadriga.

"Shut up, you fool," Victor told him. "I surrender unconditionally," he said into the darkness, addressing the heavy breathing at the other end of the submachine gun.

"I'll shoot," quavered the voice.

"Please don't," said Victor. "We've surrendered, can't you see." His throat was dry.

"Get undressed," the voice commanded.

"What?"

"Take off your shoes, take off your raincoat, take off your pants."

"Why!"

"And make it snappy!" hissed the voice.

Victor peered into the darkness, let down his hands, stepped to the side, and, grabbing the submachine gun, shoved it upwards. The robber let out a squawk and pulled back, but for some reason didn't shoot. The two of them, straining and grunting, fought for the gun.

"Banev! Where are you?" shrieked Quadriga, desperate.

Judging by the smell and feel of him, the man with the submachine gun was a soldier. He continued struggling for some time, but Victor was stronger.

"That's it," said Victor through his teeth. "That's the end. Don't move, or you'll get it in the face."

"Let me go!" hissed the soldier, resisting weakly.

"What do you need my pants for? Who are you?"

The soldier only panted.

"Victor!" shrieked Quadriga, already somewhere far off. "He-e-ere!"

A car turned the corner, for an instant casting light on a

familiar freckled face, the eyes beneath the helmet round with fear. Then it tore off.

"Wait a minute, I know you," said Victor. "What are you doing robbing people? Give me the gun."

The soldier, clutching his helmet, slid out from under the strap.

"What do you want my pants for?" asked Victor. "Deserting?"

The soldier sniffled. Such a nice young soldier with freckles.

"Well, why aren't you saying anything?" said Victor.

"It doesn't matter now," he mumbled. "They'll shoot me no matter what. I left my post. I ran off my post, I quit my post, what can I do now? If only you'd let me go, sir, huh? I didn't mean any harm, I'm not some monster, don't turn me in, huh?"

He sniffled and blew his nose and in the darkness he probably even wiped it on the sleeve of his overcoat. He was pitiful, like all deserters, frightened, like all deserters, and ready for anything.

"All right," said Victor. "You'll come with us. We won't give you away. Clothes will turn up. Let's go, only don't fall behind."

He started off, and the soldier followed, still sniffling.

Quadriga, howling like a puppy, was not difficult to locate. Now Victor had a submachine gun around his neck. The sniffling soldier clutched at his left hand, the softly moaning Quadriga at his right. A nightmare. Of course, he could always give back the submachine gun and send the little snotnose packing. No, he couldn't. He felt sorry for him, and the submachine gun might yet come in handy. We had a consultation with the people just now, and there is the opinion that disarmament at this stage would be premature. The submachine gun could prove useful in the coming battles.

"Stop whining, both of you," said Victor. "The patrols will converge on us."

They quieted down. Five minutes later, when the dim lights

of the bus terminal flickered before them, Quadriga pulled Victor to the right, muttering joyfully.

"We've arrived, thank Thee, Lord."

Quadriga, of course, had left the key to the gate in the hotel, in his pants pocket. They climbed over the fence, swearing all the while, and still swearing, floundered for some time on the wet lilac bushes. They nearly fell into the fountain. Finally they reached the entrance, kicked in the door, and stumbled into the hall. With a flick of the switch, the hall lit up in a reddish half-light. Victor tumbled into the nearest armchair. While Quadriga ran around the house in search of towels and dry clothing, the soldier quickly stripped to his underwear, rolled his uniform into a small bundle, and shoved it under the couch. After that he calmed down and stopped sniffling. Then Quadriga returned. They spent a long time briskly rubbing themselves with the towels and then got dressed.

Chaos reigned in the hall. Everything had been overturned, thrown on the floor, trampled. Books were mixed up with filthy rags and rolled up with canvases. Glass crunched underfoot, squeezed-out tubes of paint were scattered everywhere. The television stared at them with its empty square screen, and the table was piled up with dirty dishes full of rotten food. The only thing missing was excrement in the corners, and maybe there was excrement in the corners—it was too dark to tell. The smell in the house was such that Victor couldn't stand it and threw open a window.

Quadriga took up domestic duties. First he took hold of one end of the table and tipped it over, sending everything crashing to the floor. Then he wiped it with his wet robe, ran off somewhere, and returned with three crystal goblets of antique beauty and two rectangular bottles. Jumping up and down from impatience, he removed the corks and filled the goblets.

"To our health," he muttered incoherently, seizing his goblet and pressing it to his greedy lips. His eyes rolled in anticipation of the ecstatic moment.

Victor, straightening out a soggy cigarette, looked down at him with an indulgent laugh. On Quadriga's face there suddenly appeared an indescribable expression of wounded astonishment.

"Here too," he muttered with disgust.

"What's wrong?" asked Victor.

"Water," offered the timid voice of the soldier. "Plain water. Cold."

Victor took a gulp from his own goblet. It was water all right —pure, cold, and possibly even distilled.

"What are you giving us, Quadriga?" he asked.

Quadriga, without saying a word, picked up the second bottle and took a swig. His face contorted into a grimace. "My God," he said, spitting, and then, hunching over, tiptoed out of the room. The soldier sniffled again. Victor looked at the bottle labels: rum, whiskey. He took another gulp: water. It looked like an ordinary bit of deviltry—floorboards were creaking of their own volition, and your flesh crawled under the constant stare of someone's eyes. The soldier's chin disappeared into the neck of Quadriga's huge sweater; his hands ascended into the sleeves. His round eyes were fixed on Victor.

"What are you staring at me for?" asked Victor. His voice was hoarse.

"What's wrong with you?" whispered the soldier.

"There's nothing wrong with me, I want to know why you're gawking like that."

"What do you mean. It's scary. You shouldn't . . ."

"Calm down," said Victor to himself. "Nothing terrible. They're supermen. Supermen are capable of this sort of thing too. They're capable of anything, brother. Water into wine, wine into water. They sit around in restaurants and decompose. They're destroying the foundation, removing the cornerstone. The fucking teetotalers."

"Can't take it?" he said to the soldier. "Chickenshit."

"It's scary, you have no idea," said the soldier, getting animated. "You don't know what I went through there. You're on duty, it's nighttime, and he flies out of the zone, stares at you from up there, and flies off. One of the corporals even shat in his pants. And the captain kept on saying, you'll get used to it, it's your duty, you took the oath. But how can anybody get used to it? The other night one of them flew over, perched on the roof of the guard booth and stared at us. And his eyes weren't human, they were red and they glinted. And the sulfur fumes that were coming from him." The soldier took his hands out of his sleeves and crossed himself.

Quadriga emerged from the depths of the villa, still hunched over and on tiptoe.

"Nothing but water," he said. "Victor, let's get out of here. The car's in the garage, it's got a full tank of gas, all we do is get in, and off we go. How about it?"

"Don't go off the deep end," said Victor. "There's always time to escape. But all right, have it your way. You go ahead —I'm staying here. And you'll take the kid with you."

"No," said Quadriga. "I'm not going without you."

"Then stop shaking and go get us something to eat. I assume the bread hasn't turned to stone yet?"

The bread had not turned into stone. The canned foods remained canned foods, and they weren't bad canned foods either. They ate, and the soldier told them about the fearful events of the past two days, about the flying slimies, about an invasion of earthworms, about the children who had grown into adults in two days, about his friend, Private Krupman, a guy of about twenty, who was so scared he'd shot himself in order to get a discharge. And then about how they'd brought their dinner into the guard booth and tried to heat it up, and it sat on the stove for two hours but nothing happened, so they had to eat it cold.

"So this evening I went out on guard duty, it was eight o'clock and raining cats and dogs, and hailing too. There were these prohibited lights over the zone, and this weird music coming from God knows where, and this weird voice keeps on talking and talking but you can't understand a word of it. And then these tornadoes start rolling out of the steppe and right into the zone. And no sooner do they get there than who should come flying out in his car but the captain himself. I didn't even have time to come to attention, all I could see was the captain in the back seat, without his cap, without his raincoat, and he's flogging the driver in the neck and hollering, 'Speed up, you son of a bitch!' And it was like something snapped inside me, like some voice was telling me, 'Beat it, buddy, split, or you'll never know what hit you.' So I split. And not along the road either, but right across the steppe, through the ravines. I almost got stuck in a swamp, and then I left my poncho somewhere, it was a new one too, we got them yesterday. So I got to the city, and I see these patrols there. The first patrol nearly gets me, the second patrol nearly gets me, and finally there I am at the bus terminal. So I take a good look, and there are all these people running, and they're letting civilians through, but when they see one of us it's 'Show us your pass or else.' So I made up my mind."

Having finished his story, the soldier curled up in his armchair and went to sleep. The painfully sober Quadriga once again started insisting that they had to get out of there, and at once.

"Now there's a man for you," he declared, pointing his fork in the direction of the sleeping warrior. "He understands. And you're thick, Banev, you're absolutely impenetrable. How can you not feel it, I can sense it physically, there's something in the north that's pushing me south. Believe me. I know you don't believe me, but believe me now, I've been telling you for a long time, we can't stay here. Golem pulled the wool over your eyes, the long-nosed drunk. Can't you understand, the roads are clear now, everyone's waiting for daylight, and then they'll clog the bridges, nineteen forty all over again. You're incredibly thick, Banev, and you always were, even in school."

Victor ordered him to go to sleep or get lost. Quadriga sulkily finished his meal and then climbed onto the couch, covering himself with a mohair blanket. For some time he tossed around, grunting and muttering apocalyptic warnings. Then he fell silent. It was four o'clock in the morning.

At ten after, the lights flickered and then went out. Victor stretched out on the armchair, covered himself with something dry and lay there quietly, staring out the darkened window and listening. The soldier was sleeping fitfully, his moans punctuated by the snores of the fagged-out doctor honoris causae. From somewhere, probably the bus terminal, came the sound of motors starting and people's muffled shouts. Victor tried to figure out what was happening. He came to the conclusion that the slimies had broken with General Pferd, cleaned his forces out of the leprosarium, and moved their headquarters rather recklessly into town. They probably imagined that changing wine into water and terrorizing the populace qualified them for taking on a modern army. "A modern army indeed—as if they could even cope with the police. Idiots. They'll ruin the city, they'll perish themselves, and people will be left without shelter. And the children. They'll destroy the children, the bastards. And what for? What are they up to? Could it really be just another power struggle? Some supermen you are. How intelligent and talented can you be, you're the same shit that we are. Just another new order, and the newer the order, the worse it gets, that much we know. Irma. . . . Diana. . . ."

He shook himself, groped for the telephone, and took the receiver. The telephone was dead. "So once again they've failed to divvy things up between them. And the rest of us, who want nothing to do with either side, who want only to be left in peace, have to leave our homes and run for our lives, trampling each other in the process. And it could get worse, we could have to choose between them without understanding anything and without knowing anything, taking them at their word or at whatever they happen to dish out to us. And we'll have to shoot each other and claw at each other.

"Familiar thoughts in a familiar vein. It must be the thousandth time. That's the way we've been trained. Since childhood. It's either hip, hip, hooray or go to hell, I don't believe anyone. You're incapable of thinking, Mr. Banev, that's the problem. And that's why you oversimplify. Whatever complex social change you've managed to meet up with, your first instinct is to oversimplify. Either you believe in it or you don't. And if it's belief, then you'll push it to the point of stupefaction, to the devoted yelping of a faithful pup. And if it's disbelief, then you'll passionately spew your poisoned bile on all ideals, the true along with the false. Perry Mason used to say that there's no such thing as a damaging piece of evidence, what's damaging is a false interpretation. It's the same way with politics. The crooked ideologists interpret things to their own advantage, and the rest of us innocents lap it up whole hog. Because we can't think for ourselves, we're incapable of it, and we don't want to. And when the innocent Banev, who in his whole life has seen nothing but crooks, begins to interpret things on his own, he immediately falls flat on his face. Why? Because he's uneducated, because nobody's ever taught him how to think and so, not surprisingly, he can only interpret things in crooked terms. The new world, the old world—and right away the associations click into place: *neue Ordnung, alte Ordnung.* Well, all right. But the innocent Banev has still been around for a while, he's picked up a thing or two. He's not a total imbecile. What about Diana, Zurzmansor, Golem? Why should I believe that fascist Pavor, or some snot-nosed provincial dropout, or a sober Quadriga? Why am I so sure that it'll end in blood, pus, and mud? So the slimies have revolted against Pferd. Wonderful! Give him hell. It's high time. And they won't let anyone hurt the children, it's not their style. And they won't bare their chests to us to show us how sincere they are. They won't appeal to our national self-awareness and they won't rouse our primitive instincts. It's precisely what is most natural that is least fitting for man—right you are, Bol-Kunats. And it's really possible that this new world won't have any new order. Frightening? Cold? But that's the way it has to be. 'The future is created by you, but not for you.' Just look how I flared up when I broke out in those spots of the future. How badly I wanted to go back to my old world, to my eel and my vodka. Now I hate myself for it, but in fact that's the way it had to be. I detest the old world. I detest its stupidity, its indifference, its ignorance, its fascism. But what am I without all that? It's my bread and my water. Purify the world around me, make it the way I want it to be, and there'll be no place for me any more. I'm no good at glorification, I detest it, and there won't be anything to criticize, there won't be anything to hate. It's impossibly boring, it's death. This new world is severe and just and wise and sterile—and it doesn't need me, I'm just a zero in it. It needed me when I was fighting for it. But if it doesn't need me now, then I don't need it, and if I don't need it then why am I struggling for it? Oh, for the good old days, when it was possible to give your life for the creation of a new world and die in the old one. Acceleration, another instance of acceleration. But it's impossible to fight against something and not fight for something else! Well, what can you do, when you start a fire that big, you're bound to burn your own skin."

. . . Somewhwere in the huge, empty world a little girl was weeping, sobbing over and over: "I don't want it, I don't want it, it's not fair, it's cruel, how do you know what'll be better, then let it not be better, let them stay, can't you do it so that they'll stay with us, it's stupid, it's absurd. . . ." "That's Irma," thought Victor. "Irma!" he cried, and woke up.

Quadriga was snoring. The rain outside the window had stopped, and it seemed to be getting lighter. Victor brought his watch up to his eyes. The brightly lit hands showed a quarter to five. A dank cold was blowing in, and he knew that he should get up and close the window, but he was warm now, he didn't feel like moving, and his eyelids were closing of their own volition. Perhaps he saw it, perhaps he only dreamed it, but somewhere nearby trucks were driving past, one after another they were driving past, creeping along the battered dirty road and over the endless dirty field, and under the gray and dirty sky. Past the leaning telephone poles with cut-off wires, past a twisted cannon with its barrel pointing in the air, past a sooty chimney, now a perch for sated crows. And the dank air penetrated through the canvas, through his greatcoat, and he wanted so badly to go to sleep. But he couldn't go to sleep because Diana was going to come. "The gate was locked and the windows were dark, and she thought that I wasn't here and drove on." He jumped out the window and ran after the car with all his strength, and screamed until his veins burst, but just then the tanks were passing, rumbling and booming, and he couldn't even hear himself. And Diana drove off to the river crossing, where everything was burning, where she would be killed and he would be left alone. And then there came the angry piercing shriek of a bomb, right into his skull, right into his brain. Victor fell into a ditch and out of his armchair.

Quadriga was shrieking. He was convulsed in front of the opened window, staring at the sky and shrieking like an old woman. The room was lit, but not by daylight. Clear, even rectangles were traced on the littered floor. Victor ran over to the window and took a look. It was the moon, icy, small, and blindingly bright. There was something unbearably terrifying about it. At first he couldn't understand just what. The sky was as always covered with clouds, but into these clouds someone had carved a precise and even square. In the center of the square was the moon.

Quadriga had stopped shrieking. Exhausted from the effort, he was producing only feeble squeaking noises. Victor forced himself to breathe evenly and suddenly felt furious. "What do they think this is—a circus? Who do they take me for?" Quadriga continued to squeak.

"Cut it out!" Victor yelled at him, his voice full of hatred. "Never seen a square before? Fucking portraitist! Lackey!"

He grabbed Quadriga by his mohair blanket and shook him as hard as he could. Quadriga fell onto the floor and froze.

"All right," he said suddenly in an unexpectedly clear and lucid voice. "I've had it."

He raised himself onto all fours, and right from there, like a sprinter, tore off. Victor turned back to the window. In the depths of his soul he hoped that he was hallucinating, but there it was, just as before. In the lower right-hand corner of the square he could even make out a tiny star, almost drowning in the moonlight. Everything stood out clearly: the wet lilac bushes, the silent fountain with its allegorical marble fish, the latticework gates, and the dark ribbon of the road beyond them. Victor sat down on the windowsill, and, careful to keep his fingers from trembling, lit a cigarette. Out of the corner of his eye he noticed that the soldier was gone; maybe he'd fled, the poor kid, or maybe he'd merely crawled under the couch and died of fright. In any event, the submachine gun was in its former place. Victor gave a hysterical giggle, comparing the pitiful hunk of metal with the forces responsible for the square well in the clouds. "Some clowns. No, friends, the new world may perish, but the old one won't come through without a few bruises. It's a good thing I've got the submachine gun. It's stupid, but I feel calmer with it. And if you think about it, it's not all that stupid. Because one thing is clear, we're going to have an exodus, it's hanging in the air. And when there's an exodus going on, it's always better to keep to the sidelines and have a weapon."

A motor sounded in the yard. Quadriga's huge, endlessly long limousine (a personal present from Mr. President for the selfless service of a devoted brush) rounded the corner and, turning onto the lawn, headed straight for the gates. A minute later it crashed through them, flew out onto the road, turned around, and disappeared from view.

"So he took off after all, the pig," muttered Victor, not without envy. He climbed down from the windowsill, slung the gun over his shoulder, threw on his raincoat, and called for the soldier. The soldier didn't respond. Victor took a look under the couch, but there was nothing there except a gray uniform, tied up into a knot. Victor lit up another cigarette and went outside. Among the lilac bushes near the broken gates he found a bench, strangely shaped but very comfortable, and, most important, with a good view of the road. He sat down, crossed his legs, and sank deeper into his raincoat. At first the road was empty, but then a car passed, followed by a second and a third, and he understood that the exodus had begun.

The city had burst like a boil. In the beginning came the exodus of the elect: the exodus of magistrates and police, industry and trade, court and assize, finance and education, post and telegraph, the exodus of the golden shirts. They fled to the sound of backfire, enveloped in clouds of exhaust. They were disheveled and aggressive, dense and mean, the loan sharks and the moneygrubbers, the servants of the people, the fathers of the city. They fled to the howl of police sirens and the hysterical moaning of horns. The roar was deafening. The gigantic infection kept draining, and when the pus was gone the blood began to flow: the people themselves in overloaded trucks and lurching buses, in overburdened compact cars. They left on bicycles and in wagons, and they left on foot: pushing shopping carts, bent under the weight of packages, empty-handed. They were gloomy and silent and lost. They were leaving their homes, their bedbugs, their simple happiness and their ordered lives, they were abandoning their past and their future. After the people came the army. The procession was opened by a jeep full of officers, followed by an armored personnel carrier, followed by two truckloads of soldiers and our world-famous mobile field mess. In the rear came the half-track armored car with its machine guns pointing backwards.

It was getting light. The moon faded. The terrible square disintegrated and the clouds melted away; morning came. Victor waited about fifteen minutes longer, but the exodus had ended. He walked beyond the gates. The asphalt was strewn with dirty rags. Somebody's suitcase had gotten crushed—a good suitcase, too, not just anybody's. Near the suitcase was a wagon wheel, and farther off, on the shoulder, was the wagon itself, still holding its old, torn couch and rubber tree. There was nothing else. Victor looked in the direction of the bus terminal. There was nothing there either, not a single car, not a single person. Birds started chirping in the garden, and then the sun came up, the sun that Victor hadn't seen for a couple of weeks and the town for a couple of years. But there was nobody left to look at it. The silence was broken by the buzz of a motor; a bus came driving around the curve. Victor stepped out onto the shoulder. It was the Brothers in Reason, and they sailed past him, synchronizing their indifferent, imbecilic stares. "That's it," thought Victor. "I could use a drink. Where on earth is Diana?"

He slowly started back toward town.

The sun was off to the right. It moved along with him, now disappearing behind the roofs of the great houses, now appearing in the spaces between them, spraying warm light through the branches of the half-rotted trees. The clouds had disappeared, and the sky was astonishingly clear. A light mist was rising from the earth. Everything was silent, and Victor was drawn to the strange, barely audible sounds which seemed to be coming from within the earth—some sort of whisper or rustling. Then he got used to it and forgot about it. An astonishing sense of calm and security came over him. He walked as though drunk, his eyes fixed almost constantly on the sky. On the Prospect of the President a jeep stopped next to him.

"Get in," said Golem.

Golem was gray with exhaustion and somehow depressed. Diana was sitting next to him, also exhausted, but still beautiful, the most beautiful of all exhausted women.

"The sun," said Victor, smiling at her. "Look at that sun."

"He won't go," said Diana. "I warned you, Golem."

"Why won't I go?" Victor was surprised. "I'll go. Only what's the hurry?" He couldn't hold himself back and took another look at the sky. Then he looked back at the deserted street, and then he looked forward at the deserted street. Sunlight was pouring over everything. Somewhere to the south, refugees were staggering across the fields, the army was thundering its retreat, the authorities were withdrawing. They got stuck in traffic jams; they swore at one another, they shouted meaningless commands and threats. And all the while, from the north, the victors were descending on the town. In between was an empty stretch of calm and security, a few miles of emptiness, and in the emptiness were three people and a car.

"Golem, is this the new world coming?"

"Yes," said Golem. He looked at Victor from under his swollen eyelids.

"And where are your slimies? Are they coming on foot?"

"There aren't any slimies," said Golem.

"What do you mean, there aren't any," said Victor. He looked at Diana. Diana silently turned away.

"There aren't any slimies," Golem repeated. His voice was tense, and suddenly it seemed to Victor that he was on the verge of tears. "You can assume that they never even existed. And never will."

"Wonderful," said Victor. "Let's take a walk."

"Are you coming with us or not?" asked Golem wearily.

"I'd come," said Victor, "except I have to stop by at the hotel to pick up my manuscripts, and I'd like to have a look around. You know, Golem, I like it here."

"I'm staying too," said Diana suddenly. She got out of the car. "There's nothing for me to do there."

"And what's there for you to do here?" asked Golem.

"I don't know," said Diana. "But now I have nobody left except this man."

"All right," said Golem. "He doesn't understand. But you understand."

"But he has to have a look around," objected Diana. "How can he go without taking a look around?"

"Exactly," Victor took her up. "What the hell use am I if I don't look. That's my profession, looking."

"Listen, children," said Golem. "Do you understand what you're letting yourself in for? Victor, you were told: stay on your own side, that's the only way you'll be useful. On your own!"

"I've always been on my own side," said Victor.

"Here that will be impossible."

"We'll see," said Victor.

"Christ," said Golem. "As if I didn't want to stay. But you have to use your head a little. There's a difference, goddammit, between what you feel like doing and what you have to do." It was as though he was trying to convince himself. "Oh, you. . . . Well, stay if that's what you want. Have a good time." He started the motor. "Where's the notebook, Diana? Oh, there it is. If you don't mind, I'll take it. You won't be needing it."

"Of course," said Diana. "That's what he wanted."

"Golem," said Victor. "Why are you running? You wanted this world."

"I'm not running," said Golem severely. "I'm driving. I'm going from where I'm not needed to where I'm needed. Not like you. Good-bye."

And he left. Diana and Victor took each other by the hand and walked uptown along the Prospect of the President into the deserted city, ready to meet the advancing conquerors. They didn't talk. They breathed in the pure, fresh air, squinted at the sun, smiled at one another, and were afraid of nothing. The city stared at them with its empty windows. The city was astonishing: moldy, slippery, and rotten, covered with malignant stains as though eaten up by eczema. It was as if it had spent many years at the bottom of the sea, only to be dragged up for the amusement of the sun. And the sun, having laughed its full, was moving in on its destruction. Roofs were melting and evaporating; tin plates and tiles were disappearing in a rusty steam. Wet streaks appeared on the sides of buildings, penetrating the walls and revealing everything inside: dilapidated wallpaper, chipped beds, bandy-legged furniture, and faded photographs. Street lights twisted and melted, kiosks and billboards dissolved into thin air, and everything around was cracking and hissing, turning porous and transparent, changing into piles of dirt and disappearing. In the distance, the town hall tower lost its shape and merged into the blue of the sky. For some time, the old-fashioned tower clock hung in the sky, separate from everything, and then it too disappeared.

"My manuscripts are gone," thought Victor, amused.

The town was no more. Here and there were stunted bushes, sickly trees, and patches of green grass. Only in the distance, beyond the fog, you could make out the outlines of buildings, the remains of buildings, the ghosts of buildings, and not far from what used to be the road, on a stone stoop that led nowhere, sat Teddy. He had placed his crutches beside him, and was resting his wounded leg.

"Hi, Teddy," said Victor. "So you've stayed."

"Uhuh," said Teddy.

"How come?"

"Screw them," said Teddy. "They were pressed together like sardines, there was nowhere to stretch my leg, so I said to my sister-in-law, what do you need the cupboard for, stupid. And she lit into me. So I pissed on them and stayed behind."

"Want to come with us?"

"No, you go," said Teddy. "I might as well sit for a while. I'm no good for walking now, and whatever's going to happen can happen to me here."

They walked on. It was getting hot, and Victor took off his useless raincoat, letting it drop to the ground. He shook off the rusty remnants of the submachine gun and laughed with relief. Diana kissed him, and said "Great!" He didn't object. They walked and walked under the blue sky, under the hot sun, on the ground already covered with new grass, and came to the place where the hotel had been. It wasn't quite gone; there remained a huge gray cube of rough concrete, and Victor thought that it was a monument, and maybe a boundary mark between the old world and the new one. No sooner had he thought this than a jet fighter with the Legion emblem on its fuselage appeared soundlessly from behind the concrete block. Soundlessly it flashed overhead and, still soundless, banked somewhere in the vicinity of the sun and disappeared. Only then did the hellish, high-pitched roar inundate their ears, their faces, their souls.

But Bol-Kunats was already walking toward them, older now and broad-shouldered, with a streaked mustache on his sunburned face. Farther off walked Irma, also almost an adult, barefoot, in a simple summer dress, holding a twig. She followed the fighter with her eyes, and then, raising the twig as if taking aim, said, "Khhh."

Diana laughed. Victor looked at her and saw that this was yet another Diana, a completely new one, a Diana that had never been. He had never even thought that such a Diana was possible: Diana the Radiant. Then he shook a finger at himself and thought, "All this is fine, but I'd better not forget to go back."